Secret Diary of PorterGirl

The Everyday Adventures
of the Students and Staff
of Old College

Lucy Brazier

authorHOUSE®

AuthorHouse™ UK
1663 Liberty Drive
Bloomington, IN 47403 USA
www.authorhouse.co.uk
Phone: 0800.197.4150

Published by AuthorHouse   06/15/2015

ISBN: 978-1-5049-4443-4 (sc)
ISBN: 978-1-5049-4442-7 (hc)
ISBN: 978-1-5049-4441-0 (e)

Print information available on the last page.

Any people depicted in stock imagery provided by Thinkstock are models,
and such images are being used for illustrative purposes only.
Certain stock imagery © Thinkstock.

This book is printed on acid-free paper.

Prologue

Sᴇᴘᴛᴇᴍʙᴇʀ 23ᴿᴰ, ꜱᴏᴍᴇᴡʜᴇʀᴇ ʟᴏᴠᴇʟʏ ɪɴ *medieval England*

"And so, gentlemen, we are all agreed?"

"Yes, Master, we are all agreed" many voices are spoken as one.

"And we are agreed the College will uphold the scared traditions of our Order; The Order Of The Lesser Dragon; that it will honour the rites and ceremonies of our fathers and our forefathers; that it will strive towards learning and understanding and enlightenment for our members?"

"Yes, Master, we are all agreed." The voices wait earnestly for their Master to continue.

"Right! Good. Hang on, have we decided on a name for our new College yet?"

There is an uneasy quiet in the room as the assembled Scholars wait to see who will be brave enough to speak up first. The candlelight throws flickering shadows around the meeting room, as if to display their jittering unease on the stone walls. The Master is getting rather restless. He is a man of no mean proportions; there's a lot of him to get restless. The Scholars look to each other, desperately hoping one of them has come up with *something*.

"Come on, you chaps!" The Master encourages them "You're supposed to be the finest minds in England! Surely one of you has had a think about this? I did bring it up at the AGM."

Faldo, a young academic fresh out of monastic training in the West Country, coughs politely.

"Sir, I did…that is to say, I have a couple of suggestions, if Sir would like to hear them?"

"Good lad!" The Master bangs a hand like a cured ham on the table enthusiastically "It's Faldo, isn't it? Stand up then, fellow, and make sure all the old boys at the back can hear you."

There is a collective sigh of relief from the Scholars. This will give them a few minutes to try and think of something suitable.

"I was thinking of something along the lines of…" Faldo pauses for dramatic effect "College Of The Future!" A wave of his spindly arms accentuates the grandeur of the title. There is a general murmur of non-committal from around the table.

"The College Of The Future?! Didn't you hear what I was saying about upholding the sacred traditions of the Order Of The Lesser Dragon and the bit about our forefathers?" The Master is doing a valiant job of reigning in his anger. Faldo is only a youngster, after all. And it was jolly sporting of him to have a go. "Any other suggestions?"

"How about… 'Enlightened College'?" Faldo gamely has another attempt. "You did mention enlightenment, Sir."

The Master considers this, stroking several of his chins as he does so.

"Not bad, not bad. Not very catchy though, is it? I want something that sticks in the mind. Something that will stand the test of time. The bloody monasteries and churches seem to think they've got the monopoly on education these days. We need something to put their noses right out of joint."

Another young Scholar, Welby, a contemporary of Faldo's from the West Country, decides to enter the fray.

"I was thinking of something along the lines of 'Destiny College', or …"

Welby is unceremoniously interrupted by a much older Scholar, Father Walker. A former monk who couldn't get on with the itchy robes and strange haircuts so frequently demanded by the monastic lifestyle, Father Walker abandoned his calling to join The Order Of The Lesser Dragon.

"If I might, Sir, make my own suggestion?" Father Walker is a sleight man with an almost ethereal manner, which belies his cunning and ruthless intellect.

"Certainly, Walker!" replies The Master, cheered immensely by the all round feeling of participation. "Show these youngsters how it's done, eh?"

Father Walker rises elegantly to his feet and practically glides around the room, presumably to give further credence to whatever startling wisdom he is about to impart.

"I seems to me that if The Order Of The Lesser Dragon truly wishes to usurp the ecclesiastical types as the forerunners of education and modern understanding, we have to make a bold statement with regards to our new College. Wouldn't you agree, Master?"

"Yes, quite, Walker. Go on, go on" The Master is really enjoying himself now. The other Scholars are watching Father Walker with some suspicion and, it must be said, a little jealousy. He has obviously been giving this some thought whilst the rest of them have been spending more time than is strictly necessary in the local taverns. They are collectively kicking themselves for not paying more attention at the AGM.

"Of course, the designs for the building itself are as extravagant and extraordinary as the most up-to-the-minute construction techniques will allow. That is bound to irk them somewhat," Father Walker is really getting a feel for the subject now and is punctuating his performance with theatrical gestures. "But to really make our mark on the academic world, to ensure The Order Of The Lesser Dragon receives the rightful recognition and historical placement it deserves..." A dramatic pause; shamelessly stolen from Faldo's earlier presentation, "We must name the College after ourselves!"

"What do you mean by that?" Asks Welby, feeling instantly ridiculous the moment the words leave his mouth.

"Well isn't it obvious?" The Master rises to his feet with some excitement. "We shall name our establishment 'Order Of The Lesser Dragon College'! Bravo, Walker!"

Father Walker does not reply, but returns soundlessly to his seat, displaying a long-since perfected aura of smug satisfaction. The Master is delighted at the progression made at this meeting; these things have been known to go on for days.

"Just... one thing, Master, if I may?" Faldo is on his feet again. The Master fails to hide his obvious irritation.

"What is it, Faldo?"

"Don't you think it's a bit of a mouthful, Sir?" Faldo continues with caution. "And think of the size of the crest we would need to accommodate such a wordy title!"

The Scholars shift uncomfortably in their seats. They had already mentally left the meeting and now it was being prolonged. Faldo was fast becoming the most unpopular Scholar in the room. Welby comes valiantly to his rescue.

"What about an acronym, then?" suggests Welby. "It would be significant and... a bit mystical."

The Master sighs.

"I suppose it is a bit lengthy," he concedes. "So if we take Welby's suggestion we get... erm..." The Master struggles with the concept.

"OOTLD..." begins Welby "Ootelled College?"

"We can't be Ootelled College! That's ridiculous"

"If I may, Master?" Father Walker moves to calm The Master, who is keen to move onto the post-meeting cheese and wine. "The most important and pertinent letters would give us *OLD* College. Which is rather in keeping with our intentions to uphold the traditions and rites of our forefathers, wouldn't you say?"

The Scholars seem quite taken with this and make appreciative noises. Quite apart from anything else, they are also anxious for some refreshments.

"Right! Well, that's all very good" The Master rubs his hands together and starts looking around for the servants to bring the wine. "Old College, it is. Perfect. I'll inform the builders in the morning and that's all the important arrangements completed. Marvellous. All we need to do now is arrange for the sacrificial peasants to be thrown into the foundations and we're away."

"I'm sorry, Sir, what?" Faldo continues his seemingly unstoppable descent into unpopularity. "You can't surely be considering the superstitious practice of burying people under the building in order to ward off evil, or whatever it's supposed to do?"

"Well, I know it seems a little old-fashioned, Faldo," The Master responds curtly "But it's still common practice around these parts and... the rites and ceremonies of our forefathers... and so forth."

"But, Master, we are men of science! And books! And... we are scholars!"

"Yes, but you know what the workmen are like. Common chaps, you know. They get ever so uptight and nervous if you don't follow all the proper practices."

"But it's a cruel, awful, outdated *superstition!*"

"Well, it's the done thing, Faldo, and that's that." The Master will not be moved on this, especially as the servants are already preparing the cheeseboards and the wine just outside the door. "Besides, I don't think it's all about superstition, you know. It's got a lot to do with drainage, I believe. Now... where's my glass?"

Faldo is furious. His usually drawn, pallid complexion is flushed red and his spindly little hands are bunched into angry little fists.

"I will not have this, Master!" Faldo's voice has gone up an octave, if that is even possible for a voice that, despite having gone through puberty, is already on the high side. "I tell you – I am not in agreement! I shall... I shall *speak out* against this barbaric behaviour!"

"Oh, come on, Faldo," Father Walker tries to reason with him "Even the churches do it. Now, enough of this silliness and let's all sit down calmly and enjoy the wonderful spread..."

"Then I wish to leave The Order!" a cold silence falls across the room at Faldo's words. Calmer, now. "I... do. I wish to leave The Order Of The Lesser Dragon. I cannot be part of this. I thought we were progressive, I thought we would be *different*..."

The Master holds up his vast hand to silence Faldo.

"Very well. Very well, Faldo, then you shall leave." Faldo opens and shuts his mouth a few times. No words come out, so he decides to keep it closed. "But you shall not leave this room" a grave darkness falls upon the reddened and swollen countenance of The Master. "No one leaves The Order Of The Lesser Dragon, but through death. And you know that it is so."

"Errmm, actually, I wasn't aware..." Faldo's words fall away as The Master rises to his feet and the full, terrible might of his being bears down on him. A knife is produced from the folds of his coat and The Master says no more. Faldo considers the benefit of begging for his life, but it is as if the life force has already left him as terror and an overwhelming helplessness deprive him of speech and movement. Faldo is little more than a sacrificial lamb in the hands of The Master, who is at least enough of a gentleman to execute the deed swiftly. There is barely a squeak from Faldo as his slender white throat is sliced from side to side, with an unsettling deftness that suggests The Master may have some experience in this field.

With unexpected care, The Master lays the mortal remains of Faldo gently on the ground. The Scholars shuffle their feet uncomfortably as the bits and bobs that used to be on inside of Faldo's throat plop and gurgle their way out of the wound and across the floor, worryingly close to the expensive and elaborate rug commissioned specifically for the room. A respectful silence ensues, but before very long some of the Scholars are glancing expectantly towards the cheese and wine being laid out on the sideboard.

"Shame really, he was quite an able scholar" says The Master quietly. The Scholars mumble in agreement. Cheering up considerably, The Master rubs his hands together and turns away from the corpse. "Well, can't be helped, I suppose. Rules are rules and whatnot. Still, his work for Old College will continue even after his passing. He can play an instrumental role in the drainage."

The First Day

Late September, just before the start of Term...

It is still dark as I make my way towards the huge iron gates of Old College for my very first day as the new Deputy Head Porter. For the first time in what seems like forever, I am not wearing body armour or itchy trousers to go to work. The only reminders of my previous existence in the Fuzz are my trusty Maglight and a very nice pen my former colleagues gave me as a leaving present, the latter of which is sitting in my jacket pocket. I can feel it there, like a tiny security blanket, close to my heart, its very presence giving the impression that my old team are only a radio transmission away. But they are not. There is no back up. I am all alone in a whole new world and I have no idea what I am doing. I've never even been to college, let alone one of the finest universities in the world. I left school at sixteen and worked various jobs, then spent most of the last seven years being abused and threatened by drunks and drug addicts on a council estate sixty miles away. But now I am the Deputy Head Porter of Old College, an institution steeped in the traditions of learning and academia. I probably won't need back up. But I wish to God it was there anyway.

I open the door to the Porters' Lodge, and am struck by the intricate and organised arrangement of pigeonholes, ledgers, notices and stationary. It feels faintly reassuring, a bit like going into a school stationary cupboard. The air is slightly musty, I suppose from the array of paper and wood, and there is a vague sense of promptness about it. I think I like it. The Head Porter spots me and strides over in his funny stripy trousers, his College tie fastened beautifully around his neck. He is friendly and welcoming. There are other Porters milling about, eyeing me suspiciously. I swear I hear one of them whisper – "…But it's a woman". I put it to the back of my mind and get on with the awkward business of introductions, forced smiles and the empty pleasantries that come with being the New One.

The first thing that hits me is that everyone in The Lodge has been here FOREVER. The only other woman in the Lodge, the Receptionist, tells me she has been here 25 years. To begin with, the first five or six years, the Fellows didn't speak to her at all. Women in College are tolerated, it seems only because of relatively recent rules and regulations on diversity. Since the college was founded in 15th century, there has never been a female Deputy Head or Head Porter. I haven't even had lunch yet but I am already informed that my new staff do not much fancy working for a lady. Perversely, I find this quite invigorating. I am certainly not going to be put off by some grumpy old buggers and am no stranger to a bit of controversy. Time to put the cat amongst the pigeonholes!

The day continues, I meet so many people. I have no idea who they are. Invariably, they are professors or doctors and they have been at Old College FOREVER. The first words that tumble forth from all of them are acknowledgements of my womanhood. To be fair, some of them seem very positive about it. The other female staff members I meet seem amazed and delighted. I make some clumsy comments about 'girl power' at the College – these are regarded with nervous suspicion. Bugger them. I've faced up to far more intimidating people and situations than some elderly intellectuals and I've been in more scrapes than they've had hot dinners. This is not going to worry me one bit.

. . . .

Right, well, its seems I have NOT been in more scrapes than they have had hot dinners – it seems all these people DO is have hot dinners! Lunchtime is a triumph. My meals are included as part of my job, one of the primary reasons I was attracted to the role in the first place. The Dining Hall is magnificent, all wood panelling and oil paintings the size of the flat screen TVs you see in the homes of people on benefits. The food is varied, plentiful and of very good quality. Most importantly it's free. I may have the body of a weak and feeble woman, but I have the stomach of a concrete elephant and decide to make a point that even if I am not a male Deputy Head Porter, I can certainly eat like one. I look over to the High Table, where The Fellowship are guzzling away noisily. They are certainly a robust bunch, their fat ruddy faces devouring plates of food the likes of which I only usually see on Christmas Day. This is only lunch, goodness knows what they get through at their formal dinners of an evening. Their complexions suggest to me a love of port and wine and I start to feel that maybe I could fit in here after all.

I am introduced to the College Chaplain, who is also the College vet. He is a vast and jolly man whose clothes can barely contain his immense bulk. On a couple of occasions I am concerned that he is going to explode completely as he coughs and splutters his way through our brief conversation. Just as I am about to admire the man's work ethic of holding down two jobs, I am informed that pets at the College are banned, save for The Master's Cat who is in excellent health. I am unable to comprehend a need for a College vet, but that really isn't any of my business.

. . . .

Lunch over with, Head Porter takes me to the College tailor to have me measured for my 'uniform'. The tailor is much as I had imagined (in so much as that I hadn't even thought about tailors until I was informed I was being taken to see one). A small, wiry man with little beady eyes and round rimmed spectacles. He has the smallest hands I have ever seen on a man. I suppose that helps with the stitching and such like. Head Porter introduces me and explains that I need a suit made. Tailor fumbles a bit, then quietly but firmly says that he does not make clothes for women. He begrudgingly agrees to supply my bowler hat and silk (silk!) ties. Could she have a cravat? No, they don't make cravats. What size hat is she? (I'm standing, like, right here…) She must be measured for a hat. I am a size fifty four, I announce proudly – I know what bloody size bowler I am, I've worn one every day since I was twenty five. The tape measure is thrust around my forehead by Tailor's tiny little cold hands, as if he is trying to garrotte a small animal. He either chose not to hear me or outright didn't believe that I knew my own hat size. It is confirmed. I am a fifty four.

3

They don't make bowlers that small, it will have to be specially ordered. This will be expensive and time consuming. I am grateful to Head Porter for bluntly placing the order and looking at Tailor in the same manner an experienced copper looks at a petulant offender who is thinking about not moving along quietly. Feels a bit like I've got back up.

Back at the Lodge, I find a tailor online who will make me the required suit in charcoal grey and will do the necessary embroidery. It will take a week. Head Porter seems a little taken aback at my ability to find clothes for myself but I don't know why he should be so surprised. As a woman, shopping for clothes should be a finely honed skill, surely? Anyway, I've made it through my first day. The first day of the rest of my life? Maybe just the first day of a very short career that floundered because I couldn't grow a penis. Time will tell.

The Second Day

GOING TO WORK ON MY second day, I feel slightly more confident. Head Porter seems to like me (he was the one who conducted the job interview, after all) and one of the Porters was even quite nice to me. And this evening, Junior Bursar has invited me to attend the annual guided tour of Old College, which he conducts at the beginning of every academic year and is strictly by invitation only. Head Porter has *never* been on one of Junior Bursar's tours and I feel *fairly* smug about this.

If I stop to think about it too much, there is an overwhelming feeling of self-doubt that is prickling away at me; I have absolutely no idea what I am doing here. It seemed like rather a twee idea at first and applying for the job was a complete punt and not something I ever really thought about too deeply. There were many reasons for leaving my previous vocation, although it still breaks my heart I had to do it. I didn't really expect to get the job and yesterday brought the realisation that I am ever so slightly out of my depth. What if I can't do the job? What if I end up looking like an idiot? I reason that I have looked like an idiot many, many times in the past and it really hadn't been too damaging. In fact, on occasion it had worked in my favour. As the majestic gates of Old College yield to my coveted 'gate buzzer' (a privilege afforded to so precious few in the College) I decide to not be afraid of being an idiot.

I arrive before Head Porter, and am greeted by the Night Porter, just finishing his shift. I introduce myself and am a little surprised when he grabs my hand and pulls me close to kiss me on the cheek. As his greying bristles scratch my face (removing most of the inexpertly applied foundation I felt was necessary for my new role), I am grateful for some genuine affection, albeit from a dishevelled old man who has been up all night and is in need of a shave. I did not even yet know his name. It reminds me of my misspent youth.

Night Porter reaches for a ring binder, which bares the legend 'Incident Book'.

"There's a couple of bits in here you will need to look at" he says gently, as if speaking to a simpleton. Ah, more familiar territory, I reassure myself. I take the ring binder and look at Night Porter knowingly, like one old pro to another. The folder feels surprisingly light and I am momentarily confused when I open the folder to be greeted by a log dated 27th August 2007. I flick through the handwritten pages and it is apparent that the logs are filed in ascending chronological order. Why would you put the most recent incidents at the back? What benefit could there possibly be in flicking through 5 years worth of old incidents to find what is relevant? But then, that's what Old College is all about, isn't it? Remembering the past and honouring that which came before? Still, it seems bloody silly to me and the logs should be filed with the most recent first. It's only my second morning though, and I decide that this procedural amendment can wait.

It appears that there were two incidents during the previous evening that were deemed important enough to make it to the incident book. The first was a fire alarm being set off in one of the gyp rooms by a student's fledging attempts at 'cooking'. The other was a noisy party in which constituted several students (some from another College!) being found in an undergraduate's room. I ask myself how this is considered an 'incident' as, students by their very nature are noisy and prone to parties. Happily, as I am musing on this problem, Night Porter enlightens me by explaining that having other students visit your room is against College policy. He punctuates the importance of this fact by jabbing his chubby little sausage finger at his immaculately written verse regarding said 'noisy party'. Sufficiently educated, I recall the actions of Head Porter yesterday, and take copies of the incidents and put the copies into the pigeonholes of Junior Bursar and The Dean. For some unfathomable reason, Junior Bursar and The Dean are very interested in learning of not only the noisy parties, but of students burning toast. I can only imagine this is because they, firstly, wish to attend the noisy parties and, secondly, wish to avoid accepting toast from students incapable of warming bread properly. Unless it is something to do with fire alarms, at this early stage I cannot be sure.

Head Porter arrives and seems put out that I have already 'dealt with last night's incidents'. Feeling uncomfortable, I offer to make a round of tea and take solace in my solitary kitchen activity. As I fill the kettle I can hear my new colleagues having exactly the same conversation I had when I first walked in. Neither seems to notice the abject inefficiency of the 'Incident Book'. I make a mental note to sort that out as soon as I dare.

I serve the teas with a flourish. I make good tea, this I know. The look in my eyes dares them not to like the tea. The tea is well received. I know quite a bit about tea. Head Porter says I need to know about keys. Head Porter says that the American students think the Porters carry the bags. He says that Porters are not the carriers of bags, they are the keepers of keys. And, oh my lord, there are an awful lot of keys...

High Jinx In Old Court

KEYS, KEYS, KEYS! THE WALLS of the back of the Porters' Lodge are covered with keys. Many are stored in little cabinets, row after row, like little tiny forests of silver that tinkle merrily on their hooks. They are all intricately and beautifully labelled with letters and numbers that mean nothing to me. On the back walls are older keys, some of them huge and ornate, worn by years of locking and unlocking. I am intrigued particularly by an ancient looking collection, which are labelled 'Master's Lodge', 'Old Wine Cellar' and 'Old Library'. They almost look as if they are cast from some kind of magical material and have an esoteric air about them. Head Porter is carefully explaining about the keeping of keys, but my mind is conjuring wild images about what lies behind the doors these keys unlock.

Then, the door to the Lodge is thrown open and a wild-eyed woman thunders through, wheezing and spluttering in abject horror. I recognise her as the Head of Housekeeping, a brisk and blunt woman who is clearly more at home dealing with detergent than she is people.

"Head Porter! Head Porter" Her voice is raspy and accusing, she looks at him as if he has just eaten her first born. Head Porter calmly turns to regard her as one would a confused elderly relative.

"Head of Housekeeping? What ever is the matter? I won't have you carrying on in my Lodge in this manner."

"Head Porter!" her voice a strangled cry of fury, now "There is a young gentleman in the grounds… and… he is NAKED!"

"What? Where is he?!"

"He is in Old Court, running around in the all together and making a dreadful racket…"

I know where Old Court is, one of the few places I can find my way to without much difficulty.

"I'll go," I volunteer in a manner which I hope sounds confident and professional. Head Porter looks at me with his dark eyes;

"Remove him from the College" I am instructed.

I sprint out of the Lodge and head towards Old Court. This is more like it, I think happily to myself. This is running after people and removing them. This is my comfort zone. I bound over the bridge, the river rippling like a moody sheet of steel beneath me, and head through the cloisters to Old Court. I spy the 'young gentleman' in question, his little white posterior reflecting the morning sun. I call out to him and as he turns to face me, I notice how ridiculously young and nubile he is. My pace slows, along with my decision making process. As expected, the naked student makes a run for it. I can chase him, no problem, but at some point in the very near future I am going to have to grab him, quite likely in a rugby tackle, and I am going to need to employ some kind of restraining technique to bring him under control.

Perhaps ten years ago the prospect of wrestling with a nude young man would have held some appeal. Right now, I am in danger of looking like some kind of pervert. And anyway, what do I do with him then? My hat is still being made and I have nothing with which to cover his shame. The prospect of escorting a naked male student through College is not a happy one.

The young man has put some distance between us now and is heading towards the boundary wall. *Ah, that's it my boy,* I think – *get yourself over that wall and off down the street and we can all come away from this with some dignity intact.* I feign a half-hearted 'chase' towards the wall as I see him trying to get a foothold in the masonry. Bloody hell, just get yourself over the buggering wall for goodness sake, it's not even that high. Despite the early hour, some students are leaning out of their windows to watch the unfolding drama. I can't just stand here, doing nothing, so I shout, "Stop!" in an effort to appear proactive. In my previous incarnation, shouting "Stop!" at someone actually meant, "It's the Police! Run away as fast as you can!" So imagine my horror when the confounded lad actually

9

freezes mid-climb and turns his stupid head to look at me. Bloody, bloody students – no, not actually stop, run away as fast as you can! Or I will catch you! Idiots, idiots the lot of them. They can pass a series of exams to get a place in the world's finest educational establishment but have no sense of self-preservation. How will they ever survive in the real world?

Thankfully, idiot naked boy shakes himself out of his startled stupor and dutifully bundles himself over the wall and out to the streets beyond. He is now the concern of the early morning commuters and no longer anything to do with me. I make gestures of frustration for the benefit of my bleary-eyed audience and, breathing a large sigh of relief, return at a sedate pace to the Porters' Lodge.

The Master's Cat

AFTER THE EXCITEMENT OF THIS morning, I am delighted to find myself, once again, in the splendorous Dining Hall of Old College. Over lunch Head Porter is proudly telling our dining companions about Junior Bursar's guided tour this evening. Head of Catering is very interested and is asking us to take photos of this and that. I am still trying to take in the magnificence of the Dining Hall and can't help but cast furtive glances towards High Table to watch The Fellowship at feeding time. They even have waiters and waitresses attending to them. I suppose it must be quite a feat to get so much food down themselves and many hands make light work. I don't really blame them, though, the food is rather good. I am idly buttering a freshly baked roll in preparation to stuff it with slices of some very tasty floppy cheese I found on the cheese table, when a horrible though strikes me. What if I end up like them? No, I don't mean becoming a professor; that is preposterous. But a huge, sweaty, wobbling mess – gorging myself each lunchtime… It could happen. I put the roll and its cheesy content back on my side plate. On second thoughts, there is no point wasting it, it is lovely cheese…

"Head Porter! Come at once!" I look up, bread roll in hand, to see Junior Bursar scuttling towards our table. I find myself hoping that whatever has upset Junior Bursar isn't going to interfere with my lunch. Junior Bursar gestures for Head Porter to follow him and I obediently jump to my feet and cast a mournful gaze at my uneaten cheese roll before joining them outside the Dining Hall.

"A matter has arisen that must be attended to immediately!" Junior Bursar exclaims. I stand to attention, ready for whatever emergency awaits Head Porter and myself. "The Master's Cat is in danger. He has got himself stuck under a ledge by the edge of the river. Chaplain has been calling him but he won't move. You have no option but to take a punt and rescue him. The Master is beside himself with worry and wants the cat returned to his Lodge immediately."

I try to control my face as it battles with itself to display a suitable expression. I can think of no suitable expression, nor anything sensible to say, but am rescued by Head Porter who solemnly declares:

"Yes Sir, we will attend to it at once". He turns smartly on his heels and I scuttle after Head Porter towards the Boat House.

"How on earth are we going to transport a cat in a boat along the river?" I ask, feeling instantly stupid. "I mean, they aren't naturally nautical animals, are they?"

"We need some bait, something to tempt it into the boat," replies Head Porter sensibly. Clearly, this predicament is not creating the same puzzlement for him as it is for me. Obviously, this is something that happens *all the time* and will probably be something I will have to do on a regular basis. "Go to the kitchens and speak to Chef, see if he has something we can lure the cat with."

As I explain to Chef my current situation, I try to sound as blasé about it as I can. Yeah, The Master's Cat is stuck by the river, just got to rescue him, you know. Yes, we will be travelling by punt. Chef is very helpful. He furnishes me with an exquisite piece of smoked Scottish salmon, so deeply pink and so finely crumbed that I think there must be a mistake.

"I'm sure a bit of chicken leg or skin would do," I suggest. Chef just laughs and waves his hand dismissively.

"The very idea!" he says. The Master's Cat certainly has a refined palate. On the way to the Boat House I am half tempted to eat the salmon myself. After all, I haven't finished my lunch.

The Boat Master has helpfully launched a punt and has a pole ready for me.

"You do know how to punt, I suppose?" Head Porter asks, left eyebrow defiantly arched. Thank god, I know how to punt. "Good. Take us along the backs and I will look out for the cat."

It is a bit chilly for punting, really, but at least it isn't raining and the river is very quiet. Head Porter sits silent and alert, scanning the riverside for the elusive cat. He looks very dignified in his bowler and immaculate suit, his silk College tie fastened in the traditional manner. It nestles beneath a shirt collar so white and so perfectly starched you could cut glass with it. For my part, I am happily standing at the rear of the punt, carefully feeding the pole through my hands, in and out of the water, just as I was taught several summers ago. I was instructed to always punt from the rear of the boat. Pushing the punt through the water is so much more dignified than dragging it. I am by no means an expert but am fairly proficient and we are gliding through the water fairly majestically.

Head Porter calls out, pulling me from my reverie rather more abruptly than I would have liked. He has spied the cat hunched beneath some masonry on a ledge, staring malevolently at our punt. The cat is making a guttural, ungodly sound at us, making it clear that, yes, he would like to be rescued, but certainly not by a couple of common oiks like us.

I steer the punt alongside the cat's perilous perch. I can see immediately that the water level is a little too high for us to reach him easily. Head Porter is almost flat on the bottom of the punt as he reaches his arm out towards the cat, trying to gauge its level of cooperation. Cooperation is not on the mind of The Master's Cat as he flattens his ears to his head and hisses violently. I hand Head Porter the salmon, which he proffers to the cat, making encouraging noises. The cat is not interested in the slightest.

"It's no use," sighs Head Porter "We will have to try and take him by force. I can't quite reach him, you're smaller, here, come and try and grab him."

Hmm. I don't like the idea of this at all. I am envisioning being shredded to ribbons, then falling into the river, probably hitting my head on the way in. I carefully place the pole in the punt and get into position. The punt sways and rocks as Head Porter and I rearrange ourselves and I am not confident of finishing the day in dry clothing. Out of the corner of my eye I see people on the opposite bank. Closer inspection reveals Junior Bursar, Chaplain, The Master and Chef cheerfully watching our endeavours. What the bloody hell is Chef doing there? I suppose he doesn't want to miss the action.

My efforts are as fruitless as Head Porter's. The blasted animal has no intention of wilfully jumping into our punt and, at this position, we can't reach him well enough to get a good hold of him. I shake my head in frustration at the cat. He is glowering at us vindictively with his yellow eyes, demanding us to remove him from his dire situation but refusing to help us on any level.

I pick up the pole and punt us over to the opposite bank where our audience is waiting.

"What's wrong with you, man?!" Junior Bursar snaps angrily at Head Porter. "Just grab the blasted creature!" The Master looks perturbed by this comment, but says nothing.

"The difficulty, Sir," explains Head Porter "Is that we can't reach him properly. The water level is too high. If it were lower we could get a proper hold of him." At this, The Master says something to Junior Bursar that I can't quite hear from our punt. Junior Bursar nods to him and turns to go, in doing so shouts to us:

"Wait there!"

We wait patiently in the punt. Junior Bursar does not return. Head Porter removes his bowler and rubs his head thoughtfully. I am alarmed to realise that I need to visit the little girls' room. I hope we won't be here too long.

After what feels like an age, something strange happens.

"We're sinking!" I squeal.

"We are not sinking," Head Porter replies. "The water level is going down. I imagine that the locks have been opened up stream to allow us a better vantage point for reaching the cat." I am dumbfounded. The water level of the river is actually being amended to afford us a better opportunity to rescue a cat?! It appears that phone calls have been made and The Master must have sufficiently well connected friends to ask this small favour.

I am grateful that Head Porter asks me to punt and he deals with the cat. With the river suitably lowered, he scoops that cat up without too much difficulty and bundles him under his jacket for the return journey.

Back at The Porter's Lodge, there is just enough time for a cup of tea before meeting with Junior Bursar for the much-anticipated guided tour of Old College.

The Guided Tour

THE LIGHT IS JUST BEGINNING to fade as Head Porter and I make our way through Old College to meet Junior Bursar for the guided tour. Several of the Porters have commented that I should be really looking forward to this, as Junior Bursar is very knowledgeable about the College. I have learned that he was a scholar at the College as a young man and went on to be a research Fellow before becoming a fully-fledged member of The Fellowship decades ago. He has been Junior Bursar for thirty four years and must surely be approaching retirement. However, 'retirement' does not seem to be a word in the College's rather elaborate vocabulary, as the many antiquated Fellows shuffling about the place are testament to. There are some younger Fellows, too, conducting research, gradually knowing more and more about less and less. I wonder to myself what effect spending his entire life at Old College has had on Junior Bursar. The other Porters seem to fear him; he has a reputation of being exceptionally particular about how things are done. I certainly get the impression that he can be demanding, but no more so than other people I have worked under in the past. As I muse on this, a specific Sergeant comes to my mind and I smile sadly at the life I have left behind.

Junior Bursar is waiting for us by the Library, checking his watch with some agitation. Evidently we are late, but mercifully so is everyone else who has been invited to attend. Junior Bursar shakes our hands and smiles benignly.

"We haven't yet been properly introduced," he says and proceeds to ask about my background and makes small talk that isn't too excruciating. When

I have to confess to having virtually no knowledge or experience of College life, he is kind enough to explain some of the nuances peculiar to the strange new world I am inhabiting. He finishes by saying "The Bursars take care of all the money. Senior Bursar collects the money and I spend the money".

"I think you have the better end of the deal, there, Sir," I reply.

We are soon joined by the rest of our small party. There is the French Lectrice, a beautiful and willowy French woman of indeterminable age. She seems friendly, but only in the way that people of higher social standing are gracious to their inferiors. Another woman (it seems female academics are far more acceptable than female Porters) with large eyebrows and long brown hair that falls below her waist, is introduced as a Maths Fellow. With her is her husband, a tall, gangly man with equally long hair and an ill-filling suit. Neither of them look at either me or Head Porter. Finally, there is Professor F, his purpose at the College is not elaborated upon. He is younger than a lot of the Fellows, with a slender face topped by erratic, straw-like hair. He acknowledges us, but is distant.

The tour begins in Old Court and Junior Bursar talks about how the College was built, the types of bricks used and things of that nature. He points out patterns in the brickwork that were designed by the Master Mason and which are virtually invisible until they are pointed out. Then, they leap from the walls with geometric wonder and I can't help but be impressed.

We continue around the College, Junior Bursar talking constantly as we go. I am enjoying the tour immensely and am fascinated to learn of secret codes written into the cloister ceilings and even more delighted as we are all instructed on how to decipher them. Throughout the College are secret messages and esoteric writings in everything from stained glass windows to fireplaces, if only you know where to look. The very walls exude mystery and hidden knowledge, each brick placed with exacting deliberation. Spending a lifetime within these walls must do questionable things to your mental state.

Our little group is whisked through the Old Dining Hall (used for very special occasions), the old kitchens, various studies and reading rooms, each more elaborate than the last. The Old Library is my particular favourite, situated as it is at the top of one of the towers, locked away behind endless doors and iron gates. When we get there I can see why. There are shelves packed with books dating from the 15th century, including a beautifully illustrated edition of Milton's *Paradise Lost*. Junior Bursar pauses momentarily in his narrative to search the ancient shelves for a particular tome. He heaves a massive, leather bound book from the shelves and humps it unceremoniously onto a table.

"This is an 18th century medical book," he explains, carefully turning the pages. "The illustrations are printed on the pages with large plates, so all the drawings here had to be first etched in relief. The workmanship is outstanding." And indeed it is. Junior Bursar continues, "It was customary at the time for the diagrams to become more gory as the book progresses. Here, you can see how the body is stripped away of its skin and outer workings with each turn of the page." I do see. The diagrams are stunningly intricate. Junior Bursar turns to me "Do you have much of a stomach for gore, Deputy Head Porter? How far should I continue?" I smile politely.

"Let's turn directly to the last page," I reply. Junior Bursar's eyes light up and he finds the final diagram. Disappointingly, it is merely a human skull in cross section and not particularly gory at all. The book is replaced onto the shelf and the tour continues.

I learn that a complex web of secret passages weave their way throughout the College and gasp in amazement to walk through them all, up and down little stone staircases, in and out of doors hidden in wood panelling. There are secret spy holes where Masters long dead would covertly observe The Fellowship in the Combination Room, in the Dining Hall and in the studies. From every wall hang huge oil paintings of eminent figures from the College's prodigious history, staring down, insisting I appreciate the gravity of my surroundings. And appreciate I do, in spades.

As the tour comes to an end in The Master's Lodge, The Fellows prepare to join The Master for a no doubt elaborate evening meal. Head Porter and I are dismissed politely but firmly.

As we make our way back to the altogether more humble surroundings of The Porters' Lodge, Head Porter is clearly delighted.

"There were passages and doors there even I haven't seen before," he relishes.

"I wonder if we shall ever see them again," I wonder "I suppose not." Head Porter stops and looks me directly in the eye.

"Don't be so sure," he says, his eyes shining. "We hold the keys to every one of those doors. Head Porters can go where they please".

Suited & Booted

I HAVE BEEN AT OLD College a little over a week now and feel I am starting to find my feet. I can find my way around, just about, although giving visitors accurate directions still eludes me. I have a tenuous grasp on the key situation and am finding that they strangely fascinate me. There are literally hundreds upon hundreds of them, all neatly labelled and arranged in their cabinets and across the walls. They remind me, in some ways, of people. They come in all shapes and sizes. Some have limited uses; others are versatile and have infinite abilities. Some are mundane, others are desirable. But every single one of them is important in its own way, and if one single key is broken or misplaced, it has a resounding affect on the running of College.

I have met so many people over the years. Many of them came in and out of my life in a matter of minutes - another customer to be dealt with, another face in the crowd. Many of them I have chosen to forget, for innumerable reasons. Some of them will be forever etched on my memory, for reasons equally as numerous. A very few of them have made such an impression that they have changed me, sometimes for better, sometimes for worse. What I realise is, every single one leaves a tiny footprint on my psyche, whether I realise it or not. People are important. They make the world what it is. They have made me what I am. Never forget the importance of humanity; without it, we are nothing.

Right now, humanity is getting right on my wick. Although people have stopped reminding me that I am a woman, they still don't seem to like it that much. The students are faintly annoying. I have finally succumbed to the one thing I swore to myself I never would – I have forgotten what it is like to be young. I am not especially old, not even middle aged, but I am no longer in the full bloom of youthful exuberance. I am annoyed by the disorganisation, the naivety and the down right idiocy of youth. Youth burns every meal it ever cooks. Youth loses its keys on a seemingly hourly basis. Youth cannot handle its drink.

I am calculating the Porters' overtime when I hear my name from the front desk of the Lodge. A familiar figure is leaning over the desk talking to Receptionist. I recognise the small, wiry frame of Tailor. He has in his arms a box and suit carriers. Oooh!

I stride over, expectantly. Could it be?! Oh yes it is. My Deputy Head Porter's suit has been delivered and – oh my! – So has my bowler!

I sign the forms. I stamp and sign off the invoice. I take in my trembling arms my new suits and, most importantly, my new hat. I always liked wearing a hat. It gave me a sense of purpose. It dawns on me now how much I like wearing a uniform.

A uniform.

A sense of identity. A sense of belonging.

Something to hide behind? Or something to be proud of? I suppose that all have been, and no doubt will be, true for me. That said, a uniform is one thing. A bowler hat is quite another.

So let us begin with the bowler. The first time I put a bowler upon my brow, I felt like my life had really begun. Whatever had gone before had led up to that point. That was the first day of the rest of my life. At first, it hurt like buggery and stained my forehead black whenever it rained or I sweated profusely. In time, it yielded to the shape of my head and became as much a part of my job as the law itself. But always, it felt like a part of me and, from that point on, I didn't feel properly attired without it.

As I eagerly open the hatbox in the privacy of the rest area, my heart beats hard in my chest. Like a little jackhammer in my ribcage, I feel the metallic taste of rushing blood on the roof of my mouth. It's like shoes! But for your head! I hurriedly cast aside the packaging and quickly realise that this is a very different bowler indeed. Lighter and more delicate. Sleeker. Soft and black, like deep water. In place of the Battenberg is a beautiful silk ribbon, as black as night. It is tied elegantly at one side. The brim is fashioned so that it follows the contour of the head and is wonderfully peaked at a slightly jaunty angle. I face the mirror and place it slowly and deliberately upon my brow. It is a thing of beauty. But, oh, it is tight and digs into my forehead. I half expected this. It will need wearing in. No matter. I have a hat. I have a purpose.

The suit is almost as impressive. It fits perfectly and is flattering in charcoal grey. The silk lining is slightly more elaborate than I would have deemed strictly necessary, but I can certainly live with it. Embroidered on the right lapel of the jacket, and also the left pocket of the trousers, is the colourful and extravagant crest of Old College. The embroidery is a work of art in its own right. Thank the Lord for College dry cleaners, I wouldn't fancy washing and ironing this myself.

The tie will need a little practice. I haven't worn anything but a clip on tie since primary school. I have never worn a silk tie. College colours are not entirely flattering to my skin tone, but I am proud nonetheless.

I emerge from the rest room and strike a pose for Porter.

"The hat really suits you," he says "But the suit makes you look like a man".

Yes. Maybe I look like a man. But that man is James bloody Bond and I feel magnificent.

An Interesting Concept

ARRIVING AT WORK FOR THE first time in my full Deputy Head Porter regalia is exhilarating. I am feeling a little more like a piece of history with every step I take.

As I enter The Lodge I am greeted by today's Porter on duty, a stout Northern chap with a scruffy white moustache and beautifully pressed shirt.

"Morning, ma'am" he says in a wonderfully gruff accent that sounds grumpy, regardless of the tone or words used.

"Good morning, Porter!" I reply, cheerily. "Anything I need to be aware of?" There is a bit of a pause. Not quite a pregnant pause, but certainly a pause that is a few weeks 'late' and is considering weeing on a stick. "Everything alright, Porter?"

"Yes everything is alright, ma'am". I am not convinced.

"What it is? C'mon, just spit it out."

"Well, the Porters and I have been having a little chat, ma'am" I can see that Porter is choosing his words carefully. "And... we think there is something you should know."

"Oh?" This sounds ominous. "I suppose you'd better tell me, then."

"It's just that we thought you had a right to know."

"Right to know what?" I admit, I'm getting a little concerned, now.

"To know what you're doing here!" Porter is getting somewhat flustered and I cannot tell if it's because he thinks I am going to get angry or because he doesn't want to hurt my feelings.

"Well – I thought I had a reasonably good idea what I was doing here," I try to keep my voice as level as I can manage, "But perhaps I am wrong?"

"Look, look – let me start at the beginning" Porter sits himself down and wraps his sausage-y hands around an industrial sized mug of tea. I perch myself on the edge of the desk and try to look nonchalant. "You know the old Deputy Head Porter? The Old Boy who was here before you?"

I don't know him, but it stands to reason there was *someone* here before me.

"I can't say I knew him, Porter, but I've certainly heard about him." *Ah, yes. The constant comparisons to my predecessor have just about stopped grating on me.*

"Well, him and Head Porter didn't get on." Porter says bluntly.

"Oh?" This sounds interesting.

"Thing is, the Old Boy had been here for much, much longer than Head Porter. He had been serving Old College for over thirty years, man and boy. Well, man and... older man. When the other Head Porter was 'moved on', shall we say, after he was caught with his fingers in the till, it should have been the Old Boy who took over."

"So why didn't he?"

"Well, that's the strange thing. They never asked him to step up to the plate, so to speak, they just put Head Porter in the job even though he'd only been with us a couple of years."

"That's a little odd, isn't it?" I remark. Even by Old College's standards, this seems strange.

"No one ever really understood it, ma'am" Porter is relaxing considerably now and seems to be on a roll. "Some say it's a bit suspicious that some one who knew so little about College got the top job."

"Hmmm" a thought strikes me. "Or maybe he knew too much?" There is a twinkle in Porter's eye.

"Well, there's some reason or another, sure enough. The fact he's kept the job, as well, I mean... there have been... 'occasions', shall we say, over the years. Occasions and incidents, shall we say"

"Like what?" I was right. This *is* interesting.

"Let's just say that certain things have happened that you wouldn't have expected someone to keep their job afterwards, shall we say."

There's something going on, here, I think to myself *but I don't know what. And I don't think Porter really knows, either. But there's definitely something.*

"As fascinating as all this is, Porter, what has it got to do with me?"

"Ah! Right. Yes. So the thing is, obviously the Old Boy knew all about Old College; he knew about everything and everyone. Head Porter hadn't got a clue. So people used to treat the Old Boy like he was in charge, because he sort of was. And Head Porter *hated* that. Really, really hated it. He got quite paranoid, actually, convinced there was a conspiracy against him and things like that."

"And was there?" I feel I have to ask. Porter seems to debate this for a moment.

"Well, not *really*, ma'am, not as such, no." Porter takes a deep breath. "It was just easier, dealing with the Old Boy. Head Porter has some funny ideas about things." Another deep breath. "So, this is where you come in."

"Oh, good-oh!"

"So, when the Old Boy retired, I think Head Porter thought – here's my chance to finally be in control. Be properly in charge, like. There were loads of applications for your job, ma'am, and most of them from some very experienced Porters. So when you turned up, it was a bit of a shock."

"I'll say," I reply, my heart sinking just a little. I had thought it was my brilliant interview technique that had got me here. "I've never set foot in a College before now, so I can see I'm hardly the first choice."

"No offence meant, ma'am"

"None taken. My inexperience and ignorance of College life was what sealed the deal then, Porter?"

"I'm afraid so, ma'am. We think you're here to make Head Porter look good, in that you don't know anything about anything. And, not to be funny, you're a young girl and he probably thinks you'll be easy to push around, and that." I find this quite complimentary. Since I entered my thirties, references to being a 'young girl' have been few and far between.

"It's an interesting concept, certainly" I reply. "And a bit of an odd thing to do. Didn't The Fellowship kick up an awful fuss?"

"That's the other thing, ma'am" Porter continues "Head Porter held all the interviews over the Summer Vac and he gave you the job while they were all still away. They couldn't very well argue about it then, it was a done deal. I think they just sort of thought they'd see how you got on."

A thoughtful silence falls between us and I am feeling rather deflated. It's not the nicest information to receive; I got the job because I was the worst possible applicant. Oh well. I'm here now. I've got the hat and everything. Porter stands up and reaches over to pat my shoulder encouragingly.

"If it's any consolation, ma'am, we don't think you're doing too bad, considering."

"Thanks, Porter."

"Tea?"

"That would be wonderful, thank you."

Raising The Flag

A FEW DAYS LATER AND the knowledge that I am at Old College because I'm a terrible choice for the role of Deputy Head Porter is stinging less considerably. I am much more interested in the shadowy circumstances surrounding Head Porter's ascent to the top of the tree and the 'occasions and incidents' he appears to have been involved in. But I have other things on my mind right now. Today is an important day. Later this evening, there is going to be a special ceremony, which, I am told, is the 'Induction Of The Fellowship'. This ceremony is performed once, sometimes twice, a year and has been performed since the foundation of Old College hundreds of years ago. Its purpose is to formally induct the new Fellows as members of College. Apparently, I have a small but vital part to play in this ceremony, but before that I have a much more pressing task to attend to. I have to raise the College flag in honour of the new Fellows.

Part of my illustrious new role is to be conversant with the College Flag Schedule. At this moment in time, I am not conversant with the College Flag Schedule. There are several flags, which College flies at specific times; today's flag is simply the College Standard. Head Porter informs me that he will accompany me on my mission, to oversee my work and ensure I raise the flag correctly. This is a relief. I can't recall ever raising a flag before and on such an important occasion I want to make sure I get it right.

Head Porter and I make our way through the cloisters and across the courtyards, laden down with a bunch of keys so ancient and heavy I feel I am carrying the history of College in my hands. A stiff breeze tugs at my bowler, threatening to snatch it away at any moment. The hat is not worn in yet, so sits tightly and resolutely upon my head. The brim is unrelenting against my forehead, something for which I am glad under the current circumstances.

As we approach the tower, atop which the flagpole resides, I feel my pulse quicken. I am not amazingly comfortable with heights and the tower seems to increase alarmingly in size as we approach. Head Porter is talking about the significance of the flags while I am gripping the keys with ever increasing dread.

We reach the little wooden door at the foot of the tower and my hands shake a little as I find the correct key and fumble with the lock. The door is old and stiff. The tower is part of the oldest part of College and, although immaculately maintained, it has a worn and distinctly unsafe air about it. I heave the door open to reveal a delightful stone spiral staircase, twisting its way into the darkness above. As I begin my ascent I am surprised by the diminutive nature of the stone steps. My feet are barely bigger than a child's but I can only fit half a foot on each step. As I tippy-toe up and round, slowly, carefully, I think – the Porters have much bigger feet than me and they are up and down this tower on a regular basis. I'd better put a brave face on it.

The steps are worn down by centuries of footfall. The stone walls are cold and smooth to the touch. There is a length of elderly rope strung helpfully along the wall, which I cling onto for dear life. As I climb the steps, I see a small wooden door set into the wall. It is somehow adorable and foreboding all at once. Painted above the door is the legend 'Junior Bursar'. I am a little surprised and also impressed that Junior Bursar has rooms half way up the flag tower. He is a man of advancing years and I can't quite imagine him scuttling up and down this staircase. This discovery has thrown a new light on my impression of the man.

We continue up and up, until we reach a solid wooden door at the top. I fumble again with the beautiful but cumbersome keys and my white-knuckled hands find the correct one and unlock the door. I give the door a shove with purpose and determination, which belies the terror that I feel at being so high above the ground.

As I step through the doorway and onto the roof, my head spins a little and I have to take a couple of deep breaths to steady myself. It's bloody high. Head Porter is bustling impatiently behind me and I have no option but to step out onto the roof, no time to show my nervousness. The wind isn't helping, either. What felt like a stiff breeze on terra firma is a positive hurricane up here. Or maybe it's just me. I don't really want Head Porter to get the impression that I wish I had dressed in brown trousers this morning, so I chatter away merrily about the wonderful view and comment on the fabulous buttresses of a nearby chapel. I force a grin that is so fixed it looks as though rigor mortis has set in. I feel I must look positively demonic as I follow Head Porter across the lead roof to the huge chest on the far side. It is secured with a padlock so enormous I can barely lift it with one hand. I wrestle it open and fling back the lid to reveal the College flags. Head Porter selects the correct one and we unfurl it on the roof. It seems incredibly large up close; seen from below it flutters elegantly in the softest breeze. Up here, in my hands, it is heavy and coarse and gaudy. My legs are shaking as we tug and shake the flag into its full glory. I listen carefully and do as I am instructed to finally hoist the flag majestically up the pole. My spine feels like jelly, my head is swimming and my arms barely have the strength, but I raise it with aplomb and fasten it securely. The wind takes it instantly and the flag ripples ferociously in the cold morning air.

I take a moment to bravely survey my surroundings. Although my unease with heights is making me feel light headed, there is no denying the awesome and inspiring view of the ancient City that is home to Old College. I have never before seen The City from this perspective and it is unrecognisable. I can pick out many of the landmarks, but they look almost alien and foreign from my vantage point. It is like another world. I shall have to get used to these 'other worldly' experiences, they seem to be happening on an increasingly regular basis.

As we head back down the corkscrew staircase, an even more unsettling experience than climbing up it, my mind turns to lunch as a way of settling my sadly churning stomach. Lunch is still a few hours away and I still have to learn more about the impending ceremony this evening. The ceremony will be performed in the Chapel, at ground level, and as far as I am concerned, that is all I need to know right now.

The Induction Of The Fellowship

THE REST OF THE DAY passes without incident, and my mind is consumed with the task before me this evening. The day's duties done, I take a few moments to rearrange myself into something approaching fairly presentable. The male-orientated facilities in the Porters' Lodge offer scant opportunity for preening, but I barricade myself in the rest room and make the effort, all the same.

The face looking back at me in the mirror is one I barely recognise. The cynicism induced by my previous existence has left my eyes. It hasn't left my heart, but it is significantly reduced to the point that it doesn't show.

I am wearing make-up – at work! Since The First Day I have worn make-up. Not much, just smoothing out a few edges here and outlining a few others there. I'm at an age where I need a little bit of help to look fabulous. And help is at hand.

From the hatbox I gleefully lift The Bowler. I place it on my head with practiced aplomb. There! That's all the help I need. I look fabulous. I am fabulous.

Head Porter calls out to me from within the Lodge, evidently we are cutting it a bit fine.

We hurry towards the Gathering Room, near the Chapel. The new Fellows to be inducted will wait here for the arrival of The Master, who will lead them from the Gathering Room to the Chapel via Apple Tree Court. The many candles in the room throw a warming glow through the windows and the heavy oak door gives way to a welcoming heat. The room is all oak beams and wood panelling, with a glowing and regal fireplace at one end. The room is dominated by an enormous wooden table in the centre. Oil paintings of previous, long dead Masters line the walls. They appear a little disapproving at my presence. I suppose they will get used to me.

Satisfied that the Gathering Room is ready to receive its eminent guests, Head Porter leads me towards the Chapel.

"Our part in the ceremony is simple," explains Head Porter. "We set up the Chapel accordingly, then we wait by the doors. When the Tower Clock strikes seven, The Master will lead the new Fellows across the courtyard. As they enter, we must open the curtains in the Chapel to allow them in to the sacred area. We then close the curtains behind them and lock the Chapel doors. Then, we crouch down and peek under the curtains."

"Why do we peek under the curtains?" I ask. It's a reasonable a question.

"It's tradition," Head Porter replies, testily. I am clearly an idiot. "We have to kneel down and make sure we do not cast a shadow under the curtains. If The Master sees our shadows, he will know we are watching."

"Won't he know that anyway?" I am confused. "I mean, if it's part of the tradition, surely he's got a bit of an idea that we might be trying to peek under the curtains."

"That is hardly the point," Head Porter retorts, sharply. "Besides, we need to know when the ceremony has ended so we can open the curtains again and unlock the Chapel doors to allow The Fellowship to make their way to The Feast."

"Can't we just listen in?" I feel I am beginning to dig a hole, here. "Isn't it obvious when the ceremony has ended?"

Head Porter barely changes his expression, but I sense that he is exercising every ounce of patience in his being.

"The service is conducted in Latin," he explains wearily. "We won't know it's over until we see The Fellows' feet moving towards us."

Right. College servants throughout the ages would probably not have had much of an education in the way of Latin. Actually, I studied Latin at school (it's a long story) but I wasn't brilliant at it, so I let the moment pass and proceed with setting up the Chapel.

It would be a travesty and a dishonour to Old College to reveal the setting up of the sacred area and the ceremony itself (what little I saw). All I will say is that the clock strikes seven and the curtains are opened, as they have been by Porters for hundreds of years previously. When the curtains are closed behind The Fellows, I take my place on the stone floor, my knee nestling in the concave masonry worn down by centuries of knees before me. As it happens, this performance is unnecessary as the ceremony ends with a Latin phrase that should be easily recognisable to anyone in my Latin class at school.

I rise to my feet a few seconds before Head Porter (who was clearly not in my Latin class at school) and reach for the elaborate and weighty curtains. Head Porter unlocks the Chapel doors and we stand like sentries as the newly-inducted Fellows make their way to their feast.

As we make our way back to the Porters' Lodge, I can't help thinking to myself; I didn't really do anything at all. But, the few actions I did perform were of such vital importance to this place that they have been repeated exactly for centuries. I'm a strong believer in the 'if it ain't broke, don't fix it' mantra but this is something else. Then again, I think of all the ways I could be earning a living and I think to myself – it sure could be a hell of a lot worse.

The Night Watch

I PULL INTO MY PARKING space at Old College, the parking area unusually deserted. This is due to the fact that it is nearly ten o'clock at night. I am starting my first night shift. The ancient behemoth of brick that is Old College looms darkly over the city, light spewing like fire from its many windows. Shadows fall at unnatural angles, distorting the familiar into unnerving things that seem to leap and dance in my peripheral vision. The Porters' Lodge looks almost sinister as it lurks menacingly at the mouth of Old College. The late evening air is chilled and sharp but mercifully still and dry. I make my way to the door of the Lodge and the warmth within.

Porter looks pleased to see me. I imagine he is rather looking forward to discharging the responsibilities of the College to my good self and getting home to a nice warm house. Maybe some cheese on toast, perhaps a stiff drink. He looks like a man who enjoys a stiff drink.

There is nothing noteworthy to report from the day, there is a small dinner in Old Dining Room this evening and the heating in Dr R's room has broken. It is shaping up to be a quiet night as I wave off my colleague.

The first few hours fly by as students come in to borrow keys, ask ridiculous questions and post letters. Some Fellows come and go in much the same vein, albeit less politely. Around two-ish, one of my preferred Fellows comes into the Lodge. Dr J is a few decades younger than most of The Fellowship and hasn't yet succumbed to the cosseted and entitled mindset that comes from years of being cocooned in College life. He has been out in town and evidently feels like a chat before retiring to his rooms.

31

We talk jovially about all aspects of College life. He seems interested to know what a newcomer makes of it all. We discuss the mealtimes at length. I am stunned to learn that Dr J is tired of attending banquets. I listen wide-eyed as he bemoans the fact that banquets happen so frequently that he can barely muster the enthusiasm to pick up his knife and fork. I offer to attend in his place. I would certainly tackle banquets with gusto and delight. We laugh at the very idea. College servants would never be tolerated at High Table.

"Have you seen all the secret nooks and crannies yet?" Dr J asks, lowering his voice and leaning conspiringly over the desk. I tell him that I have. "What did you make of the Crypt?" he enquires.

"What Crypt?" I reply, my interest piqued.

"There's a secret Crypt underneath the Library," Dr J informs me. "Well, it's not all that secret, the Porters and most of The Fellowship know about it. The students don't, of course, they would be trying to break in to it all the time."

"Where in the Library? How on earth do you access it?" I know the Library well, I can't imagine where a Crypt would be hidden.

"There is a trapdoor hidden under the carpet, near the neo-classical section. The key for the lock is on the Library bunch. You should have a look when you lock the Library up later."

Hmmmm. This sounds intriguing. I will give this some thought.

"What time do you finish?" asks Dr J.

"I'm off at eight thirty tomorrow morning."

"Marvellous! I'll pop in and see you before I go cycling. I shall be wearing lycra!" This last statement makes me wince; it is doubtful that the podgy physique of Dr J will lend itself well to lycra. It is certainly a mental image that will keep me awake all night.

Old College is a completely different place after the moon comes up. I thought the old place would be spooky and macabre, like a haunted house. Instead, it feels more like I've stepped through the back of a wardrobe into a Nania-esque dreamscape. The cloisters are moonlit paths to places unknown; the courtyards are stunningly draped in starlight and all around my footsteps echo cheerfully on the stone floors. My night time patrols are verging on the magical, the illusion only occasionally dispelled by the raucous banter of students returning to their lodgings.

In the dead of night, The Master's Lodge dominates the north wing of Old College. Many of the lights and candles are still alight and throw a warm glow through the stained glass windows. The affect is akin to a midnight rainbow, scattering coloured shafts towards the ground below.

The hours tick by and I lock up the Chapel, the bar and the gym. The last to be locked up is the Library, beneath which is concealed, supposedly, the Crypt. Perhaps I shouldn't venture down there without speaking to Head Porter first. There is probably a good reason why he hasn't mentioned it to me before. Maybe it is dangerous or structurally unstable in some way. Then again, it couldn't hurt just to have a look for the trapdoor. Maybe see if I can work out which key opens it. I could just, maybe, open the trapdoor and shine my torch down there, see if there is anything down there. Yeah, it seems almost rude not to. Just a really quick, tiny peek. Just for a minute.

The bunch of keys for the Library is populated by keys of all sizes and origins. It clangs and clatters ominously at my side as I make my way to the door. The Library is in the oldest part of Old College, but has had some form of modernisation over the years in order to provide a world-class studying environment. The stone walls and oak beams have been lovingly maintained over the centuries and it is set over an incredible four floors. The books on the shelves are far more serviceable than the relics in Old Library, but impressive nonetheless. There is an entire room dedicated to dictionaries and thesauruses. No student of Old College has any excuse for anything less than perfect spelling and grammar.

I check each room on every floor and evict three bleary-eyed young academics, each diligently studying for their PhDs. I inwardly applaud their work ethic as I usher them out into the cold courtyards and they go their separate ways. I can't help but admire these young people, barely out of childhood, working so hard to make a better future for themselves. Maybe better futures for the world. There is no telling what some of these young, brilliant minds will become. Certainly not chefs, I think to myself as I bring to mind the daily activations of fire alarms from fledgling attempts at making toast. The other day, one chap even managed to burn eggs. Eggs! How on earth do you burn an egg?

I lock myself in the Library and set about looking for the neo-classical section. I must confess to not really knowing what 'neo-classical' is. Maybe sexed-up Homer, or Tacitus with swearwords. I'm half expecting to find works by Julius Caesar translated into rap.

As I am searching the Library, the duty mobile phone in my pocket emits a poor impersonation of an old fashioned telephone. I answer it.

"Hello? Is that Old College?" an urgent voice in clipped English twitters into my ear.

"Yes, this is Old College" I reply.

"Ah! Good. Hello, this is Hawkins College here, good evening"

"Good evening Hawkins College, what can I do for you?"

"We have just turned out a rowdy group from our Junior Combination Room, they're heading your way. I heard one of them say he was a student of yours. I watched them go down Prince's Lane, I think they are heading towards Sprockett Gate."

"Thank you Hawkins College, I will attend to it immediately."

I end the call and slip the phone back into my pocket. I will have to resume my search for the neo-classical section later. Sprockett Gate is at the rear of Old College, the furthest entrance from the Porters' Lodge. The most logical entrance for a 'rowdy group' hoping to avoid detection from the Porters. I am sure they would appreciate a warm welcome from my good self on this chilly evening.

Showdown At Sprokett Gate

Sprokett Gate towers before me in the moonlight, a masterpiece of wood and iron. It has a smaller pedestrian gateway within it, which I open to receive my guests. I lean nonchalantly in the heavy wooden frame and listen to the sounds of The City at night. Sirens sound in the middle distance and the cries of late night revellers echo through the ancient winding streets. The moon is bright tonight and casts its silvery light along Prince's Street and spills into the courtyard.

I do not have to wait long. I soon hear drunken voices raised in song – although I use the term very loosely. It could be a bastardisation of the old favourite 'The Good Ship Venus' but I wouldn't want to put money on it. I guess at there being approximately seven males heading towards me, accompanied by what sounds like a couple of horses clip-clopping along the pavement. That can't be right. A quick glance around the gateway and I realise my mistake. Accompanying the young gentlemen are four hefty young ladies of considerable girth in vertigo-inducing heels, snorting and giggling as they totter along in outfits clearly destined for much smaller persons than their good selves.

When the sounds of merriment are almost upon me, I step from the shadows with palms outstretched and a broad grin.

"Good evening, ladies and gentlemen," more of an announcement than a welcome "And welcome to Old College. May I see your student identifications?"

Eleven pairs of bleary eyes peek at me in horror. A couple of the 'ladies' giggle nervously. One of the young men fumbles hurriedly through his pockets and eventually produces his College ID card. I make a mental note of his name and nod approvingly. "And your guests?" I enquire.

"They are from Hawkins College," the youth replies as politely as one can when slurring ones words. "We – um – we are celebrating the first night of a play we put on there this evening."

"How marvellous!" I beam patronisingly. "And I suppose Hawkins College has no facilities for celebrating such an event?" This awkward moment is having the desired sobering effect on my little band of thespians. "Or, perhaps, you have already abused the hospitality of Hawkins? Outstayed your welcome, so to speak? And you thought that Old College would be more tolerant of your celebratory techniques?" Very awkward now. I feel a bit guilty about ruining the party atmosphere.

There are explanations, there are protestations. There are even apologies. For a moment, I think there would be tears. I relent a little. I was young once, not so very long ago. They have been putting on a play, not stealing cars or breaking into houses. They at least have something to celebrate. I take down all of their names and issue stern words of advice about disturbing the peace of Old College. Suitably chastised, they are permitted to enter and I escort them to the lodgings of our student, under no illusion that I will return at the slightest hint of disturbance. I remind them that I have the keys to the lodgings and will not hesitate to use them if I deem it necessary. The solemn looks and nods do not convince me entirely, but I haven't the heart to throw them all out. I'll keep an ear out, certainly, but I am far more interested in finding the Crypt...

Tales From The Crypt

MY YOUNG CHARGES SUITABLY SUBDUED and ensconced in the safety of our student's rooms for the evening, I make my way back across the moonlit courtyards towards the Library. I am determined to find the entrance to the Crypt mentioned by Dr J, but strangely *not* mentioned by Head Porter or anyone else. As my footsteps become increasingly more urgent, I haven't yet decided whether I will actually enter the Crypt or not. It's not that I am scared, no, I am a practically thinking person and not especially given to superstition or matters of an ethereal nature. And my experience of dead bodies is fairly extensive thanks to my previous employment, so it's not that. I cannot quite put my finger on just what is causing my hesitation. Nonetheless, I am curious to at least find the trapdoor and see if I can work out which key opens it. Mind you, we all know what they say about curiosity, do we not?

As I reach the imposing wooden door of the Library, I find myself musing on that last thought. *Curiosity... it killed the cat. What cat? Why a cat? Were any dogs ever seriously injured by curiosity? Could curiosity maim a fish?* This train of thought strikes me as rather odd and I put it down to the very late hour and sleep deprivation.

I grapple with the ancient and heavy bunch of keys for the Library. The familiar smell and sound of old metal seems even more pronounced in the chill, dark air. The physical weight of the keys is somewhat muted by the intangible gravitas possessed by certain instruments, that only age and experience can acquire. With some effort, I turn the key in the lock and let myself into the Library.

I would love to say that the Library at night is a mystical, haunting place – but it really isn't. It is much the same as it is in the daytime, just darker. It does feel a little unusual without its studious inhabitants, sprawling books and papers and laptops all over the place, but the books seem to have a presence all of their own which somehow makes the place seem occupied. I set about finding the neo-classical section. Obviously, it must be on the ground floor. Although - I am learning not to be surprised by anything at Old College, so a trap door to a Crypt on any one of the four floors would not be so far from the realms of possibility.

It does not take me too long to discover the neo-classical section, tucked away in an alcove at the rear of the Library. A cursory glance at the books suggests to me that neo-classical is a type of architecture. Some sculpture, too. You learn something new every day. Dr J said the trapdoor was under the carpet. I get down on my hands and knees and tentatively feel around the edges of the worn floor covering for any inconsistencies. It doesn't take me long to find a loose corner at the base of one of the bookshelves. I give it a bit of a tug. There is some give there, but it doesn't feel like it will come away all that easily. *Bugger it. In for a penny, in for a pound.* A short, sharp tug produces a louder-than-expected tearing sound and the corner of the carpet comes away unhappily from the floor.

I stop.

All of a sudden, this doesn't seem like such a good idea. I am on my hands and knees in the middle of the night, tearing up a carpet in one of the oldest libraries in The City. This is more like vandalism than exploration. For a moment, I consider running along to the Maintenance sheds to find some super glue to repair the damage I have caused. That thought is actually quite encouraging, so I decide to tear up the rest anyway, I can always repair it later on.

The carpet makes a protesting screech as I liberate it from the floor. But it is worth it. There, laid in to the cold stone floor is a wooden trapdoor. My intake of breath would be audible, if there were anyone there to hear it. There it is! It doesn't look as old as I thought it might. It must have been replaced at some point in the relatively recent past. The lock looks fairly new, as well. I reason that the trapdoor would have to be well maintained for safety reasons, what with it being in such a regularly used location, so I shouldn't be quite so surprised. This makes finding the right key a straightforward task – it is the most modern-looking key on the bunch. The key is in the lock before I have even thought about it. It turns easily and I am able to lift the trapdoor with unexpected ease. All the films you see about people heaving open ancient secret doors in a cloud of dust accompanied by dramatic creaking and groaning sounds have somewhat let me down.

The open trapdoor reveals some rickety wooden steps leading down into the gloom. These steps do look incredibly old and have not received the same attention as the door that conceals them. The air coming up through the hole is warm and dank and has a smell I cannot quite describe – somewhere between musty and acidic. I shine my torch down and see that there are about eight steps leading down to a stone floor. Well, I'm here now; I can't very well *not* go down there. I move into a sitting position and test the strength of the steps with my feet. I am not totally confident that they will take my weight, but I am only small so it will probably be alright.

With the greatest of caution, I make my way down the steps. My torch offers me tantalising snapshots of the room below; stone walls, old broken furniture, huge tarnished candlesticks bereft of wick and wax. It feels more like a cellar than a crypt. I reach the bottom of the stairs and swing my torch around expectantly. I am in a narrow-ish room scattered with odds and ends that the College clearly has no further use for but didn't want to throw away. I can see why. Although no longer useful, the artefacts are still beautiful. Something catches my eye. Somewhere ahead of me I think I can see a flicker of light. The gloom prevents me from being able to ascertain the proximity, but it is there, right in front of me.

The hairs on the back of my neck prickle. An ancient and survivalist instinct surfaces at the base of my skull. It is an instinct I have finely tuned over the years, but its basis is ingrained into creatures of all types since the dawn of evolution. It is the instinct *that you are not alone.* I stand so still my heart almost stops beating. I strain my ears to the very limit of their ability. There is something. The faintest, softest, almost scratching sound. It is irregular, not consistent. All my other senses immediately leap into action and I am suddenly very aware of the thick, unpleasant smell and taste in the undisturbed air; the menacing shadows that are now bearing down upon me; the feel of the oppressive dampness cloying my skin.

39

The effects of adrenalin on the human body in a stressful situation are well documented and have been drilled in to me through training and experience. I recognise and over-ride the *fight or flight* instinct and wrestle back some logical thought processes. There can be very little in Old College that could do me any real harm, especially as I am in possession of a heavy, blunt object in the shape of my torch. Anything that is not susceptible to the considerably convincing aspects of a Mag-Light is probably not worth being too frightened of, on the grounds that it doesn't exist. Come on, then. Let's go and check it out.

I move slowly and soundlessly towards the source of the light ahead of me. The faint scratching sound becomes a little more discernable... I recognise the sound, it is so familiar... what is it? As I get closer, I can make out a small, narrow stone archway in the wall. The light is coming from beyond. There must be another room. I switch off my torch so as not to bring attention to my presence; the element of surprise may be useful. Unconsciously, my grip on the torch alters and I move carefully to the mouth of the archway. Peeking through, I can see that there is, indeed, another room. It is illuminated by several candles, which are placed on... blimey. This really is a Crypt. This second room is larger than the one I entered. Wider, deeper and, I don't mind admitting, a little spookier. Why spookier? I don't know, it must be the tombs. There are about twelve stone tombs, all beautifully ornate, lined like sleeping sentries throughout the room.

Mesmerised, I walk through the archway and into the sepulchre. It is actually quite beautiful in the candlelight, the warm glow on the carved stone giving the feeling of being in a rather macabre sculpture gallery. Hang on, that's a point – the candles. Who lit the candles? There can be very few people in Old College who have the key to the trapdoor. The little scratchy sound that led me in here has stopped. Whatever is in here, knows I'm in here too. My heart is in my mouth. Only one thing for it.

"Hello?" I venture.

"Hello, Deputy Head Porter" I nearly jump clean out of my own skin at the measured, not entirely friendly reply that is delivered in rich, clipped tones. My torch flicks on and I scan the room wildly.

"Who's there?!" I reply, trying to keep my voice steady, automatically adopting a defensive stance. My torchlight falls on a figure, hunched in a battered old chair between two of the tombs. As the harsh, battery-operated beam falls upon my unseen companion, the figure raises a hand to deflect it as it unfurls itself from the chair and stands up. It is a tall, thin, immaculately dressed man with carefully coiffured white hair. I let the beam of my torch drop to the floor. It is The Master of College.

"Deputy Head Porter, this is indeed a surprise."

"Yes, your Lordship, this is a surprise." The Master is both a Professor *and* a Lord of the Realm. This is impressive, even by Old College standards.

"Won't you join me? I am just doing some sudoko puzzles." *Pen on paper! That was the sound!*

"At this late hour, Sir? In here?"

"The hour is actually rather early, I feel" The Master replies, kindly. And I suppose he is right; we are at that rather confusing point in time that could be either very late at night or very early in the morning, depending on your point of view.

The Master returns to his worn old chair between the tombs and gestures to a less inviting wooden stool, abandoned near the archway. I pull up the stool and join him between the tombs. In the candlelight, The Master is a striking man. He is aged and withered, but his eyes are sharp and alive and as clear as night. A fierce intelligence sizzles behind them, and it is not simply the academic intelligence of one who has stuffed their head with books for years, but a genuine, frightening, brilliance. The delicately lined skin on his face clings to his skull with grim determination. The passage of time has not completely hidden the fact that this was once a very powerful, handsome face.

"What brings you here at this hour, Deputy Head Porter?" The Master's words are spoken beautifully, but with an underlying air of razor wire.

".... Security patrols?" I offer, feebly. "How...?"

"There is a passageway from The Lodge that allows me access to The Crypt," The Master replies, anticipating my question. Of course. I remember from The Guided Tour that The Master's Lodge has secret passageways to almost all of Old College. The Master continues "Back from the days when The Old Masters where interred here after their deaths." It is they who occupy the tombs that surround us.

"But what are you doing down here, Sir?" I ask.

"I told you. Sudoku. It is peaceful here. I am never disturbed. Until now."

"But isn't it a little... spooky?" I ignore his last two words deliberately.

"Spooky? Deputy Head Porter, I am a man of science! I do not get... spooked"

He is a Professor of Economics, but maybe that is a type of science. I feel it is not my place to point this out, nor to pursue it further. And, actually, the dead bodies aside, it isn't that spooky. It is, in fact, rather beautiful down here. A thought strikes me.

"Your Lordship, I share your pragmatic view. But in a place as ancient as Old College, surely there must be some ghost stories from over the years? If such a thing were to be true, could Old College be haunted?"

The faintest of smiles appears on his thin lips and he waves an elegant, spindly hand dismissively.

"Oh, you would think so, wouldn't you? But no. Old College seems to be completely without ghost stories. Do you find that strange?"

I must admit that I do. You would think, at some point in the last six hundred years, there would have been someone with an over active imagination and prone to mystical dramatics. Particularly when you consider the amount of drink consumed on the premises, by students and Fellows alike.

"It is a little odd, Sir."

"But then, I believe ghosts, if there are such things, only appear following violent or unexplained deaths." I am not qualified to confirm or deny The Master's theory, so merely shrug. "I understand that there needs to be some kind of trauma surrounding the death. Nothing of that ilk has happened at Old College."

"But people must die here, surely" I ask, reasonably.

"Oh, certainly!" The Master replies. "It is not unusual at all for elderly Fellows to pass away here. Occasionally students, but it has been very rare. But Fellows... I remember dear old Dr D. Fellow of English, as I recall."

"He died in Old College?"

"Yes, in his chair by the fire in the Senior Combination Room. It was nearly a full twenty-four hours before anyone realised he was dead. The latter part of his career was spent asleep in that chair and it was only when he failed to turn up for lunch the following day that we realised something was wrong."

"He doesn't come back for hauntings, then?"

"Not that I am aware. His passing was like his life. Very peaceful. He probably doesn't even realise he has died." This last statement is unnervingly devoid of humour.

"It does seem strange there have been no ghostly sightings *at all*" the disappointment in my voice is barely concealed.

"Yes, well, perhaps" replies The Master. Then, "Although... there was something, when the Porters' Lodge was rebuilt. The ground..."

"When was the Porters' Lodge rebuilt?" I ask, surprised. I didn't know this.

"Oh, many years ago, when I was an undergraduate" The Master's eyes, for the briefest of moments, mist over and a darkness seems to fall upon him. "When the ground was dug for the new foundations... it was..." The Master seems to catch himself and simply shakes his head. I am intrigued.

"What about the ground? Was there something there?"

"It... was just very old ground, that's all. Very... old ground."

An uneasy silence falls between us.

"Deputy Head Porter, you must get about your business," The Master's voice cuts through the musty air of the Crypt. "Daylight will soon be upon us."

"Yes Sir. Thank you for your time."

I leave the Crypt the way I came in and head to the Maintenance sheds to find something to repair the vandalised carpet in the Library. What was in the ground beneath the Porters' Lodge, I wonder? Something The Master does not deem communicable with a College servant, such as myself. A chill wriggles its way up my spine, and I feel it has little to do with the cold morning air. Old College obviously has a few skeletons in its closet. Skeletons? Hmm. I make a mental note to be more perceptive of the darker side of Old College in future. I also decided that this conversation is best kept to myself for the time being. My tired mind is racing and I feel that I will not be sleeping very easily when I finally make it to my bed.

Private Eye

I AM HAPPILY SIPPING TEA in the Porters' Lodge when I hear a commotion at the front desk. Mug in hand, I go to investigate and find Porter frantically tiding the front desk and emitting four letter words, not quite under his breath.

"What's up?" I ask, a little concerned. Porter is the epitome of cool, calm efficiency and I wonder what has caused him to panic so.

"Junior Bursar has just been on the phone, he is on his way down to The Lodge," he replies, her cheeks flushed above his bristling moustache. "He does not sound happy."

I roll my eyes and huff. Junior Bursar rarely sounds happy, but I have learnt that he is rather prone to dramatics. I am faintly amused and interested to know what minor catastrophe he has in store for me today. I tuck my mug of tea into one of The Fellows' pigeonholes behind me as Junior Bursar throws open the door of the Lodge, almost liberating it from its hinges in the process.

He has that look on his face. The look of barely-concealed glee of one who takes great pleasure in departing bad news. The mask of concern he wears does a poor job of hiding the macabre smile playing across his lips. I have seen this look before, generally just before he allocates to me a task he deems too testing for me.

"Good afternoon, Junior Bursar," I greet him with a bright smile. This seems to unnerve him a little. "I do hope you are well,"

"Yes, yes, indeed, Deputy Head Porter" comes the irritated reply. "Listen, there is a matter you must attend to immediately."

44

Ah, yes, I thought as much. A matter I must attend to immediately. Why are there never matters that must be attended to by the end of the day? Or by a week next Tuesday? I am becoming a specialist in Matters That Must Be Attended To Immediately. I wonder if Old College offers a PhD course? Hmmm.

"Deputy Head Porter, you're not paying attention!" Junior Bursar must have noticed my eyes glaze over.

"Sorry, Sir, I…"

"Well! I expect you to listen when I'm… I say, what's that in The Dean's pigeonhole?"

I realise, with mild horror, that it is my mug of tea.

"It's a mug of tea, Sir," I reply, having a lack of anything more substantial to say.

"Well! If The Dean can have his tea delivered by the Porters I expect to be offered the same privilege,"

"…Certainly Sir, it's a new procedure we are testing, just to see if it takes off, you know, I thought The Fellowship might like to have their beverages delivered along with their post." It is a weak explanation, I know, but Junior Bursar seems to be considering it.

"Hmm! Yes, I suppose… what about biscuits? Would the Porters bring biscuits, too? Because I don't want crumbs all over my post. I suggest a secondary device for transporting the biscuits."

"Duly noted, Sir," I reply, as solemnly as I can. I see an opportunity, albeit a tiny one, to avoid the rest of my conversation with Junior Bursar. "Well, I suppose I should be getting this tea to The Dean…"

"Deputy Head Porter, have you forgotten that I have an urgent matter for you?" Junior Bursar sounds furious, but I am guessing mainly at himself for becoming sidetracked by tea-envy. "There has been a crime, well! A series of crimes, really, committed in College these last couple of weeks. The crimes are of a fairly serious nature and Dr F is incandescent with rage!"

Ha! 'Incandescent with rage'! I've only ever seen that phrase written down, I didn't think people actually said it. Anyway.

"What's happened?" I ask, getting a little worried now.

"Every week, Dr F has his copy of *Private Eye* magazine delivered to the Senior Combination Room for his perusal. Today is the third consecutive week that *Private Eye* has not reached the Senior Combination Room.

Clearly, it is being stolen and the miscreant responsible must be exposed and removed from Old College at once."

A thought occurs to me.

"Have you spoken to The Fellowship, Sir? Perhaps someone has been borrowing it…"

"Don't be so foolish, Deputy Head Porter," comes Junior Bursar's agitated reply "The Fellowship don't borrow each others' newspapers. It is being stolen, I tell you, and I want you to find out who is responsible. I want a preliminary report by the end of the day."

When Junior Bursar has stamped his way out of the Lodge, I retrieve my mug of tea from The Dean's pigeonhole and turn to Porter, who is looking at me sympathetically.

"What do you think?" I ask him "Do you think someone is really stealing Dr F's copy of *Private Eye*?"

Porter shrugs. "It doesn't seem likely," he replies. "The Fellowship would know it belonged to Dr F, the only other people with access to the Senior Combination Room are the Porters and the Bedders."

"I can't see any of our chaps being avid readers of *Private Eye*," I conclude, somewhat cynically, I feel.

"I can't see any of the Porters being avid readers, full stop" Porter confirms my conclusion.

"Hmm, and the Bedders even less so," I agree.

"It must be going somewhere," says Porter, little cogs in his head evidently turning. I take a long sip of tea.

"Maybe it's not making it as far as the Senior Combination Room," I muse "Perhaps it is going astray somewhere on the way."

"Well, you'll have to come up with something to put in your report to Junior Bursar"

I think a little on the conundrum, until my desk phone interrupts me.

"Deputy Head Porter? It's The Dean here"

"Good afternoon, Sir, I hope you are well," my enquiry is uninspired and insincere, my mind on weightier matters.

"Very well, thank you. Junior Bursar tells me you have made me a cup of tea? Bring it up, will you, I'm parched."

I close my eyes. I sigh.

"Yes, Sir. Right away Sir…"

To Catch A Thief

I MUST SAY, THE DEAN was very appreciative of having a cup of tea delivered to his rooms. It was a bit tepid by the time I had carted it across the river and up two flights of stairs and, on reflection, he thought it would have just been easier for him to make it himself in his office but – he seemed quite pleased nonetheless. My hastily invented, and then abandoned, tea delivery service idea was deemed charming but impractical. Thank God. I have no idea how I would have explained to Head Porter that our staff are now tea maids for The Fellowship.

More frustratingly, I had wasted valuable time that I should have been spending investigating the mysterious disappearance of Dr F's copy of *Private Eye*. I make the obvious enquiries with the newsagent who supplies Old College, I speak to the humourless but surprisingly helpful Head Of Housekeeping. Abrasive at the best of times, Head Of Housekeeping is not amused at the finger of blame being pointed at her staff, but once I explain that, actually, the finger of blame is merely being waved in their general direction, she relents a little. She will look into it, but is of the same opinion of Porter and I. It seems a little unlikely. (By the way, I am not sure why we are all making the same sweeping judgements on the average readership of *Private Eye*, for all I know housekeeping staff absolutely love it).

I speak to the Porters responsible for delivering the papers these last few weeks. All confirm that Dr F's reading material was safely deposited in the Senior Combination Room on each occasion. I have no reason to disbelieve them.

The pink-tinged fingers of dusk are creeping across the sky and I am painfully aware that Junior Bursar will be requiring a report any minute now. I stare at my keyboard and huff and puff a little, enough to attract the attention of Porter.

"Did you find out anything about our mystery thief?" he asks.

"Not much," I reply "Nothing we didn't know already. The magazine is definitely being delivered to College from the newsagent. The Porters delivering the newspapers are all adamant that it was there and that they put it on the reading table in the Senior Combination Room. Head Of Housekeeping is looking into things but their rota means that the Bedder has already cleaned the room before the papers are delivered. That would mean a Bedder going back especially to steal that publication, which seems a little strange. Particularly as the Bedder responsible for that floor is Eastern European and has limited English."

"I don't think it's the Porters. I have known most of them for over fifteen years. I know they're not always the most reliable of people, but they are certainly not thieves."

"I don't think it's the Porters, either," I reply. "But clearly someone is taking the bloody thing."

"Junior Bursar is going to want something a little more elaborate than that," Porter sniffs.

"Yes, don't worry, he'll get his report. I have a feeling I'm making this more difficult for myself than is necessary. There could be a simple explanation I have over-looked."

"Oh? What's that, then?" I don't reply, but starting tapping feverously away at my keyboard. Within five minutes, Junior Bursar has his report and I have a plan. I feel more optimistic about the matter entirely. The thing with having a plan is, it doesn't have to be a particularly good plan, it just has to be a plan. It is far better than having no plan at all, and my plan has been so sketchily outlined to Junior Bursar that it is very open to interpretation. But it looks like I know what I'm doing and actually, like all the best plans, it is simplicity itself.

Case Closed

It is early Wednesday morning and I am waiting by the window of the Porters' Lodge. It is still dark and there is a frost. The ground twinkles coldly, a mirror of the star studded sky above. The City's early morning populous are going about their business, while the commuter classes are still sleeping. It is that interesting part of the day, just after the night people have finished their labours, but before the day people begin theirs.

I see people shuffling along, coats buttoned up against the cold, heading to who knows where. Some look like labourers, burly chaps in multiple layers topped off with high viz jackets of all kinds. Others have the appearance of late night revellers doing the Walk Of Shame, their flimsy outfits ineffective and ridiculous at this sober hour. One figure catches my eye. The many layers of mismatched clothing make it impossible to tell if their wearer is male or female. A well-worn and filthy woolly hat completes the cocoon effect. The figure walks slowly and without purpose, illuminated briefly by the streetlights as it passes beneath, like some sort of wretched performer on an unforgiving stage. I wonder where he or she might be going. I suspect he or she wonders the same thing.

Approaching the imposing iron gates of Old College is the man I have been waiting for, the newsagent. He has in his arms The Fellowship's newspapers, including, I hope, Dr F's copy of *Private Eye*. I exit the Lodge and meet him at the gates, taking his burden from him. I make a cursory check of the bundle. Sure enough, there it is, nestled between *The Independent* and *The Financial Times*.

Back in the Lodge, I flick back to the magazine that has caused so much uproar in Old College recently and stare at it sternly, as if to admonish it for the part it has played in recent events. *Don't you dare go missing today,* I think to myself. I realise that trying to send my thoughts telepathically to an inanimate object is fairly pointless, but it is early and I haven't had enough tea yet. I take my trusty pen from my jacket pocket, and carefully write two words on the top right hand corner of the front page.

I transport the papers myself to the Senior Combination Room, placing them carefully on the table. Another, last, final check. Yes, *Private Eye* is now safely delivered. The Senior Combination Room is eerily quiet, its usual occupants still tucked up in their beds. The well worn, but still sumptuous, leather chairs are scattered haphazardly about the place, standing forlornly in the same places their incumbents left them last night. The Bedder obviously hasn't been in yet; she must be running late. No matter. I return to the Lodge, and wait for my plan to take effect.

Several hours later and I haven't heard any rumblings from The Fellowship. This is a very good sign. Just to be sure, I ask Porter to call Dr F and see if he is in receipt of his weekly publication. Praise the Lord, he is. Marvellous. All that remains, is for the culprit to reveal himself.

I have to wait several days for my cunning plot to reach fruition. I am on the phone when Dr J bounces into the Porters' Lodge, his scarf and jacket fluttering wildly. The much-vaunted lycra cycling suit is happily omitted from today's outfit. He waits patiently by my desk for me to finish my conversation.

"Good afternoon, Dr J, I hope you are well."

"Yes, thank you, all good here," he replies cheerfully, one hand absent-mindedly twisting locks of his curly brown hair. "I wondered if you could do me a favour?"

"Of course, what is it?" I ask, hoping that I already know the answer.

"Could you arrange for another copy of *Private Eye* to be delivered along with the papers? The one I've been reading apparently belongs to Dr F, so I thought I'd better make arrangements for one for myself. Can you do that?"

The smile that breaks across my face must have been a little confusing and unnerving for Dr J, who looks at me strangely as I reply, with the utmost enthusiasm,

"Certainly, Sir. That will be no problem at all. I will see to it right away!"

I relay the tale to Porter over a cup of tea later that afternoon.

"So, all you did was write Dr F's name on the top of the magazine?" he asks.

"Yes! Can you believe it? Bloody Fellowship, all they had to do was ask around and it would have resolved weeks ago. Why won't they ever do anything for themselves?"

Porter laughs and shakes his head.

"You still have an awful lot to learn about life in College!" he exclaims, the disbelief in her voice plainly evident.

Clearly, I do. But I'm starting to get the gist of it, just about.

The Committee For The Prevention
Of Drunken Behaviour

I FLICK ON THE KETTLE in the Porters' Lodge and drag my mug from the sink to the counter. My churning stomach and aching joints are telling me that I may have overdone the cabernet sauvignon last night. My head feels like it has a family of Mexicans living in it. Why, why, why did I drink on a school night? It wasn't intentional. A chat with a friend turned into dancing round the kitchen with a friend which turned into staying up too late and putting the world to rights over a bottle (maybe more than one bottle) of red. Stupid, stupid, stupid. The tea bag takes three attempts to make it into the mug. Most of the sugar ends up on the kitchen counter. Some of the milk makes it into the mug to complete my morning cup of salvation.

Frank Sinatra once said, "Alcohol may be man's worst enemy, but the Bible says love your enemy". It is true, that of all the Gods, Bacchus is probably my favourite, but I normally reserve my indulgences for times when I am not required to do much the day after. Seeing the students (and quite a few Fellows, come to that) in the undignified throes of intoxication on a regular basis has tempered my relationship with the demon drink. Or so I thought.

That said, I'm not sure I entirely understand those who do not drink at all, at least not those who, for some sort of self-righteous reason, think they know right from wrong better than the rest of us. The steadfast refusal to get drunk suggests to me a fear or loathing of something deep down inside and you cannot trust a person who is afraid of that. Although there is no dignity in the stumbling and heaving that excess alcohol induces, it at least teaches you something of humility. It is a reminder of the foolishness and failings that come with being human. It is pretty difficult to take yourself too seriously when you are face down on the bathroom floor.

Three cups of tea and one of Chef's celebrated bacon and sausage sandwiches brings my operational levels up to 'functional'. By the time the other Porters arrive, all that remains of my over-indulgence is a dull ache in my head. The Mexicans have moved out.

I have been thinking about the 'very old ground' comment during my conversation with The Master. It was a bit of an odd thing to say, surely. Isn't all ground 'old'? Strange. I also begin to wonder exactly how many people have died at Old College over the years. I feel I am in danger of becoming a little morbid.

The phone on my desk bursts into life. I pick up the receiver to be greeted by the softly-spoken tones of Senior Tutor, a gentle and kindly man whose conciliate manner belies his past as a decorated officer in the Special Forces.

"Deputy Head Porter, it is Senior Tutor here, I trust you are well?" I confirm that I am (a little white lie) and enquire after his own health. He is resplendently well, thank you.

"Deputy Head Porter, I would like you to cast your eye over a document I have produced. I am setting up a new College Committee which I would very much like you to be part of. I have produced a little aide memoire to facilitate our work and I would like you to read it and make any suggestions you see fit."

"Certainly, Sir, I would be pleased to. May I ask what Committee I will be joining?"

"Oh yes, how remiss of me. It is The Committee For The Prevention Of Drunken Behaviour" The irony is not lost on me. "The alcohol related incidents this term are far more numerous than we are used to at Old College. Our reputation could be endangered if these antics are allowed to continue. I would very much appreciate your input on this matter."

I assure Senior Tutor that I would be delighted to join The Committee and would head up to his office shortly to collect his document.

A little under an hour later and I am reading the 'aide memoire' at my desk in the Porters' Lodge. The document offers such priceless advice as

"...prod the intoxicated person regularly" and "...do not force vomiting but encourage them to eat food, if possible." Interestingly, Senior Tutor insists that on finding an unconscious intoxicated person, the first course of action is to contact the Porters' Lodge. I can think of many actions to take when coming across someone who is unconscious and they involve checking airways and the recovery position. An ambulance is often a consideration. I add some helpful first aid advice to the document and make a mental note to tactfully question the wisdom of constantly poking someone and offering them food whilst unconscious, then hurry back to Senior Tutor's office. You would think an email would be the more obvious approach; Old College prefers the personal touch.

Senior Tutor has been joined in his office (which is functional, but beautifully presented) by the other members of the newly-formed 'Committee For The Prevention Of Drunken Behaviour'. I am greeted by the Chair of the Student Union, a youth who looks about twelve and bares a striking resemblance to Harry Potter. He shifts uneasily on the Chesterfield, his solemn expression telling me that he is not relishing the prospect of having to curtail the student past time of choice. Also present is College Nurse, a formidable Scottish lady of about sixty-five whose delicate frame belies her fiery and out-spoken nature. Sat next to Nurse, theatrically brandishing a tea cup, is The Dean. I am quietly in awe of The Dean. I am fascinated with his attire. Last week he wore a purple v-neck jumper with a bright pink shirt and royal blue trousers. Today, he is wearing yellow trousers and a mustard-coloured roll-neck. His age is indeterminate due to carefully dyed hair and a generally well maintained appearance. He is of a jolly disposition, although I have heard tales of him losing his patience on occasion. Today, though, he seems to be in fine spirits and is talking loudly with Senior Tutor. No sign of Junior Bursar. I didn't think this would be his scene, somehow.

"Let us begin the meeting!" Senior Tutor announces cheerfully. "Now, I'm sure we are all aware of recent incidents in College involving some of our First Years over indulging in drink,"

The nods and murmurs around the room are dripping in over-dramatised concern.

"I, like you all, I'm sure, hoped that these incidents would reduce significantly after Fresher's Week. This is sadly not the case and several of our students have required medical attention following an evening's revelry. My concern is that sooner or later we will have a serious incident on our hands, possibly even a fatality. I have called this Committee together to find ways to reduce the risk of this, and to better educate our students about the risks they are taking."

Chair of the Student Union looks crest-fallen. Under his careful guidance, Old College has built up the reputation of throwing some of the best theme parties in town. Students from other colleges flock to Old College events from across The City. This achievement was the one and only thing the scholarly young man had ever done that was 'cool'. After years of being bullied for being over-achieving and bad at sports, Chair of the Student Union has masterminded a series of legendary parties, which had made him a sort of geeky demi-god. And now it was all going to be taken away from him.

Nurse suggests some basic first aid advice, which Senior Tutor scribbles down furiously. Then commences a debate of the recovery position, and the best use thereof.

"What if the person is conscious but clearly drunk?" asks Senior Tutor "Should we try and get them into the recovery position anyway?"

"That would be a good idea, if they are compliant," Nurse replies.

"What if they're not compliant?" suggests The Dean

"We should probably try and force them into the recovery position anyway," Senior Tutor replies, somewhat unexpectedly. "Better to be safe than sorry".

"What if the drunkard is a girl?" The Dean continues. "We can't have our Porters wrestling drunk young ladies to the floor and forcing them to lie on their sides, think of our reputation!"

"Well, that would need to be a consideration, but the Porters should be able to physically persuade them into a position where they will be less of a danger to themselves..."

I decide to interject. "I think," I say as politely as I can "That if the person is upright and able to physically fend us off they are probably not in need of urgent medical attention. Our main concern should be getting them to their lodgings with as little disruption as possible. I feel trying to force them onto the ground, male or female, will only inflame the situation."

"That is one way of looking at it," says Senior Tutor "But I think it should be thought about. It would be easier to prod them repeatedly from the recovery position."

"I don't think…" I begin, but am cut off by Nurse.

"Yes, and it's important to keep talking to them, as well," she explains, beginning a brief brainstorming session of how to arose one from a drunken stupor. I feel that the distinction between conscious and unconscious drunkenness have been horribly blurred and the whole procedure appears that it will consist of getting people down on the floor and poking them incessantly. Maybe it's the hangover, or maybe I've missed something, but this doesn't make any sense to me at all.

The meeting closes with Senior Tutor having made endless notes and a promise to update us shortly. The next meeting will be about how to prevent the students from getting into such a state in the first place.

I simply cannot wait to find out what ideas The Committee For The Prevention Of Drunken Behaviour come up with for stopping students doing what comes as naturally to them as breathing and long division.

It seems not very many, as The Committee is not recalled for the rest of Michaelmas Term. This is faintly disappointing, especially as I do not even get a chance to execute the all-new 'recovery position' with its added extras of prodding and force-feeding. And I had such high hopes for the festive season, as well.

An Uninvited Guest

I AM SO FED UP with having my meals interrupted. If eating is such an important part of College life, why do crises always happen at mealtimes?

Today, it is the Full English that will lie sadly uneaten on its plate. Junior Bursar, the constant factor in my mealtime disruption, is bearing down on me, incident book in hand.

"A student in Old Court was caught smoking in his room in the early hours of this morning," Junior Bursar smells of fried eggs and black pudding. "The substance he was suspected of smoking is cannabis!"

Well, I suppose that smoking cannabis is actually against the law. More importantly, it seems, it is also against College policy. The problem with College policy being law is that it only operates during office hours (this is something that strikes me as in need of reform). When the offence was committed, College Justice was safely tucked up in bed. In the cold light of day, the scene is cold but justice must be seen to be done. Head Porter and I are to conduct a search of the student's bedroom.

Now, any sensible person caught smoking cannabis in the wee small hours has plenty of time to dispose of the evidence before The Fellowship roll up. Even an insensible person would probably have smoked their stash by now, anyway. Still, I am rolling up my sleeves and putting on latex gloves stolen from the first aid box.

Mercifully, Head Porter agrees to search the bedroom / bathroom area, leaving me to search the living / study area. Although I have been up to my elbows in far more hideous scenes than this, somehow sorting through a teenager's boxers and toiletries is unthinkable. We are supervised by the watchful eye of Junior Bursar, who evidently is enthralled with the drama of the scene, but doesn't fancy getting his hands dirty. I cannot say I blame him.

I focus on the task in hand. My search technique is methodical and thorough. I am naturally nosey and have always loved sorting through the mundane personal effects of others. In past times it has made me feel so much better about myself. As I sifted through the grubby personal effects of suspected drug dealers on their filthy bare floors, I would feel so lucky that life had not led me down that path. This gives me almost the same feeling, but in such a different way.

The student in question (a nineteen year old white male with the obligatory floppy blond fringe, retreating jaw line and over-fed mid-drift) is studying politics. He writes neatly, but ineffectually. He banks with Coutts. He is ashamed of his sexual conquests. How to I know all this? I've read his essays. I've seen his cheque book. I have found his secret stash of used condoms and their wrappers! I shudder to think what he will eventually grow into. The over-pampered educated classes of our society are a real worry.

So obviously, I find no cannabis. What I do find is even more shocking (to Junior Bursar). Another item banned by College legislation.

It is badly hidden under a discarded coat. The main giveaway is the telltale squeak of the wheel. I discard the coat to reveal the expected hamster cage. I realise that the hamster is suspected of no offence, so therefore I really shouldn't be searching his house. Then again, It's only a bloody hamster so why not?

The hamster is not concealing a consignment of drugs. However, it is still an illegal immigrant in itself. Seeing an opportunity, I usher out Junior Bursar with the promise of dealing with this incident. The student is clearly a good friend of Mary Jane, judging by the stack of king-size silver Rizla I find in his room. (The only thing that is king-sized, I might add). Then again, kids will be kids and the student is obviously a posh boy away from home for the first time. Easily sorted.

Junior Bursar returns to his office and Head Porter returns to the Lodge. I wait in the room for the arrival of the student. He arrives back soon after the departures of my superiors. He doesn't seem that alarmed to see me. While we were conducting the search, he was being read his rights by Senior Tutor. He is just praying that the College don't call his parents.

As he walks through the door I am sitting at his easy chair near the desk. I introduce myself. He asks if we found any drugs in his room. Like he needed to ask. I tell him that we didn't. I tell him what we did find. The look on his face is priceless. Then I tell him about the hamster.

"What's his name?" I ask "What's the hamster's name?"

"His name is Murray" the student replies, already on the back foot.

"Murray? Nice name for a hamster" If I had an over-sized cigar I would have taken a drag. "You know pets are banned, right?"

"Umm, well, I don't really know..."

"Well they are. If you don't want Murray passed into the custody of The Master's Cat I suggest you find somewhere outside of College to smoke your weed." I take a breath and look into his eyes. Cocky little bastard. "I'm serious. If I hear your name in College again I'm feeding Murray to the fucking cat. Stay out of the Porters' way."

With that, I stride from the easy chair and out of the room, never letting my gaze leave that of the student. I know it. He knows it. For both of the incidents of copulation he has engaged in since the start of term, he has used extra small condoms. Killing Murray is one thing, destroying his opportunity of sexual gratification for his entire student life is quite another. I feel confident he will pose no further problems.

Christmas Eve At Old College

It is Christmas Eve at Old College. I am alone in the Porters' Lodge, College is closing down for a few days over the festive period and all that remains is to lock down the place. I cannot complete the lock down until after four o'clock, which is when the Library closes. I cannot fathom why the Library has to be open until four, there is almost no one left in College at all. The students have long since departed to their families for Christmas and the last of the Fellowship left this morning. There were a couple of the chaps from Maintenance in earlier today, but right now I am the only soul in the whole of Old College. Apart from, quite possibly, The Master's Cat, who I am sure will not be going out of his way to visit the Library.

I have several tasks and errands to run to while away the few remaining hours of my shift. They mainly involve checking and locking many of the doors and gates, but I also have several hand-written notes of instruction from some of the Fellowship. Dr G, for example, wants me to move his car for him. Dr J has asked for his wine delivery to be taken to his rooms, ready for his return in the New Year. The Dean wants some files moving from his rooms to the Tutorial Office. It's almost like they've given me errands for the sake of it.

It turns out that my demanding Fellows have actually done me a favour. I haven't visited many of the Fellowship's rooms before and it is fascinating to see their little dens of academia. The rooms all have familiar heavy, dark wood furniture – enormous desks with angled lamps as their centrepieces. The curtains are heavy with garish embroidery. All the rooms also have bookcases, like huge wooden monoliths, dominating walls from floor to ceiling. Books bulge and tumble along the shelves, jostling for position with their neighbours. They seem almost animated. I must confess to lingering longer than I need to, just to take in the characters of the rooms. In the still and silent College I can almost hear the echoes of its illustrious past. The whole building feels almost alive. I wonder idly if, when things have been around for such a long time, they acquire some sort of vitality of their own. Maybe it rubs off over the centuries or something.

The Dean's request proves to be the most problematic. His rooms are a chaotic black hole of papers, files, books, notes and letters. Finding the required files takes me nearly an hour. He does have a couple a lovely leather sofas, which I discover during my epic search.

I run my various errands and enjoy the beautiful artwork in Dr C's rooms, gaze in awe at Dr F's book collection and am open mouthed when I discover Junior Bursar's rooms are even worse than The Dean's. Senior Tutor's rooms are, by stark contrast, spectacularly well ordered and neat. His furniture is far more simple and serviceable than the heavy, overly ornate collections favoured by the other Fellows. It seems Old College has not dampened the tendencies of his military past.

I take my time locking up the fabulous and beautiful halls and rooms of Old College. I linger in the oak panelled splendour of the Gathering Room and move slowly and deliberately through the Old Library, which is, I think, my favourite part of Old College. The organ loft is the ideal vantage point to view the Chapel in all its glory. I sit there for a while, feeling quite small and insignificant among the sombre magnificence.

I decide to check that the Senior Combination Room is all in order. The Senior Combination Room is the place to which The Fellowship retreat from time to time (some are more regular visitors than others, it has to be said) to relax and… do whatever it is Fellows do when they are not eating or causing me problems. Like a rather elaborate snug.

The Senior Combination Room is located very close to the Dining Hall. This, I feel, is due less to luck than some very careful planning. I don't come in here much. For a reason I cannot quite put my finger on, I feel happier to give this room a wide berth. The last time I was in here, I was ensuring the safe delivery of Dr F's *Private Eye* magazine. Somehow, it seems like a long time ago. Then, I notice something a little strange. Well, very strange. The fire is still lit. I cannot imagine why this is. I make my way towards the yawning great stone fireplace, which is being huddled by several worn and elderly leather chairs. I stop. One of the chairs appears to be occupied.

"Ahem!" A theatrical cough: the universal sign of politely saying 'I'm here!'

The figure shifts a little in the chair, the aged leather creaking and complaining at the movement. There then follows another sound, which I suppose could be blamed on the chair but I suspect it is emanating from the occupant.

"Sir?"

When a voice finally comes from the chair, it is as creaky and complaining as the chair itself.

"Who is it that disturbs my sleep?"

"Sir, it is Deputy Head Porter. I am sorry to disturb you…"

"Is it time for lunch?"

"No, Sir, the kitchens are closed. I am shutting down Old College for Christmas…"

"No lunch! I say…" the rest of the sentence is lost in something between a mumble and a gurgle. It is a little troubling that I have a snoozing Fellow who doesn't seem to know what day it is before me, but then again it wouldn't be for the first time. As I am trying to formulate a suitably emphatic argument for him vacating the Senior Combination Room, I am distracted by a pile of magazines seemingly flying across the room behind me. I spin round, more perturbed than anything. Ah. One of the windows is still open. It must have been the breeze.

I skip over and shut the window, a little annoyed. I return to the fireplace to deal with my dozing Fellow. And here's the thing. *He isn't there.* The chair is completely empty, save for a rather threadbare cushion and some toffee wrappers. And here's the *other* thing. *The fire isn't lit.* It doesn't look as if it has been lit for a day or so. Not a smoulder, not an ember. I swear I can detect the faintest whiff of woody smoke in the air. An icy chill slowly drip-drips its way along my spine and I shudder involuntarily. Was that… I mean, it couldn't have been. There are no ghosts in Old College, The Master had said. I stop. Still. Think. I recall my conversation with The Master in the Crypt, not so very long ago. Dr D? Had he come back for

Christmas Eve? It sounds a little daft even as I say it to myself. But then...
but then, it is time to lock the Library.

Unlike the Old Library, which is more akin to an ancient book shrine
of some description, the Library is probably about as slick as you can get
using a 600 year old building. It covers four floors, with the rather smug
sounding Law Library at the top. It gives me the impression that it looks
down on the rest of the Library.

The locking up passes without incident. My work is complete. As I
make my way through the cloisters and courtyards towards the Porters'
Lodge I feel almost a little sad to be leaving. I pause to enjoy the beauty
of The Master's Lodge and reflect upon my place in the grand scheme
of things. Just a simple caretaker of this fascinating seat of learning,
one of many others, our simple tasks echoing back through time almost
unchanged. Even The Fellowship, aged as they are, are positively embryonic
compared to Old College itself. If Old College had eyes, their presence in
its company would have passed in the blink of one. Even the most eminent
and long-serving members had barely ever stopped by long enough for a
cup of tea, from Old College's point of view. No matter what minor trifles
occur within its walls, Old College will always be Old College. Stoic,
unchanging, it's got *staying power*. All the pomp and circumstance is just
a bit of a smoke screen to cover up the fact that the world around it has
changed and it doesn't want to. And no one can make it.

It is Christmas Eve and I am all alone in Old College. If there were any
poetic justice in the world, flakes of snow would start to fall and a distant
choir would start to sing. Needless to say, neither of these two things occur,
but I still leave Old College feeling very festive and eager to recount the
marvels of the day to those waiting for me.

Resolutions & Revelations

THE CHRISTMAS BREAK IS NOTABLY shorter for College servants than it is for students and The Fellowship. This is to be expected, of course, but I still feel a little hard done by nonetheless as I waddle into the Porters' Lodge from the cold January air. I say waddle, as it is simply the only way to describe my recently acquired gait, following the fairly indulgent festivities of my family Yule time celebrations. My beautifully tailored trousers pinch reproachfully at my bloated, pallid flesh in such a way that I begin to wonder just who these trousers where originally tailored for. Me, obviously, but a pre-festive me who had not yet succumbed to the complacent attitude towards alcohol and pabulum that is so common during the twelfth month.

My eating prowess is well documented, but I am usually fairly sensible about *what* I eat, if not how much. But even my metabolism, so efficient as to verge on the psychotic, has been no match for the rich and delicious festive fare produced in abundance by my overly generous friends and family (brilliant cooks, one and all). I rather feel the free-flowing availability of my Grandfather's wine collection has contributed significantly to the bloating. We are a family of modest means, but my Grandfather's long-standing passion and appreciation of a good, rich red has produced a collection even Old College would have to begrudgingly admire.

Regardless, the New Year is a time for resolutions and I resolve, here and now, to eat and drink less. Or, at the very least, better.

I give it a week.

College remains almost deserted as the students are still enjoying their break. I dare say some of The Fellows may venture in occasionally here and there to work or take advantage of the peace and quiet of the Senior Combination Room. I don't expect to see many of them, though, as the kitchens are closed for another week. I would be unusual to find a Fellow too far from readily available refreshments.

The Lodge feels chilly. My newly acquired fat reserves do little to protect me. There is, however, something to warm the bones of a still hung-over, festively plump Deputy Head Porter. The Porter on duty with me today is, perhaps, my very favourite. Middle-aged, robust, and reassuringly Northern; he reminds me of Father Christmas, had he enjoyed an extensive military career. He is not overly jolly, but is courteous and hard working and has helped me out on more occasions than I care to mention. It was he, of course, who was kind enough to explain the reasons behind my employment.

"Good morning, ma'am!" comes Porter's greeting. "Happy New Year."

"Happy New Year, Porter" I reply. "Did you have a good one?"

"Thank you, ma'am, I did. You?"

"A little too good, I think" is my rueful reply. "Is Head Porter in?"

"Haven't seen him, ma'am." I nod in acknowledgment and make my way to my desk and switch on my computer. There are probably aren't any emails requiring my attention, but I feel obliged to check any way.

I admit to being more pleased than I should be at the news that Head Porter isn't around. After an initially warm welcome, his attitude towards me has been decidedly cooler in recent weeks. Quite why this is so, I cannot be sure. Maybe he has got word that I've found out that he is using me as a pawn in whatever game he is playing. He hasn't actually said anything, not verbally. But his eyes… there is a darkness there. Something I can't quite read. No matter. I have other things on my mind. For example, The Master's comments in the Crypt. About… something… in the ground beneath the Porters' Lodge.

"Hey, Porter" I call across the Lodge.

"You wanting a cup of tea, ma'am?" This stings a little. Surely I requisition the attention of Porters for more varied reasons than the acquisition of cups of tea? Maybe, maybe not.

"No, Porter… well, actually, yes please, if you're putting the kettle on" I rarely refuse a cup of tea. "But I was going to ask you about the Lodge."

"What about it?"

"Do you know anything about it being rebuilt?"

"Rebuilt?" Porter looks like he is thinking, very hard. "When was that, ma'am?"

"I'm not sure, exactly. Must have been decades ago, it was when The Master was an undergraduate."

"Can't say I know anything about it." There is more thinking going on. "I tell you who might, though. Professor K. He might have been knocking around then. Why are you so interested, anyway?"

"Sudden interest in…er… architecture, Porter" it's the best I can manage. "It's part of my New Year's resolution to better myself" I smile. Porter seems convinced. Or at least uninterested enough to move on to tea making.

Professor K, ah yes. I have only met him a couple of times. He is ancient, even by Old College standards. A tiny, wrinkled little bag of bones and genius with, perhaps, the naughtiest twinkly eyes I have ever seen. And I have seen some very naughty eyes, let me assure you. He does not pass through the Lodge very much; I imagine he does not pass anywhere very much any more. I like him. I like his naughty eyes.

"You could try the Senior Combination Room, ma'am" Porter returns with a proper mug of steaming, dark tea, just the way I like it.

"Hmm?"

"Senior Combination Room. Professor K rarely ventures outside of College these days. No family, you see. He might be up there, or he'll be in his rooms."

"Oh, it's not urgent, really…" I begin, framing my words in such a way that what they actually say is 'it isn't urgent, but I'm quite keen to get on with it anyway'. Porter allows himself to be taken in and smiles indulgently.

"Don't worry, ma'am. I'll keep an eye on the Lodge."

I am a little nervous about returning to the Senior Combination Room, I must say. A part of College I avoid at the best of times, the slightly spooky incident on Christmas Eve has done nothing to endear the place to me further. I try to walk in confidently and look like I have some kind of purpose.

The Senior Combination Room is almost unbearably warm, and the fire is roaring away merrily. I recognise Gustav Holst's *Planet Suite* playing on the record deck, I'm pretty sure it is *Mars*. Today, the room does not feel deserted and, indeed, it is not. The very real and very much alive Professor K is encumbered in one of the huge battered armchairs by the fire. A skeletal finger on his left hand is vaguely keeping time to the music and his thin, drawn lips are softly humming. I don't think they are humming Holst, but that is hardly my business.

I do not wish to startle the old chap, so glide as elegantly into view as I can manage, in over-tight trousers.

"Good morning, Sir" I offer, politely. Those naughty, twinkly eyes take a moment to focus and still a moment more to recognise me.

"Ah! Deputy Head Porter! Good morning, dear girl. Did you have a splendid Christmas?"

"Yes thank you, Sir, lovely. Yourself?"

"It was… quiet, thank you, Deputy Head Porter" There is the very suggestion of sadness in his voice, but it doesn't make its way to those twinkly eyes.

"I wondered, Sir… do you have a moment? I have something I wish to ask you about, if it is not an imposition."

"I cannot see that it would be, my dear girl, why don't you come and sit with me here by the fire?" Professor K gestures delicately, invitingly to the chair next to his. This is quite an honour of no small consequence, to be invited to sit with a Fellow.

I make myself as comfortable as I dare and return Professor K's thin lipped, yet still cheeky, grin with a slightly more conservative smile of my own. I don't want to give the old chap any ideas. Or a heart attack.

"Sir, I wanted to ask you about when the Porters' Lodge was rebuilt," I begin cautiously. I suspect that there may be any number of delicate issues, here.

"What a thing to want to ask about!" Professor K seems surprised, but not offended, as yet. "What has piqued your interest, dear girl?"

"I happened to be talking to The Master recently. Actually, we were talking about the possibility of Old College being haunted…"

"Oh! You were? I expect he told you a tale or two?" *Interesting. The Master was fairly clear that there were no tales to tell. Perhaps I should delve a little deeper...*

"Well, he was a little... vague about the ghost situation," I reply, tactfully. "I did sort of wonder, though, what with the place being so very old and the occasional passing of Fellows in College and suchlike..."

"Yes, quite a few of the old boys and girls have breathed their last here, certainly. One or two of the youngsters, too, as I recall..." Professor K trails off and it appears he has meandered into uncomfortable territory, as he quickly brings me back to my original question. "But what of the Porters' Lodge? You had a question?"

"Yes, Sir." I feel a need to proceed delicately. "The Master mentioned, when the Lodge was rebuilt that there may have been something... wrong with the... foundations...or something...in the...ground?"

Professor K is now ill at ease. The naughty twinkle has slipped; a steely wall in its place. And something else. Is it... fear?

"Tell me, dear girl, do you believe in ghosts?" Professor K is leaning close to me now and it is hard to tell if it is indeed fear, or malevolence in his eyes. Whatever it is, I am not afraid. If anything, I am more curious than ever.

"I'm not sure that I do, Sir. I prefer to concern myself with things of a more solid nature" *Although Christmas Eve in this very room gave me reason to reconsider...* "The Master tells me ghosts, if such a thing exist, tend usually to follow a traumatic death. He said there had been no such deaths..."

"Old College has ghosts, Deputy Head Porter," Professor K's reply is matter-of-fact, not superstitious. "Maybe not the kind you think. Maybe some of those, too. The thing with ghosts, I find, is that it doesn't matter if you believe in them or not, they go about their business all the same."

I really don't know how to respond. Professor K holds my gaze for a few moments longer before turning back to his fire and his music. The conversation is evidently over. I ease myself gently out of the chair and leave the room swiftly, feeling like I have been chided in some way.

My intelligence gathering skills are obviously getting a little rusty as I have come away from this with more questions than answers. Very academic, that. But not terribly useful to me. Without doubt, something or other has gone on within these walls - *gone on? Still going on?* And I would be bloody interested to know exactly what.

Spooky

IT IS THE SECOND WEEK of January and Old College is slowly rousing itself back into action. Like a giant, ancient beast awakening from hibernation, the stirrings are laboured and delayed and College has the annoyed and cantankerous air of an elderly gentleman forced to get up before he is properly awake. The Fellowship have been trickling back in, the trickle increasing to a steady stream now that the kitchens are open again. Although term doesn't start for almost two weeks, some of the overseas students have returned and are shuffling around, generally making the place look untidy.

The Porters' Lodge is a hive of activity once again and I am keeping busy with the day-to-day nonsense of post, overtime forms and random tasks from crotchety Fellows.

The morning is progressing nicely when I receive a telephone call from Head Of Housekeeping. It is always an uncertain affair, answering the phone to Head Of Housekeeping. She is as helpful as she is hostile, but quite often she is just hostile. I pick up the receiver and hope for the best.

"Good morning, Deputy Head Porter, Head Of Housekeeping here. Look, one of the students in Apple Tree Court has barricaded himself in his bedroom. My Bedder can't get in there to clean, sort it out, will you?"

It appears that Head Of Housekeeping has been taking telephony etiquette lessons from The Fellowship.

"I'll see what I can do" I reply in the most non-committal manner I can muster. "Which room?"

I write down the name and room number of the student and frown. Apple Tree Court is in the oldest part of College, so kicking doors in willy-nilly is certainly not an option. Junior Bursar would have an absolute fit. No, gentle persuasion is the preferred method here. That said, I do not yet know the nature of the barricade, so I call for Porter to join me. There might be some heavy lifting involved.

"These bloody students are all bloody drama queens," grumbles Porter as I try to hurry him along through the cloisters to Apple Tree Court. "As if we haven't got better bloody things to do…"

As Porter curses the entire student population of the world, I am acutely aware that what we find on the other side of that door might be more unsavoury than your average student bedroom. Students are prone to overindulgence of drink and sometimes drugs. Some are also prone to depression, brought on by the stress of heavy workloads and pressure to perform well in their chosen subject. Chances are, our student is playing silly buggers, and he will be getting the dressing down of his pampered little life if that's the case. But if it's not…

Porter is so wrong. We really don't have anything anywhere near better than this to do right now.

As is often the case when trying to get somewhere in a hurry, our destination is located as far away as physically possible from our departure point. I am less than impressed to discover the room we want is on the top floor. *Ah*, I think to myself, *a classic example of Sod's Law. I could be a Doctor of The Law Of The Sod.*

I unlock the door to the student's rooms, which opens up into the living/study area. It all looks fairly typical, actually a fair bit tidier than I was expecting. The bedroom door is on the left wall of the room and I try to open it. The door bangs against a large wooden dresser that has been placed directly in front of it. I experimentally put my body weight against the door to see if there is any movement. There is no give at all. The dresser is too heavy.

I shout to the student, there is no response. The room on the other side of the door is very quiet. I feel something ominous stirring in the pit of my stomach. I don't recognise it at first, it is something that hasn't stirred for quite some time. Then I realise. It is *instinct*. The silence from the other side of the door isn't your regular, ordinary silence, which is simply the absence of noise. This is a different kind of silence. The type of silence that suggests that no noise *could* be heard, even if it wanted to.

Porter motions for me to stand aside and he shouts, informing any occupant in no uncertain terms that we are coming in. There is a sterling struggle, in which Porter performs valiantly; Man versus Furniture, flesh against wood. He manages to force the dresser back enough to make a gap large enough for me to squeeze through.

I scramble up onto the dresser through the gap and tumble into the room with all the grace and poise of a baby giraffe. Making an elegant entrance has never been my forte. I pick myself up and look wildly around the room for the student. He isn't in here.

The bedroom is not large, there is the bed at the far end and behind me is a small sink and cabinet. The dresser should be occupying the spot underneath the window on the far wall. I scoot to the window. Although not original to the building, the window is still bloody old. It doesn't have a lock, as such, but the catch is fastened in place. I open the window and stare down four floors to see the river directly below me. Beyond the river, the grounds of Hawkins College. I certainly hope he didn't go out this way.

"He's not in here," I shout to Porter "Have someone at the Lodge check if he has signed back into College yet." I heave the dresser laboriously out of the way of the door and begin searching the rooms for anything unusual or of concern. Before long, the Lodge call us back to inform us that the student is not due back in College for another week and his key and spare key are hanging up in the Lodge. I am relieved that the boy is safe. But then I get thinking...

How did the dresser come to be pushed up against the bedroom door? It is certainly very heavy. Who put it there? Not the student, certainly, he isn't even here. Only the Porters and Bedders have access to his room keys. It is conceivable that someone could have got in the room, but how did they get *out?* There are no loft hatches or secret tunnels in the student quarters. To get out unscathed through the window and down into the river would have been quite a feat. I know that student pranks are legendarily ingenious and cunning, but there are hardly any students in College right now. Porters and Bedders are not known for their love of pranks, ingenious or otherwise.

I am sure there are a hundred ways a huge piece of wooden furniture could come to be shoved against a door in an empty room behind a locked door, but I cannot summon one to mind as I return thoughtfully to the Lodge. I am sure people far cleverer than I will, with withering looks, recount several examples of how this could have occurred. Whatever, it plays on my mind for a while.

Spooky, huh?

By the way, this incident doesn't make it into the incident book. I wouldn't know what to write.

A Reasonable Explanation

My New Year's Resolution to cut back on the hard stuff is being seriously tested at the moment. Apart from the unlikely spookiness that seems to be occurring on an alarmingly more regular basis, I have received a note informing me that The Committee For The Prevention Of Drunken Behaviour is due to reconvene very shortly. I am fond of Senior Tutor, I really am, but the last of these meetings of his was arduous to say the least.

I am amusing myself today by auditing the College keys. I say amusing myself; this is a rather generous turn of phrase for such an onerous task of mind-numbing monotony. It must be said, some of the keys are fairly interesting. The older ones are like little works of art, in their own way. But however attractive some of them may be, there is no getting away from the fact that the task in hand goes like this: Is such-and-such a key on its hook? If the answer is 'yes', all good. Tick the box. If the answer is 'no', check the signing out record and check where it is. Don't tick the box. And so on. I think to myself, this is what comes of not paying attention in school.

Obviously not learning the lesson of what comes from not paying attention, I now find myself not paying attention to the dark art of key auditing. My mind wanders to the stranger goings on in Old College of late. It all started with that conversation with The Master in the Crypt and I haven't been able to shake it from my mind since. *It was just… very old ground.*

I will give the unsettling incident on Christmas Eve no further thought as, in the cold light of day, I cannot convince myself whether it happened or not. Likewise, the bizarre incident in the student quarters in Apple Tree

Court. What was it Professor K had said? *Old College has ghosts. Maybe not the kind you think…*

Right. That's it. My pen and tick sheet are placed carefully on the side and I turn my back on the keys. My naturally enquiring mind, coupled with my straightforward, pragmatic approach, will not allow me to leave this mysterious state of affairs unchecked. I enjoy an innocuous riddle as much as the next chap, but it's about time I asked some straightforward questions and got some straightforward answers. Or, at the very least, get rebuked sternly and told to mind my own business. These ridiculous, ethereal half-answers and cryptic clues simply will not do. Not even at Old College.

I make my way to Professor K's rooms. I expect he will be a better bet than The Master, who no doubt will not take too kindly to me bursting into his Lodge unannounced and uninvited. Professor K is ensconced in the newer part of College, presumably because there is a lift and more effective heating. His door is slightly ajar and I knock politely.

"Come in!" Professor K sounds in good spirits.

"Good afternoon, Professor!" I say cheerfully as I enter his rooms. The Fellows' rooms in the newer part of College are more like contemporary studio apartments and do not have quite the same charm (in my opinion) as the ancient rooms on the other side of the river, swathed as they are in the kind of dark opulence only the passage of time can deliver. Still, they are comfortable and beautiful nonetheless.

"Ah! Deputy Head Porter!" The naughty twinkle of the eyes is on full display, today. "This is a nice surprise. Won't you sit down?"

Professor K shows me to his settee as he shuffles over from his writing desk to join me. I make myself comfortable and note that the Professor has a remarkably modern taste in décor. I also spy some Alan Moore books on his (very well-ordered) bookshelves. Who would have guessed! They look surprisingly comfortable next to the endless tomes on chemistry.

"Do you like my rooms?" Professor K asks, obviously noticing me having a nose round.

"I do, Sir" I reply. "Might I say, we share some familiar reading material!" This is a phrase I never thought I would utter to a Fellow of Old College. Or, any College for that matter. Professor K chuckles and looks delighted.

"Reading is very important," he says "But just as important is variety of reading. You'd do well to remember that."

"I will, Sir." I take a deep breath. "Sir, you know what we were talking about the other day?"

"Ghosts and ghoulies?" I don't recall ghoulies coming into it, but there you go.

"...Yes. You see, since joining Old College I have become rather interested in the history of the place and, of course, I have read the College website and learned all about when it was built and the famous people who have passed through its cloisters, but... I get the feeling I might be... missing something?"

"I see you have an admirable thirst for knowledge, Deputy Head Porter. It is a precious thing to have; you must make sure you treasure it and never lose it."

"I will, Sir, certainly, yes. But, come on Sir, a place as old and as illustrious as Old College..." I am interrupted by Professor K's keen and somewhat passionate reply.

"Old College is like a beautiful woman, Deputy Head Porter. She has a past. And, in my experience, the more beautiful the woman, the more thrilling the past she has, wouldn't you say?"

"I'm not sure I can confirm that one way or another, Sir" I cannot help but chuckle as I become convinced that Professor K has an absolute authority on this.

"But you can, Deputy Head Porter, I am sure of it" Professor K leans a little closer and the years seem to fall away as – horror of horrors – I think he is going to make some kind of a move on me!

But no. He is a gentleman, it seems. He stops short of physical contact and simply says

"I imagine your past is... shockingly colourful!" I am not sure if he means this as a compliment, or that I look like a fallen woman – one that has fallen pretty far, at that. "And so all I will say to you, Deputy Head Porter, is that Old College is an exquisitely attractive woman. And there is a reasonable explanation for everything, if you know where to look. Well, an explanation, at least. Even if it doesn't seem very reasonable!"

I sigh and am irritated.

"Professor K, you Fellows are too fond of talking in riddles for my liking. I thought you were teachers? The more I talk to you the less I learn!"

"Really? Is that how you see it?" Professor K seems positively delighted at my frustration. "You'll never make an academic with an attitude like that..."

I open my mouth to reply, but we are interrupted in spectacular fashion by The Dean, who comes flying through the door, arms flailing. He looks particularly annoyed, as usual, and I am delighted. The Dean is fabulous when he is annoyed. He stops in mid-rage when he sees me, obviously not expecting to find me here.

"Good afternoon, Sir!" I announce cheerily, unable to stop myself giving him a little wave.

"Oh! Deputy Head Porter! Yes, good afternoon, nice to see you. What are you up to in here?"

"We were talking about ghosts and ghoulies!" Professor K answers before I can even open my mouth. "And discussing Deputy Head Porter's thirst for knowledge."

"What? What?" The Dean is uncharacteristically dumbfounded. "Thirst for knowledge? In a College servant? Are you mad?"

"Not as mad as you appear to be, my dear Dean" replies Professor K. "Tell me, what has upset you so?"

Ah! Brilliant. Things that upset The Dean are always entertaining.

"I'm not... upset" The Dean wrestles his anger down quite successfully. "Look, can you two continue this... lesson... or whatever it is, another time? We have College business to discuss, Professor."

Bugger. That's my cue to leave, I expect. I rise reluctantly to my feet, and turn to Professor K with one of my best smiles.

"Thank you for your time, Sir, this has been most enlightening."

"I thought it might be, dear girl. Think on everything I have said."

And with that, I give a little grin to The Dean and leave them to discuss their College business. And do you know, this has been quite enlightening. Thinking over the words of Professor K, I realise just what he is getting at. But it will have to wait. I have my own College business to attend to and I really should be getting on with it if I don't want to incur the wrath of Head Porter.

The Committee Meets Again

WITH LESS THAN A WEEK to go before term starts again, Senior Tutor is starting to get twitchy about the inevitable drunken gatherings of our dear students. He has summoned The Committee For The Prevention Of Drunken Behaviour to meet once again.

The Chair of the Student Union is still languishing at home with mummy and daddy, but present in Senior Tutor's rooms are the usual suspects of Nurse, The Dean and Senior Tutor himself. As I enter the room, The Dean is hurriedly exiting it.

"Oh do get out of the way, Deputy Head Porter!" he chastises me as if I were a small child. I sidestep smartly to avoid the flourishing arm of The Dean as he bundles through the door grumpily. Today's outfit consists of a lovely blue jumper (with a hole just below the collar) and brown trousers. I didn't quite catch a glimpse of the shirt, but I suspect it may be yellow.

"The Dean is feeling unwell," Senior Tutor offers by way of an explanation.

"Ha! He has been feeling 'unwell' since Formal Hall last night!" Nurse snaps distastefully.

Ah. Formal Hall. An unusually elaborate meal held once a week for The Fellowship. It's the one where they get the really good wine out.

"Shall we begin?" Senior Tutor asks tactfully. "The Dean will be back momentarily, I have no doubt."

Nurse and I sit down. After the last meeting, I am filled with nothing but fascination as to what will happen next.

"As you are aware, we are here to deter and protect our young charges from the evil of succumbing to over-indulgence,"

Yes, I think to myself, *And to prod them mercilessly when they are unconscious, as I recall.*

Senior Tutor continues: "I believe strongly that Fellows and staff should lead by example at all times. However, I have growing concerns regarding this, following the staff Christmas party..."

Ah, yes. The staff Christmas party. I have hazy memories of this. The day preceding the evening of the staff Christmas party involved, for me at least, *two* lunches – both of which offered complimentary wine, one of which included venison – and a general 'festive' atmosphere. If you know what I mean. The party itself was gatecrashed in spectacular style by several members of The Fellowship. I recall being in the bar, enjoying a fabulous glass of red and sophisticated background music, the general scene being more akin to an upmarket hotel than a College drinking establishment. The band were tuning up but had not yet started to play. All of a sudden, the doors where thrown open and careering through them came a selection of Doctors and Professors, some very elderly – all drunk as lords. They hit the dance floor immediately and flailed around wildly, even though the band hadn't started playing.

What happened next, I only have a patchy recollection of, at best. There was dancing. There were funny coloured drinks in very small glasses. There was a general tendency to falling over. I remember dancing inappropriately with Dr C then him urging me to take some A-Levels. Or something. Ah, the staff Christmas party...

The Dean returns, looking pale and a little sheepish.

"Have I missed much?" he asks, collapsing into a sturdy and practical leather chair near the door.

"We were just discussing the unfortunate antics of the staff Christmas party," replies Senior Tutor. The Dean brightens up a bit. He was not one of the gatecrashers, but had heard the rumours.

"Ah! Yes, an absolute disgrace by all accounts," states The Dean. "We should do away with it all together."

"The point I'm making," Senior Tutor continues, with a patience that has every sign that it is being stretched, "Is that *we* should be setting a good example of responsible drinking."

There is an audible sigh from The Dean, as he rests his head in his left hand and sinks a little lower into his chair. I gaze resolutely at my shoes and shift uncomfortably in my seat. Only Nurse sits proud and upright, a shining beacon of abstinence and sobriety.

"We can't expect our students to behave in a respectable manner when we ourselves are roaring drunk, rolling through the cloisters. This will not do" Senior Tutor is determined and resolute, and is staring intently at The Dean. My heart goes out to The Dean at this moment, these meetings are impossible with a hangover. I should know.

Senior Tutor rises swiftly from his seat behind his desk and strides purposefully over to the window. He seems to contemplate the view for a while, before finally turning back to the assembled Committee.

"What I have in mind," his voice is soft, low and even. Each word is spoken as if it is floating on a cushion, quite apart from its neighbours, "Is something quite radical for Old College. I will not tolerate the acceptance of this increased level of intoxication by Fellowship or staff." The gaze of Senior Tutor falls squarely on me. "And the Porters will be my essential tools in accomplishing this!"

I realise with horror that Nurse and The Dean have also focussed their attentions in my direction.

Oh dear. I do not like the sound of this at all…

Bouncers

"BOUNCERS!" CRIES SENIOR TUTOR EXCITEDLY.

"Bouncers?" comes my meek reply.

"Yes, Deputy Head Porter, I want you to have all the Porters train as bouncers. And I want you and Head Porter to lead by example and be the first to qualify as doorme... door... people?" Senior Tutor looks to me for assurance. "Door people. Can you arrange that?"

My reply to Senior Tutor is, of course "Certainly, Sir. I will attend to it immediately."

The reply inside my head is somewhat different. I'm not sure I could verbalise it. It would be a type of unrestrained laughter that clearly demonstrates my feelings that this is the most hilarious thing I have ever heard in my life. And quite how this will deter The Fellowship (who pay little attention to us at the best of times) and staff from drinking too much is beyond me. Still. I am sure that this all makes perfect sense in the undoubtedly brilliant mind of Senior Tutor, so I will do as I am told.

Whilst spending the rest of the day researching the world of professional bouncer-ing, I begin to think that it might not be such a bad idea. The required license is quite sought-after and expensive to obtain. You would think that getting training and a recognised qualification should cheer the chaps up no end. I also know the Porters and it dawns on me that it will just give them a whole new other thing to moan about.

With my proposal and costings for the training and licenses in hand, I head towards Junior Bursar's office, to plead with him to pay for it. I haven't got much of a pitch worked out, to be honest. I glumly wonder how I am going to sell the idea of training (mainly) elderly, grumpy old buggers to work as 'professional security', as the training company so proudly (and frequently) boasts. Don't get me wrong, I adore the Eeyore-like temperament of the Porters and they do a good job. But The A-Team they certainly are not.

Junior Bursar is in a jolly mood as I sit down in the chair he indicates by his desk. The surface between us is covered completely in a comical-looking pile of paperwork, which partially blocks my view of him. There are little yellow post-it notes on almost every surface. I even spot one on my *chair leg*. There are books and books and books everywhere, much like the other Fellows. But there is a difference between Junior Bursar's books and everyone else's books. At least three quarters of Junior Bursar's books appear to be in the midst of being read. They are off their shelves and propped open in ingenious ways all around the room. Perhaps if he read fewer books he would have time to clear up some of this paperwork. But anyway.

"This looks like a very interesting idea," Junior Bursar seems mildly delighted by the proposal. "I imagine that the Porters would be extremely pleased to gain a qualification. Make them feel more like the rest of College."

I put to one side, for the moment, the spectacularly pompous terminology and muse on the idea. I don't think the Porters will be especially pleased to be 'more like the rest of College'.

"And the other good thing," Junior Bursar continues, really getting a feel for the idea now, "Is that they can do a bit of moonlighting on their nights off, if they want. They can earn themselves a bit of extra money!"

The Porters working the doors of the City's pubs and clubs? I feel this to be even more unlikely. But, then again, you never know with these chaps.

I lean slightly to the left in order to get a clear view of Junior Bursar.

"Do you want me to go ahead and book the courses, Sir?" I ask. Junior Bursar doesn't look up from the proposal before him. He throws a cursory glance in the direction of the costs.

"Yes, absolutely, I think you should make the arrangements as soon as possible. Keep me updated!"

Well, this is an interesting turn of events. As far as I can tell, the Porters have never had any formal training at Old College before. This will be breaking new ground. And you know how Old College feels about breaking new ground. On the upside, in a few weeks time I will be a fully qualified and licensed 'security professional'. In the case of The Fellowship deciding that I am the worst Deputy Head Porter of all time, this could come in very handy for finding alternative employment.

What The Professor Said

WITH THE PLANS FOR THE slightly controversial new training scheme for the Porters well under way, I am finding myself at a bit of a loose end. I say 'slightly controversial' as the Porters are not happy at all about becoming 'security professionals'. I suppose I can sympathise somewhat. These chaps came to Old College to see out the last of their working days (ideally by doing as little as possible), not to embark on new ventures. Particularly not new ventures that involve restraining techniques and conflict resolution. Even so, I am a little disappointed at their lack of a sense of adventure.

As happens often when I haven't much to occupy me in the Lodge, I am patrolling the grounds of Old College. I say patrolling; that is a generous term for the superfluous ambling that has led me to the perimeters of the gardens and not much further. I feel a little guilty about using my time so gratuitously, but not much. It is nice to have time to have a think.

My mind is turning over the words of Professor K. Although it felt like he was talking in riddles, I feel certain he gave me all the information I need to pursue my interest in whatever mysteries Old College has to offer. I suspect they will not be half as interesting as I imagine, but it is certainly a pleasant distraction. Having assembled in my head all the information gathered so far, I have reasonable grounds to suspect that the following is true:

Something was discovered in the ground when the Porters' Lodge was rebuilt some fifty years ago.

It was something bad; no one wants to talk about it.

Whatever is was, it is still having repercussions of some description all these years later.

The Master lied about 'ghosts' in College. What else could he be lying about?

There seems to be a question mark over Head Porter. Why did he get the job and not my predecessor?

That's a point, Head Porter was been notably conspicuous by his absence recently. I rarely see him these days. This is not a bad thing, from my point of view; I am far happier left to my own devices. But I thought The Fellowship might have said something about it, particularly one of The Bursars. Is it normally acceptable for the Head Porter to be practically invisible? Maybe so, Old College has certainly done much to challenge my views of 'normal'.

A thought strikes me. Professor K had made a pointed comment about reading – and the importance of a thirst for knowledge. Of course! There must be reams and reams of written history about Old College, it stands to reason. If I want to know more about the history of the place perhaps all I need to do is look further than the end of my own nose.

I mentally kick myself for not coming to this conclusion before. I am surrounded by learning and study and didn't for one minute think that it might apply to me. Idiot. Self-recrimination out of the way, I believe that the best place to start would be the Old Library. I do not carry these keys as a matter of course, unwieldy as they are, so a quick detour to the Porters' Lodge is required. Whilst I'm there, I make a cup of tea to accompany me in the Old Library. From what I gather from the students, studying is thirsty work.

As I have mentioned before, the Old Library is probably my favourite part of College. Despite my lack of formal education, I do like books. I am also very fond of old things, so this tucked away little dusty oasis of papery antiquity is just perfect. As I make my way carefully up the wrought iron spiral staircase, I am not exactly sure what I expect to find, or even what I should be looking for. If nothing else, it will be a nice way to while away an hour or so.

The lock requires a certain amount of jiggling and persuasion to convince it to release, but once I have wrestled the ornate and cumbersome door open, the wonderful smell of wood, paper and leather greets me like an old friend. The floor is warped and uneven and I am grateful that this job requires me to wear sensible shoes. I wonder where to start looking; this is not a library that is intended for everyday use and therefore does not seem to have a clearly defined index or labelling system. I'll just have a little wander round and see what I can find.

Ah! There is the stunningly illustrated manuscript of *Paradise Lost*. It is in a glass case, so I can't really read it, but just to be able to look at it feels like quite an event in itself. I have, of course, read *Paradise Lost*, but I'm guessing the copies we had at school were a lot newer than this one.

With all of these strange goings on recently, I idly wonder if the Old Library has any ghosts lingering? This is in the oldest part of College, after all. I am rather morbidly considering how many people might have died in this room over the centuries. It is quite surprising how recent events have changed the way I am thinking about Old College. This fascination with people dying all over the place is probably quite unhealthy.

I am quite enjoying my own little private tour, but haven't found anything very useful. I decide to take a seat at the back by the medical books and, at the very least, enjoy my tea. I remember from Junior Bursar's Guided Tour several months ago that the medical books are quite interesting, so I heave a random one out from its resting place on the shelf and pop it on the reading table to peruse while I finish my tea.

As I shuffle my chair closer to the table, my foot makes contact with something very solid. I shuffle back quickly and see to my dismay that my highly polished practical shoe is scuffed. Bugger. I hope that whatever I kicked has come off better than my shoe.

I bend down to see a fairly large wooden chest, tucked under the table and right up against the wall. The aged oak panels suggest it is pretty old and the lack of ornament or decoration give the impression that this is designed to be serviceable rather than aesthetic. Well, the obvious thing that springs to mind is – what's in it? There are metal handles on either end and I give the one nearest to me a tug. The chest doesn't move an inch, it is very heavy. I shift myself into a squatting position and wrap both hands around the handle. Using all the strength in my arms and legs I manage to move it by maybe three inches. The build up of filth and the contrasting conditions on the floor around the chest indicate it hasn't been moved for a very long time.

The benefit of being small is that I can wriggle into tiny places. Under the desk I go and decide to see if I can open the chest from where it sits. To my immense surprise, there is no lock or fastening of any description; just a flip top lid. It opens easily, although the underside of the table prevents me from opening it very far. Squinting through the gap I can see there are a lot of very old-looking books stacked neatly in the chest. This looks interesting.

I scoot out from under the table and drag it out of the way of the chest. With the lid fully open, I can see an impressive-looking collection of very, very old books. Well, I might as well have a peek.

I carefully lift the first book that comes to hand out of the chest and rearrange the table so I can read in comfort. As I delicately open the cover and slowly turn the pages, I wonder if I should be wearing gloves of some kind. I don't have any gloves with me, so it's a bit of a pointless thought. The book appears to be the records and accounts of an enigmatic-sounding organisation called The Order of the Lesser Dragon.

To be honest, I am struggling to understand a lot of what is written here as it is in what I can only assume is old English (or, 'Ye Olde English, to give it its improper name). From what I can gather, The Order of the Lesser Dragon was a wealthy gentleman's society, in a similar vein to the Masons. They seemed to have had a lot of meetings and spent quite a bit of money on wine and cheese. The names of the past members appear to be listed periodically throughout the book, alongside the roles they played within the organisation.

This is all very interesting but I do wonder what this book is doing in the Old Library. Did The Lesser Dragons have something to do with Old College? Ah… here we go. There's a whole bit here about them setting up an academic institution… it's really difficult to understand most of it… but I recognise the names of 'Apple Tree Court' and 'Old Court'. That's a bit odd. If it's a brand new building, why name it Old Court? This is obviously the record of an embryonic plan for Old College! There must be some explanation here about the naming of it, but it really is very hard to comprehend. There are lists and records of the artisans and craftsmen and their costs and materials. Some of the labourers appear to have been paid in mead! Fantastic! And what's this? A long list of names… some of them seem very unlikely... There's one chap here called Faldo! Who were these people?

Oh. I am able to decrypt this rather unhappy excerpt relating to the list of names. They were peasants, 'sacrificed' using some kind of ancient protection rites and cast into the foundations of Old College. This is unpleasant and a little unexpected. Mind you, now I think about it, I do recall something of this nature from my history lessons many years ago. For some reason I thought it was just bridges; I remember learning that people were buried in the foundations of bridges in the belief that it would stop them falling down. It must have been same principle used here. I do quite like that these Lesser Dragon chaps had the decency to at least make a list of the unfortunate sacrifices and credit them in this weighty tome. That seems more than fair, in the given circumstances.

I expect the peasants are still there! Tucked up for all time beneath the ancient walls; eternal watchmen for Old College.

Oh. My. God.

Well. I think I may have solved the 'mystery' of what was discovered under the Porters' Lodge, half a century ago. It must have been a fairly grisly unearthing, a whole pile of human bones. And a real pain in the backside, too, as I am sure there are all sorts of rules and regulations concerning the discoveries of human remains. I wonder what they did with them? I will have to find time to have another chat with Professor K. But not now, I think to myself sensibly. I've already spent far too much time away from the Lodge.

I replace the books and make sure I leave the Old Library as I found it. As I hurry back to the Porters' Lodge I hope I haven't missed too much. Rather irritatingly, I will be away from College for a few days while I train to be a bouncer, so I will have to take this up with Professor K upon my return. He was right, though. A thirst for knowledge certainly is a wonderful thing.

Back To Reality

I AM SITTING IN A classroom in an ugly purpose-built facility, about a mile from Old College. There are eight strangers in the room with me, all looking as apprehensive as I feel. We are here to train as bouncers. Once I have completed the course, I will report back to Junior Bursar about its suitability for the Porters.

I must say, it feels very strange to have escaped the cosseted confines of Old College and to be operating, once again, in the real world. The eight other people in the room appear to come from all walks of life. What has brought them here to join the world of 'professional security' is not clear. It will be interesting finding out, I am sure.

We are all casting furtive glances around the room, trying to weigh each other up and look for potential allies and foes. Before anyone is brave enough to break the uneasy silence, the door opens and in walks our trainer. He is a short, stocky man in his early sixties. His bare forearms are adorned in faded tattoos, some of which I recognise as being from the military. His white hair is cropped close to his head and crowns a face that has clearly seen it all.

"Good morning, guys," he says in a thick Scottish accent. "My name is John and for the next few days I will be training you to become licensed security professionals!" John goes on to introduce himself and gives a brief history of his military and, latterly, his security career. Both are impressive and, although he comes across as a very gruff, blunt man, John seems to me to be a perfectly reasonable person to listen to for the next few days.

We then indulge in the training course tradition of going round the room, introducing ourselves and revealing an 'interesting fact'. I have always found this a particularly humourless task and I can rarely think of anything interesting to say about myself. That is not to say that I don't have interesting points, just that I don't generally like to share them with rooms of strangers. But I digress.

This onerous task at least reveals to me the identity of my new chums. We have Paul, an Irish gentleman who is soon to retire from his job as a prison officer and is hoping to do some casual bouncering in his twilight years. There is Pavel, who worked as an inspector in the Bulgarian police force before moving his family to the UK. He is tall and broad and looks a little like David Beckham. I also notice that his trousers are a little too short for him and he is wearing socks so white I have to shield my eyes. Jamie and Simon are two young barmen who have been sent here by their employer. There is a man in his fifties called Steve, and an African man I can barely understand called Samuel. James is an intense and serious-looking young man who for some reason appears to have the weight of the world on his shoulders. Lastly, there is Tim. Tim seems to me to be the most unlikely security professional I could possibly imagine. He has greasy, dyed black hair, a straggly ginger beard and would weigh barely seven stone soaking wet. He looks uncomfortable and says he is here because his girlfriend wanted him to get a proper job.

And so our little band of trainee bouncers is formed. John rouses and cajoles us along and we are soon noisily and enthusiastically engaging as a group. Well, some of us are. Some of us are sitting sulkily and pretending to make notes. Mainly Tim and Samuel. Samuel can be partly excused, as English is obviously not his strong point. Tim regards the class with barely-concealed suspicion and distaste. Or perhaps it is just the thought of getting a 'proper job' that he finds distasteful.

We soon discover that John can be easily sidetracked by getting him to regale us with stories from his military days. With gentle coaxing, we can elicit all sorts of gory details and tales of derring-do, which he relays with relish. There is a deliciously schoolboy-like atmosphere as we do our best to distract from our lessons as often, and as for as long, as possible. It amuses me to note that the vast majority of people, when faced with a learning environment (any learning environment) will revert to the juvenile behaviour of their schooldays; in which they exert twice as much effort trying to avoid learning anything as they would actually learning. The Fellowship would be horrified, I am sure.

Eventually, we reach the point of the inevitable role-playing scenarios. Samuel is given the role of unconscious male, who is to be discovered by Pavel during his tour of duty. Samuel performs his role with great aplomb and lies prone on the floor, every inch the unconscious vagrant. Pavel enters the scene. On seeing Samuel, he strides over and you can see his mind assessing the threat to the security of his imaginary workplace. Pavel then leans down and grabs Samuel by his lapels and starts to drag him towards the classroom door. This is a surprising tactic and no one is more surprised than Samuel himself who looks around in confusion and mild terror.

"No, no Pavel," cries John, jumping up from his seat. "Use your communication skills like we talked about, remember? Try it again."

Pavel unceremoniously drops Samuel back to the floor and restarts his scenario. Samuel keeps one eye open as he awaits the return of Pavel. The scene replays in exactly the same way, but as he is manhandling Samuel, Pavel announces in heavily-accented but perfect English "My name is Pavel. I am the security guard for this place. And now you must leave!"

As Pavel is trying to force Samuel out of the classroom, John intervenes as kindly as he can.

"Pavel, what were we saying about communicating with our customers? About showing empathy? Do you remember what we said about empathy?" John asks desperately. Pavel nods his head.

"Yes," he replies "It is when you wear the shoes of the customer, yes?"

In my periphery vision I can see Paul desperately trying to suppress laughter. Jamie and Simon don't bother to suppress it and are giving Pavel a warm round of applause for his performance. Samuel is looking deeply uncomfortable and appears relieved when John announces that it is lunchtime.

The following days pass pleasantly enough and all the talk of patrol plans, reasonable force and 'high risk situations' find me on much more familiar ground than the seemingly random and esoteric ways of Old College. Being back in the real world, back within my comfort zone – I can't deny that it feels good. I am reminded that I am not a heathen idiot who has no idea what she is doing. I have skills and knowledge that are relevant and respected. That said, the real world does not provide you with hot meals on a regular basis and certainly doesn't offer the surreal entertainment provided by College life.

I make my way back to Old College to find out what I have missed while I have been away. To be honest, I am toying with the idea of giving this 'security professional' lark a go. But when I see the iconic and ancient gates looming before me, I realise that there is little chance I will go down that road. The promise of hot meals on a regular basis is too strong to resist. Cursing the weak resolve of my stomach, I return to the Porters' Lodge and hope that at least some of Old College has missed me. Just a little bit.

But, alas, they appear not to have missed me very much at all. The only remarks passed are that the supplies of tea are notably less depleted than usual and the kitchens have more leftovers from lunch. It is nice to know my presence makes an impact, no matter how small.

Buried Things

I CANNOT FOR THE LIFE of me see what the benefits of training our Porters as bouncers will be, but I suspect that Junior Bursar and Senior Tutor will be expecting something a little more comprehensive in my report. In almost any other working environment I can imagine, I would say that staff training is a positive, if not essential, use of time and resources. Here at Old College, the Porters' Lodge in particular, I would say that it is less so. I decide that the best thing to do is to present an even-handed report of pros and cons and let The Fellowship make up their own minds. This should give me plenty of breathing space; coming to a decision has been known to take The Fellowship months, if not years.

I decide to deliver my reports by hand, as it will give me an excuse to be out of the Lodge for a while. I am hoping to pop by and have a chat with Professor K about my discovery. Something tells me he will know all about this already. What I really want to know is – *what did they do with the bodies?*

As I am not really in the mood for talking about my experiences of 'security professional' training, I decide to slide the reports under the respective doors of Senior Tutor and Junior Bursar. This turns out to be a good decision, certainly in the case of Junior Bursar. When I reach his door I can hear what can only be described as an almighty row going on in his rooms. I cannot be sure, but it sounds very much like he might be arguing with Head Porter. This is certainly not a situation I want to get myself involved in, so I hurry away once the report is under the door. I am curious as to what the argument is about, but I am sure it can wait until later.

At this hour of the afternoon, I cannot be sure whether Professor K will be relaxing in The Senior Combination Room or having a snooze in his rooms. I hope he is in his rooms. It will be easier to talk there.

My luck is in. Professor K is shuffling around his rooms and seems pleased to see me.

"Deputy Head Porter!" He welcomes me through the door with open arms and a broad grin. "Would you like a drink?" The Professor is pouring himself a large whiskey.

"Not while I'm on duty, but thank you, Sir"

"Oh, go on. Just a little one," the twinkly eyes seem even naughtier than usual today. "I promise I won't tell Head Porter!"

"All the same, I'd better not" I reply. "I haven't got long, I shall be needing to get back to the Lodge. I've come to say you were right!"

"I am invariably right, my dear girl" Professor K looks very pleased with himself. "What was I right about this time?"

"A thirst for knowledge and reading," I lick my lips a little nervously. "I found a book in the Old Library"

"Well done you. A book in a library? Who'd have thought it!"

"You know what I mean. The one about The Order of the Lesser Dragon."

Professor K takes a valiant gulp of his whiskey and makes himself comfortable on the sofa.

"Ah! Yes. The Order of the Lesser Dragon. The forefathers of Old College."

"Yes… I say, don't you think it's rather strange they would name their brand spanking new establishment 'Old College'?"

Professor K bursts out laughing and twitches excitedly in his seat. Maybe it was the mention of spanking?

"Dear, dear Deputy Head Porter!" He shakes his head in mock despair then fixes me with a sympathetic gaze. "Do think about it, girl. It isn't difficult to fathom."

I can see I won't be getting a straight answer on this one. Another puzzle for me to go away and think about, no doubt. So I continue,

"I know what they found under the Porters' Lodge, when it was rebuilt. It was the sacrificial peasants, wasn't it?"

Professor K seems to light up with pleasure from the soles of his battered boots to the very tips of his ice white hair. He nods slowly and smiles broadly.

"Clever girl. Of course, we couldn't be absolutely certain, but it was a common practice of the age and the amount of – remains – discovered certainly suggested that was indeed the practice we stumbled upon."

I knew it! And I do feel like a very clever girl.

"So tell me, Sir, what happened to the remains? Are they interred somewhere? On display? I would love to visit and pay my respects, as a servant of Old College."

"Ahh... well, that's the thing, you see, Deputy Head Porter" Professor K has adopted a sombre tone but I can tell he is itching to tell me whatever it is he is about to impart. "There was some – disagreement – at the time regarding the discovery. Having the bones removed and studied would have cost College a lot of time and money. Not to mention inconvenience."

"Yes, but, there are quite specific procedures for the removal of human remains..." I trail off as the realisation sinks in. Old College doesn't much care for the rules and regulations of the world outside its walls. "What happened?"

"As far as I know, they were dug back into the ground and simply built over" his voice is a little shaky now, but Professor K goes on "It was a very unpopular decision with a couple of the Fellows at the time. They threatened to go to the police, you know."

"That would have been disastrous for College!" I exclaim. "I mean, that's a crime! How on earth did they wriggle out of that one?"

There is a long pause, punctuated only by a long sigh from Professor K. It is a sigh that sounds like it has been waiting to be exhaled for a very long time. He spits out his next words with such disgust, it is almost as if they taste bilious in his mouth.

"As luck would have it, the two Fellows who were so perturbed died 'peacefully in their sleep' before they managed to make it to the authorities," I can hear the inverted commas in his speech. "That was a stroke of luck for Old College, wouldn't you say, Deputy Head Porter?"

Before I can answer him, a sharp knock at the door makes us both jump. This is followed immediately by Head Porter, face like thunder, striding through the door. Professor K is furious at this imposition and rises to his feet far more swiftly than I would have imagined for a man of his age.

"Head Porter! Is it not customary to wait to be invited into a Fellow's quarters? How rude of you!"

Head Porter is unmoved by this and I am very surprised to see him stare stonily at Professor K.

"My apologies, Professor" Head Porter replies. His tone is distinctly unapologetic. "My Deputy has been neglecting her duties and I require her to return to the Lodge." I wonder how he knew I was here?

"She has been assisting me with some important work," Professor K snaps back "And I have not kept her away long. The Master will hear of your impudence!"

"I will remind you, Sir, that Deputy Head Porter belongs to my staff, not yours. And she has her own work to attend to" I really am shocked at Head Porter's bravado. Speaking to a Fellow in this way is completely unacceptable. I can see Professor K becoming increasingly enraged and I cannot imagine that this is a good thing for a man of his advanced years.

"I am sorry, Head Porter," I interject quickly. "It was wrong of me to be away for so long. Professor, I will speak to you on another occasion."

"You have not heard the last of this, Head Porter!" Professor K says, darkly. I can still see the rage in his eyes as Head Porter practically drags me out of the room.

Once the door is closed behind us, I twist my arm out of Head Porter's grip and turn to face him, my own anger burning hotly on my cheeks.

"There's no need for that!" I say crossly. "What's the matter?"

"I'm not happy with the amount of time you have been spending with Professor K," Head Porter's voice is like lead. "You need to realise you are here to do a job, not to be spending your time chatting up old men." This is a most un-gentlemanly insult, no doubt designed to either enrage or insult me. It does neither.

"What's the matter, are you jealous?" A childish reply but, hey, he started it. The look he returns leaves me in no doubt that if we weren't getting on before, we are certainly not getting on at all now.

As Head Porter just stands there and looks at me, in a manner I assume he believes is intimidating, I cannot even be bothered to respond. I turn my back on him, making sure I flick my ponytail in the most derogatory way I can manage as I do so and make my way back to the Porters' Lodge.

The walk calms me down a little. I didn't appreciate his manner, but Head Porter was correct that I shouldn't have been away from my post for so long. And I have been letting myself get a little distracted with all this mysterious nonsense recently. Perhaps I should keep my head down for a while and keep my mind on the job in hand.

Senior Bursar's Biscuits

THINGS ARE TICKING ALONG NICELY in the Porters' Lodge. The very first signs of Spring are emerging around the grounds and it is indeed a sight to behold. The delicate, drooping little heads of armies of snowdrops are peeking out from the ground in great, haphazard smatterings all along the riverbanks and around the courtyards. Things that have seemed grey and dead for an eternity are sprouting fledgling flecks of green from the ends of their brittle extremities. Today, a watery-yellow sun casts tentative shafts of warmth from an ice-blue sky. The air is crisp and bright and it feels as though the world has, finally, shifted its great clunking seasonal gears and is edging itself slowly into the early stages of Spring.

I am trotting subserviently alongside Head Porter through the cloisters, on our way for a meeting in the Gathering Room. As I try to keep pace with his long, brisk stride, I try to remember what meeting this is that I am attending. It is obviously a fairly important one, as both Senior Bursar and Junior Bursar will be there. As will Head Of Housekeeping and Head Of Catering, each with their respective Deputies.

Inside the Gathering Room, the fire is lit and the great wooden table set out with tea, coffee and biscuits of all descriptions. Housekeeping and Catering have already arrived and are helping themselves to refreshments. I take a seat next to Head Porter at the far end of the table, opposite Deputy Head Of Housekeeping. Unlike her stern and uncompromising superior, she is a warm and humorous Spanish woman with beautiful Latin features and a colourful dress sense. She smiles at me across the table and gives a little wave before leaning across to speak.

"Quick!" she says "Get the biscuits down this end before the Bursars arrive!" I catch the attention of Head Of Catering and indicate furiously at the tray of biscuits in front of him. Head Of Catering dutifully slides the tray to me and I place it between Deputy Head Of Housekeeping and myself. Her big brown eyes shine with delight as she starts rummaging through our hoard. The biscuits are all individually wrapped in their own packaging, so this is not as unhygienic as it sounds.

All the biscuits look fabulous and any one of them would have beautifully complimented the steaming cup of tea I have helped myself to. But I know that one will never be enough. And I really want those four big chocolate ones. I'm going to have those four big chocolate ones. I deftly swipe my prey from the tray to my lap with a sleight of hand that would make a magician weep. I reason that the best way for my consumption of four large chocolate biscuits to remain undetected, is to eat the evidence as swiftly as possible. This I manage with ease, and, I feel, a certain grace. I fold the wrappers neatly by my notebook and usher the crumbs into a neat pile in their centre. The perfect crime.

The heavy wooden door bursts open and the tall, sturdy frame of Senior Bursar strides into the room with a gravitas most mortals can only dream of. He is a vision in expensive, bright tweed and his booming, cut glass accent greets the room magnificently.

"Good morning all!" Senior Bursar says, taking his seat at the head of the table.

Behind him comes Junior Bursar. Shorter of stature and slighter of build, he still somehow manages to exude the menace of a man twice Senior Bursar's size. Junior Bursar says nothing and takes a seat to the left of his colleague.

Senior Bursar is pouring himself a generous cup of coffee and looking around the table for some unknown object.

"I say," says Senior Bursar "Where are the blasted biscuits?"

All eyes search the table and eventually come to rest at the tray laying, notably depleted, between myself and Deputy Head Of Housekeeping. Without saying a word, Junior Bursar thrusts his hand out in my direction and fixes me with a gaze that could melt steel. Clumsily, I reach across as far as I can and apologetically nudge the tray of biscuits towards him.

Once in possession of the tray, Senior Bursar still seems unsatisfied as he examines the contents.

"Oh, for Heaven's sake!" he exclaims "I specifically asked for the chocolate ones, where are they? They're my favourite. Head Of Catering, what's going on here? I remember making this request distinctly."

Head Of Catering shoots an accusatory glance in my direction but, mercifully, does not give me away.

"I apologise unreservedly, Sir, there must have been some dreadful mistake…"

"There aren't any of the cherry ones, either!" Junior Bursar joins the fray with aplomb. I look across to see him fishing out unsuitable biscuits and tossing them out of the tray. From the look of distaste on his face, you would think he was sifting through some unpleasant waste product. *Well, it wasn't me that ate the cherry ones* I think sullenly to myself. I meet the gaze of Deputy Head Of Housekeeping across the table. Oh dear. So that's what happened to the cherry ones.

I realise, with mounting fear, that the four wrappers and chocolate crumbs are sitting directly next to me. I am vaguely aware of Head Of Catering receiving a stern chastising from the Bursars, then the meeting beginning. I make a mental note to thank him sincerely for not exposing my biscuit theft. When the meeting ends, he comes up to me and offers me his coffee cup.

"Here, put the wrappers in here, I'll get rid of them" he whispers. I give him a grateful look and thank him as I crumple my shameful wrappers into the cup. At the very moment I do this, Head Of Catering seems to lose his grip on the handle and I force the cup from his hand sending crumbs, wrappers and cold coffee tumbling all over the beautiful and elderly rug beneath us.

The entire room turns to look at us and I make embarrassed apologies and try to salvage some of the mess from the rug. Head Of Housekeeping pushes me to one side.

"Leave it! I will have one of my team attend to it," she says brusquely.

Head Porter is looking at me like I have just eaten his children.

"Come on" he says, darkly. "We're going back to the Lodge".

Something tells me I have not heard the end of this. For the time being, at least, life rolls on with no further mention of The Biscuits. But it's in the post.

The Great Feast

OLD COLLEGE IS BUSTLING AND alive with anticipation. Tonight, The Great Feast is to be held and we all have our instructions. Many of tonight's guests are esteemed and generous benefactors of College and an awful lot of them are decorated and titled to within an inch of their lives. They must be treated as if they are Gods. In fact, the Gods themselves would be jealous of the veneration and obeisance awaiting our guests.

As I go about my business around College, I can almost taste the decadence in the air. The resonance of bygone life is unusually strong today. This is obviously a propitious event and Old College *knows* it. The ebullience is tangible, the very walls exude the aura of a child at Christmas. Old College must have seen *thousands* of feasts – I have seen quite a few in my short time as Deputy Head Porter. But this is obviously a really special one. I try to adopt a pious and respectful temperament fitting for the occasion, but it is a constant struggle to maintain. I rather fear I am giving the impression of being bi-polar.

I pop my head round the huge wooden doors of Old Hall. The place is teeming with immaculately presented Catering staff, who are artfully dressing the room for The Great Feast. They are setting the tables with the very best china, exquisite crystal and silver cutlery so delicate it appears to have been born from angels' hair and babies' breath. Each place setting has five wine glasses. *Five!* I feel a sharp pang of jealousy. This looks brilliant. This is why parents want their kids to do well at school. They get to go to the best parties. I am mightily impressed, and I decide to go and tell Head

Of Catering so. I haven't really spoken to him since the incident of Senior Bursar's Biscuits and I feel the need to show my appreciation.

I reason that the obvious place to find Head Of Catering on a day like today, would be the kitchens. As I push back the cumbersome metal doors to the kitchens, a world of chaos, four-letter words and exquisite aromas pushes and shoves it's way into view. If Dante had seen the kitchens of Old College at this very moment, he would have known ten layers of Hell. Possibly eleven.

The heat and noise overwhelm me. The aggression and passion coursing through the kitchens like white water rapids is ferocious in its desire for perfection. The atmosphere is vaguely threatening. I make my way through the steam and expletives in search of Head Of Catering. On every side, the blades of a variety of knives flash and glint in the glare of artificial lighting. Smoke and flame punctuate the scene, accompanied by the roars, hisses and crackles that assault the ears like some kind of audio vandalism.

My ears are drawn to the booming, terrifying voice of Chef in full flow; his combination of encouragement and threat perfectly balanced, like a delicate jus. I make my way through the steam and hostility to Chef in as dignified a manner as is possible. As his considerably dominating countenance comes into view, I proffer a friendly wave. He doesn't look especially pleased to see me. Oh well. This is not an unfamiliar reaction to my presence. Hide behind the uniform, just like I know how to. Big smile.

"Good afternoon, Chef!" More a statement than a greeting, I feel. "Everything is looking wonderful! How are you?"

"How the BLOODY HELL do you think I am?! Get OUT of my BLOODY kitchen before I ..." The rest of Chef's rhetoric is unrepeatable, but I am left in no uncertain terms that I should find somewhere else to be, very quickly.

"Before I go, just one more thing," I venture, Columbo-style. "Where is Head Of Catering?"

"Preparing the Dining Hall! OBVIOUSLY!" With that, I am completely disregarded and Chef continues where he left off, as if I had never existed. The Dining Hall? Fine. I'll go there.

The Dining Hall is an oasis of calm in comparison to the rest of College. The tables are already set out in an even more tremendous style than Old Hall. The only audible sound is the gentle tinkling of glass and silver as I spy Head Of Catering fussing over tiny details. I weave between the tables towards him. On hearing my approach, he raises his head and smiles.

"Hallo, Deputy Head Porter" he greets me warmly. "What can I do for you?"

"Oh, nothing at all, I just had to pop by and say how marvellous Old Hall is looking… what's all this in here? I thought The Great Feast was being held over there." Head Of Catering laughs.

"Yes, part of it is," he chuckles "I take it you haven't been given the full run down on The Great Feast?" I shake my head, interest piqued. "Well, it all kicks off with a drinks reception in Old Kitchens. Of course, most of the senior Fellows have pre-drinks reception drinks receptions in their rooms, so the drinks reception itself is usually quite a rowdy affair. They are usually fairly merry by this point."

Pre-drinks reception drinks receptions?!

Head Of Catering continues, "Then everyone goes to Old Hall for the first three courses. They then 'promenade' to The Dining Hall for a further three courses, before making a final 'promenade' to The Gathering Room for the port and cheese course. They usually call it a night at about half past two."

"Bloody hell!" I reply. I try to think of something more intelligent to say, but am stunned into stupidity. So I just say "Bloody hell!" again.

"I don't know how some of the old boys manage it, to be honest. I can't believe we haven't had any deaths, actually." Head Of Catering looks thoughtful for a moment. "We've had a few heart attacks, over the years. They all survived. Didn't make it to the port and cheese, though."

"That is a shame," I reply. I would be very disappointed to miss out on the port and cheese. "It's a bit of an elaborate affair, isn't it? Even by Old College's standards, it seems a bit excessive. And what's the idea behind wandering around College between courses? That must be rubbish if it's raining." Head Of Catering shakes his head and smiles.

"It's how it's always been done! Oh, it's all good fun, you'll see. Now, if you'll excuse me, I have quite a bit to be getting on with!"

"Yes, of course. Good luck!" I reply. "Let me know if there's anything the Porters can do to help."

"Oh, you chaps will have your hands full enough once they all start arriving," says Head Of Catering, ominously. "I'll catch up with you later."

Alone in the Dining Hall, I gaze around me in wonder at the sheer opulence and decadence of it all. Amazing. And in the middle of a recession, too. I check the time on the wall clock and decide to head back to the Porters' Lodge. It can't be long until our guests start arriving, what with all the pre-drinking they have to fit in before the actual feasting. I imagine they must be a very hungry, thirsty bunch. I simply cannot wait to meet them.

Lords & Ladies

THE CARRIAGES OF THE VENERABLE guests of The Great Feast are already arriving, conveying, no doubt, those fortunate enough to be attending a pre-drinks reception drinks reception. It's a little bit like a Hollywood red carpet event, but in place of the glitz and glamour is understated elegance and old school resplendence. Instead of stars of the stage and screen there are Lords and Ladies, doctors and professors and all kinds of collegiate aficionados. It quickly becomes evident that the Rolls Royces and Bentleys are struggling to squeeze into the distinctly average sized parking spaces of Old College. The gleaming, stately vehicles are a mixture of stunning classics and brand new, top of the range leviathans. All chauffeur driven, of course. I take pity on the chauffeurs and invite them for tea and biscuits in the Porters' Lodge. A few take me up on my offer, but most look down their perfectly chiselled noses at me. Even the chauffeurs are of better breeding than College Porters, it seems. Then again, I am not entirely surprised at this. These chaps, in their impeccable suits and peaked Parker-esque caps, look like pedigrees. The Porters and I are mongrels, at best.

As I am contemplating putting the kettle on, a gentleman who looks like a 1950's catalogue model wearing a chauffeur's uniform strides into the Lodge with the arrogance and allure of a Siamese cat. He casts his gaze distastefully around the assembled staff – that is, myself and Porter, who is halfway through eating an elderly meat pie.

"Good evening," I venture, as superciliously as I dare "Can I help you?" The Chauffeur sniffs at me and narrows his eyes, as if I am the most unpleasant article he has come across recently. I probably am.

"Lord and Lady B-K have arrived. I believe you have instructions to escort them directly to Senior Bursar's rooms." This is a statement of fact, not a question, or a polite request. Porter wipes his greasy paws on his trousers before removing rather a lot of short crust pastry from his mouth with the sleeve of his already heavily soiled jacket.

"Oh aye, Senior Bursar rang down about that earlier," he says "'Ere, give us a tick and I'll show you up…"

"It's fine!" I interrupt quickly, jumping to my feet "I will show them to Senior Bursar's rooms. You – you finish your pie, or whatever it is,"

"Well, that's very kind of you, Deputy Head Porter, if you're sure you don't mind…" Porter swivels his eyes between The Chauffeur and his half-eaten supper. He is obviously slightly torn between his duty and his pie, but only slightly. The draw of the pie is far stronger.

"Not at all, it will be my pleasure. Please, take me to Lord and Lady B-K."

Porter gives me a grateful look and waves me off as I scurry after The Chauffeur as he stalks across the car park towards the awaiting Rolls Royce. *Well, that's kept the Porter happy,* I muse to myself. *How to make friends and influence Porters; never separate them from their pies.*

Standing by the Roller (with the 80's style doors that open backwards) are, evidently, Lord and Lady B-K. To describe Lord B-K as rotund would be generous. Corpulent, would be getting closer to the actuality of this gentleman's stature; exorbitant would be better still. But, I am generous by nature, so 'rotund' it is. Like a beautifully attired little planet, I half expect nearby shrubbery to yield to his gravitational pull at any minute. His beady eyes stare at me beneath monstrous eyebrows that give the impression of two white woolly caterpillars engaged in a fight to the death. His countenance is that of abject fury, but when he greets me, he is full of blustery charm.

"Ah-ha!" he exclaims, loudly "A girl Porter, what? Marvellous idea! Old College will get up to anything these days!"

"Good evening, your Lordship. I am the Deputy Head Porter. Welcome to The Great Feast."

"*Deputy Head Porter?!*" Lord B-K explodes into obstreperous laughter "Bloody good show! The old boys knew what they were doing when they employed you, what?" he gives me a conspirative wink. "Something pretty to watch skipping through the cloisters, no doubt? Ah-ha! I like their thinking!"

I console myself by thinking, *there's a compliment in there somewhere.* Lord B-K gestures grandly to the willowy and beautiful woman-of-a-certain-age loitering, slightly embarrassed, behind him.

"This is my wife!" as if he has revealed some hitherto unknown and shocking information. "We are pleased to meet you, Deputy Head Porter. Now, where can a man get a good stiff drink?"

"I will take you directly to Senior Bursar's rooms," I reply. I cast a glance at The Chauffeur, who looks at me with disdain. I throw him a derogatory air-kiss to annoy him, which it clearly does.

Lord B-K strides purposefully towards the bridge, enthusiastically regaling me with tales of his commute and enunciating beautifully as he does so. I struggle to keep up, and notice with dismay that Lady B-K is trailing several feet behind us, the combination of ancient uneven flagstones and expensive vertiginous heels conspiring to hinder her progress. She gathers the folds of her swirling silk gown in her delicate, bejewelled hands and totters along as best she can. I am caught between the two of them, trying to keep pace with the eager Lord, both in stride and conversation, and with the Lady; trying to politely hurry her along to rejoin her husband. As I stoop to gather the flowing material of her gown as we ascend the bridge, I feel I must make some effort to converse with her.

"What a beautiful dress!" I remark. Always a safe bet when engaging a Lady, I feel.

"Oh, do you think so? Thank you so much!" she seems genuinely delighted at the compliment. "One never knows what to wear this time of year, the weather is so unpredictable." Ah, the weather. The comfortable main stay of polite conversation.

Once across the bridge, we enter the building that is home to Senior Bursar's rooms. Rather annoyingly, they are situated on the top floor and there is nothing for it but to climb the enormous wooden staircase. Lord B-K bounds ever upwards, with a grace and vigour that belies his robust physique. Lady B-K is displaying that familiar look upon her face, one that transcends all forms of race, class and birthright. It is the look of she who regrets the choice of ostentatious shoes; the shoes that, when admired in the mirror lengthen the leg and create an elegant poise, but when have been walked in for more than a dozen steps cause discomfort beyond measure. I feel her pain, as every woman has, as I observe her painful, ungainly gait as she hauls herself up step after agonising step. I hear the unspoken cursing of the footwear and silently urge her onwards. *It will be worth it. They are, after all, fabulous shoes.* She will be just fine after a few drinks, I'm sure.

Half way up the staircase, the sounds of a most uproarious and decadent party reach my ears. I am very experienced in all aspects of partying. Whether as a guest, a hostess or the one kicking in the door and closing it down, I have attended, in one way or another, pretty much every kind of party you can imagine. Even some kinds you can't imagine. The sounds invading my peace at this moment tell me that if I were a guest at this particular soiree, it would be time to consider getting a taxi. If I were the hostess, it would be time to consider calling the police. If I were the police, it would be time to call for back up, roll up my sleeves and give everyone a bloody good kicking. And this is the *pre-drinks reception* drinks reception. I admit, I am a little jealous.

Lord B-K makes it to the top of the stairs before me, and long before his staggering wife. The door to Senior Bursar's rooms is open, but he waits for me to knock. I very much doubt a knock on the door could be heard above the racket going on within, but I knock anyway. No point in standing on ceremony. It never stood on me. Without waiting for a reply, Lord B-K bundles in, loudly demanding a drink. A drunken *'Hurrah!'* is heralded from somewhere inside and he is lost forever to this posh version of the last days of Sodom and Gomorrah. Lady B-K smiles apologetically at me, and totters unsteadily after him.

I shake my head forlornly and make my way back to the Porters' Lodge. There are endless more guests to greet and escort about Old College, I am sure. Part of me is comforted to know that class and social standing do not necessarily guarantee moderation and morality. When it really comes down to it, excess and depravity is in the person, not the breeding. No matter the education, or lack of it, the demon drink levels us all. By the time the starters are served, I doubt most of this lot will be able to spell their own names.

Happily for me, my shift finishes long before The Great Feast reaches its climactic conclusion and I am able to get to my bed at a far more decent hour than the revellers of Old College. Which is just as well; I have an early start and a busy day tomorrow.

A Friend In Need

This morning is feeling earlier than is strictly necessary. I don't know whether it is the later-than-usual finish last night (in order to accommodate The Great Feast) or the gloomy, leaden sky above me that is making me feel like it is still the middle of the night. I suppose sometimes mornings just come around too quickly, and that is that.

As I make my way through the courtyards to the Porters' Lodge, Old College somehow feels like it agrees me with me. The morning after The Great Feast and the old place has a 'hung over' atmosphere about it. Even the bricks are looking a little paler than they should and I swear the shadows falling beneath the windows are longer and darker than usual.

Crossing the bridge, I am surprised to see Professor K walking unsteadily towards me. It certainly is unusual to see him out and about on his own, particularly at this early hour.

"Good morning, Professor!" I call out with as much cheer as I can muster without having had at least three cups of tea. His twinkly eyes are lifted from the ground and meet mine. I quicken my step towards him; his eyesight isn't that great and I wonder if he can recognise who I am from a distance. "Professor, you're up early, is everything alright?"

"Oh, yes my dear! Certainly," is his chipper reply. He sounds a little weary to me, though.

"What are you doing out and about so early?" I ask "Breakfast won't be served for another half an hour yet."

"Truth be told, Deputy Head Porter, I had terrible trouble sleeping last night, what with The Great Feast. I was woken a couple of times during the night by my revelling colleagues and their guests and it disturbed my sleep to such an extent that I couldn't really settle. Eventually I thought the best thing to do would be to take a breath of morning air before breakfast and maybe have a snooze mid morning."

"You didn't attend The Feast?"

"No, no. Gracious, no. I have been to quite a few over the years, but they are a bit excessive for me these days." Professor K reaches out and takes my arm in a gentlemanly fashion, although from the weight he then shifts in my direction it is clear that he is in need of a little support. "Mind you, back when I was young roister-doister, my chums and I used to have a whale of a time at The Feasts!" The very thought of it brings a broad smile to my face.

"Yes, I have no doubt of that, Sir!" I laugh.

"Ooh, I could tell you a tale or two, I really could. Those were the days!" Professor K is lost for a moment in misty-eyed reverie. "Do you know, Deputy Head Porter, I'm sure the girls were better looking back then."

"Do you think so, Sir?" I ask. I can sense he is struggling a little on his feet this morning; it must be the lack of rest. "Why don't I escort you to your rooms and make you a nice cup of tea while we wait for the Dining Hall to open?"

"You can escort me anywhere you wish, young lady!" he announces cheekily. His body may be bending under the weight of the years but his mind and spirit are more virulent than a man a fraction of his age.

Once I have him settled on his sofa with a hot cup of tea and a biscuit, Professor K seems much better. I have made myself a cup too, at his request, and make myself comfortable next to him. I realise it is rather inappropriate for a College servant to be quite so familiar with a Fellow, but I have become so fond of Professor K and I know he enjoys 'teaching' me about the mysterious side of Old College.

"You haven't been to see me recently," the Professor says, rather ruefully. "Not since Head Porter barged his way in here. I do hope you didn't get into trouble." I shake my head and sip my tea.

"Don't worry, Sir. Head Porter has been rather – difficult – shall we say, for a while. I am sorry I haven't been along since. He has kept me quite busy and I thought it best to keep my head down and get on with things."

Professor K gently taps my knee and leaves his hand there while he speaks.

"You are welcome in my rooms any time, my dear girl, and Head Porter is not to tell you that you cannot visit. I rather feel that we have become... friends"

I stop mid-sip and look wide-eyed into the sincere and smiling face of the Professor. This does not merely warm the cockles of my heart; it wraps them in a rug and puts them snugly by the fire. Momentarily lost for words, I take his hand in mine and give it a little squeeze.

"We are friends" I say, emotion cracking my voice just barely. He squeezes my hand back and taps it again before readjusting himself on the sofa.

"I did speak to The Master about Head Porter's rudeness, not that it will do any good," the Professor continues.

"Why do you say that?" I ask.

"Head Porter is a man *some* of The Fellowship are keen not to upset."

"Oh really?"

"Really. But do not let it trouble you. I am an old man now, and no longer hold much sway at Old College. But there are those that are firm supporters of you. Powerful people."

This comes as something of a shock. It had never occurred to me that I would have come to the attention of anyone in The Fellowship, one way or the other. I hadn't realised they had been paying that much attention. My natural inclination is to ask who these people are, but Professor K carries on talking so I drink my tea and listen.

"I have been here a long time now and seen many things. Some of those things I wish I hadn't seen but I didn't have much choice. Sometimes, a man cannot be proud of everything he has done but he cannot ignore it, either. It would be... such an *injustice*"

I rather fear Professor K is going off at a rather odd tangent. His eyes are distant and I get the feeling he is speaking to someone else, unseen. He is an elderly man, who did not sleep much last night, it is possible he just needs a bit of a rest.

"Are you alright, Professor?" I ask gently. "Maybe you should get some rest. I can arrange for Chef to keep a breakfast back for you if you sleep over breakfast."

The Professor hears my words but still seems to be in another place.

"Sleep! Ah, yes…" He speech is becoming slurred now and the colour has drained from his cheeks. I'm no doctor, but I can see he isn't well. I pull out my mobile and dial Nurse's number. It is ringing. Professor K mumbles incoherently and I hold his hand and make soothing noises.

"Good morning, Nurse's Office" the clipped Scottish tones of Nurse twitter in my ear.

"Nurse, it's me. I'm with Professor K in his rooms, he seems quite unwell"

"I'm on my way!" The phone in replaced sharply and I know that Nurse will be here in no time. I turn my attentions back to the worryingly pale Professor.

"Professor! My dear friend, Nurse is on her way. You are going to be fine"

"Just a little sleep, my dear," a moment of lucidity "Peacefully in their sleep… didn't I tell you?" I think he is referring to our last conversation.

"That's right, Professor. You did tell me" why I say what I say next, I'm not really sure "Is this something else my thirst for knowledge should be applied to?" The faintest of twinkles in the eyes.

"A thirst for knowledge is a wonderful thing," the Professor's voice is as dry as bones "Remember that. And this – not all sleep is as peaceful as it seems!"

Nurse bursts through the door with a bag of equipment almost as big as she is. With concern etched on her face, she politely but firmly pushes me to one side to examine the Professor.

"You'd better call an ambulance, just in case" she says under her breath. As she attends to my new best friend, I give her some space and dial 999. I then call down to the Porters' Lodge to let them know what is happening.

Arrangements in place, I nervously turn back to Nurse and Professor K. Nurse has him lying on the sofa with his legs propped up on the arms. His colour looks a little better but he is very quiet.

"Is he going to be alright?" I whisper to Nurse.

"Och, he should be fine," she replies. *Big, big sigh of relief* "I'm sure it's just a temporary drop in blood pressure but he's as well to go to hospital for a proper check over anyway. You can't be too careful."

111

"Thank God," I say. "He did say he didn't sleep well last night."

"Has he had anything to eat, do you know?"

"I don't think so, he was waiting for the Dining Hall to open when I came across him by the bridge."

"That's probably it, then" Nurse nods confidently and I am instantly put at ease. "The hospital will give him some fluids and no doubt he will be back on his feet in no time."

I check with Nurse before I finish for the day and, indeed, Professor K has made a full recovery and is expected to be released from hospital first thing in the morning. I make a note to ensure I collect the finest breakfast Chef can possibly muster and deliver it to the Professor's rooms upon his return. The perfect welcome back, I feel!

The Hairdryer Treatment

I TAKE PROFESSOR K HIS epic breakfast first thing this morning, as planned. Actually, it is my breakfast that I am kindly donating to this worthy cause. It is a bit of a feat, I feel, to transport the towering pile of expertly grilled (not fried – I specifically requested it not to be fried. I have the Professor's health to consider) mountain of meaty delights from the kitchens to his rooms.

When I arrive, Professor K already has half The Fellowship visiting him and showing varying degrees of concern. I am delighted to see that he looks much, much better than yesterday so I deliver the breakfast and make a hasty exit.

I keep in mind his puzzling comments from the day before, but it could have been his semi-conscious state causing him to ramble. That said, there is definitely something rather suspicious about the Fellows from fifty years ago dying before they could report the unsavoury activities of their colleagues to the police. What could be done about it now, after all this time, I really have no idea. But it would be nice to find out a little more, if I can.

By mid-morning I am happily conducting one of my many daily patrols of Old College. Once such an alien experience, the old place is now feeling familiar and almost homely to me. If I close my eyes, I can identify my location and find my way just by the feel of the ancient ground beneath my feet. Apart from being one of the most beautiful and inspiring places I have ever had the fortune to be caretaker of, my patrols almost always result in the general feeling that everything is well and as it should be. I stop and

113

speak to all manner of staff and students, making small talk with everyone from Bedders and Gardeners to Doctors and Professors. I feel I am now just coming to terms with my new life as Deputy Head Porter in the strange and Wonderland-like world of Old College. I can now understand why Junior Bursar has spent his entire adult life here. I feel a spell has been cast and I have succumbed to it. Quite when this happened, I cannot say. All I know is that somewhere along the line I became part of Old College.

I can hardly believe that my six-month probationary period is mere weeks away from completion. The initial struggle to prove my worth as a woman in a traditionally male role seems a lifetime away. I feel quietly proud of being the first female to wear College Deputy Head Porter colours in over six hundred years. The contrast to my previous life could not be starker. Although everyday a small part of me mourns everything I left behind, I believe this is simply because my new life has felt so unreal to me. And maybe because I felt that I didn't deserve it. But now, I feel part of the rich and vibrant tapestry that echoes through every wall and cloister, across every perfect lawn and every immaculate flowerbed. I am still an outsider, but I am wiping my feet on the way in.

I check my watch; it is almost time for my review meeting with Head Porter. I have had a couple of these meetings since my appointment at Old College and they have always been overwhelmingly positive. I have made mistakes along the way and my ignorance of College life has been commented upon, but these things I have learnt from and in some instances have even had an endearing quality to them.

I have never been a religious person, but as I find myself in Apple Tree Court I decide to visit the Chapel before making my way to the Armingford Room for my meeting. By no means is the Chapel the grandest of The City University's Chapels. Our proud neighbour, Hawkins College, has probably the most awe-inspiring Chapel in all the land. However, I will happily settle for the comparatively modest yet beautifully crafted Chapel of Old College for my moment of reverie and reflection.

The Chapel is empty, yet still feels as though it bustles with the activity of hundreds of years of worshippers, mourners, brides and grooms, choirs and good old-fashioned fire and brimstone. While the spirituality of the place completely eludes me, the basic humanity and everyday need for higher understanding does not. Although I have never really understood organised religion (seemingly the cause of almost every significant conflict throughout history. That and oil), I do understand the human attribute of needing to find reasons and answers outside of our own egos. There is not one of us that, at some crucial point in our lives, has not cast out eyes to the sky and asked "Why?' or "How?" or "When?" Whether or not we know to whom we are talking does not matter. We still ask.

I have only a few minutes to drink in the heady, pious atmosphere, but it is enough. Sometimes we need to feel small and insignificant to appreciate the bigger picture. The smell of elderly wood and fresh candle wax is just what I need to clear my head and centre my thoughts. I make my way to the Armingford Room.

Head Porter is already waiting for me. He rises from his seat as I enter the wood panelled room. He indicates a plush wooden dining chair set by a coffee table, opposite his own identical seat. As previously mentioned, I haven't seen much of Head Porter in recent weeks due to us now apparently working opposite shifts. I am not really sure when my training ended (or, for that matter, when it began,) but at some point along the way he deemed it appropriate for me to work independently. It would have been nice to have been notified of this arrangement, but you can't have everything. I greet him cheerily and take my seat. I am not prepared for what is to come.

Head Porter takes a deep breath. And goes straight for the jugular.

"I have to let you know, Deputy Head Porter, that I have received several complaints about you. There are several things I have to bring to your attention."

This throws me completely off kilter. I come from a world where complaints and mistakes are brought to attention immediately. Where has this come from? Head Porter continues...

"Several weeks ago, a student came to the Lodge to collect a package. You enquired if she knew what the package might be and when she said she was expecting some new shoes, you squealed and jumped up and down. You then *skipped* to the postal room and *skipped* back, before asking to see the shoes. This is unprofessional."

Involuntarily, I make a derisorily annoyed facial expression and regard him as if I have an idiot before me. This is a reflex reaction but, all the same, not a wise move. I compose myself within seconds.

"Simply an example of tactical communication; engaging with the student at her own level," I reply, trying to keep the annoyance from showing. Head Porter looks at me blankly. This is not an acceptable response.

"There are several other instances of your unprofessional behaviour that have been brought to my attention," he continues. He lists them. Endlessly. Asking advice from Head Of Catering; laughing loudly at the front desk; wearing my hair down on TWO occasions, jumping up and down, being noisy, being *too enthusiastic* in my job... the 'charge sheet' went on and on. Head Porter concludes...

"Not to put too fine a point on it, the Porters don't like you and The Fellowship don't think much of you either. You need to make some drastic changes if you hope to get through your probationary period."

Inside, I am torn apart. This feels like a personal attack, not constructive criticism of my professional ability. Devastatingly, all of Head Porter's remarks about my behaviour are all aspects of my personality that I will find very difficult to change. I will always share in the delight of a new pair of shoes. When I laugh, I laugh with my heart and soul. Whatever I do, I do enthusiastically. (I am bloody noisy, I'll give him that). I struggle to contemplate why events from months ago are being used as a stick to beat me with. I struggle with the notion that *absolutely no one* likes me. Only the other day, The Dean asked my opinion on his new trousers. Then, I say the stupidest thing I could possibly say...

"Is this because I ate Senior Bursar's biscuits?"

Head Porter looks at me with the coldest, darkest look I have seen in a long time. I have looked into the eyes of criminals of every discription. But never have I felt the aggression and coldness I feel when I return the gaze of Head Porter. For a second or three I feel my world crumble and my heartbreak in a way that it has never been broken before. But then my senses regroup and I feel my back against the wall, but most of all I feel outrage. I have achieved much since coming to Old College. Every task I have taken on with relish and glee. Every obstacle placed in my path I have demolished with aplomb and finesse. Backed into a corner, I am dangerous. Especially, I am a danger to myself.

"These things you say to me," I say slowly and carefully "Are all things about myself that are part of my personality. Have you considered that maybe I am not the right person for the position of Deputy Head Porter?"

Head Porter seems taken aback. He shuffles his paperwork ineffectually.

"I just think there are a few changes..."

"These things are who I am," I reply with a composure that I impress myself with. "I am not prepared to suppress who I am. If the Porters don't like it, and The Fellowship don't like it, well" *deep breath* "Well then maybe you need to find a new Deputy Head Porter."

The bombshell has been dropped. I cast my gaze through Head Porter. He looks as shaken as I feel, but, despite the catastrophic collapse I feel within me, I know my countenance is displaying the perfect mask of outraged indignation. I have travelled too far along my own path to take this kind of nonsense.

"I don't think you should make any hasty decisions," Head Porter is on a completely different tact now.

"It is not my decision to make," I answer back with the petulance I learnt as a teenager. "The decision is yours. If I am not what College wants, I will go. Let us not waste any more of either of ours' time."

I stand up to leave. Head Porter holds up a barely-noticeably shaking hand.

"Just... promise me one thing," he pleads. I barely nod my head. "Please... just speak to me before you speak to anyone else. I would hate to come in and find your keys and a note on the desk."

I shrug nonchalantly, before turning on my heels and striding out of the room as fast as my shaking legs can carry me.

They carry me beyond the walls of Old College and into The City streets. For all I care they can carry me to the moon. My legs and I don't quite make it to the moon, but we do make it to a quiet back street drinking establishment with a questionable reputation. And, for all I care, we can stay there.

Contemplation

I SIT, SADLY NURSING A large glass of red, ridiculously over-dressed and looking quite out of place in this dark and scruffy public house. The whole place appears to be in urgent need of repair and restoration; indeed, parts of the building look like they are about to collapse at any minute. However, I get the impression that it has been this way for quite some time and if it was going to fall down, it probably would have done so by now. The upholstery is faded and threadbare; most of the chairs, tables and other associated furniture seem to be held together by will power alone. Quite how strong the will power of a table is, I have no idea. I try to avoid resting too much of my weight on mine, just to be on the safe side.

My few fellow patrons seem in better spirits than my good self. There is a wiry, elderly gentleman sitting precariously on a rickety-looking stool at the bar. He has skin the same colour and texture of an old boot, an old boot that has had a particularly hard life, at that. He is wearing a vest top and shorts that leave little to the imagination. To complete the look, he has opted for a sock and slipper combination for his foot attire. The old man chatters happily to himself, seemingly without a care in the world. He catches the attention of the shaven headed, purple-bearded bar tender who dutifully furnishes him with further refreshments. *What am I doing here?* I think to myself.

The first glass of red does nothing to ease my wounded pride and feelings, so I order another. I do not expect the continued imbibitions to resolve my current situation, I just hope they can take the edge off a little. I smile wryly to myself and wonder what The Committee For The

Prevention Of Drunken Behaviour would say if they could see me now. I allow myself to wallow a little, and let the feelings of loneliness and rejection swim self indulgently round and round my head. *But I've worked so hard! Put in so many hours! Nobody loves me, everybody hates me, I might as well go and eat worms...*

I quickly realise that feeling sorry for myself is going to get me nowhere. And something just doesn't feel quite right, somehow. I turn Head Porter's words over and over in my head and the more I think about them, the more petty they seem. As I contemplate the scenario further, I feel my hurt and heartbreak subside to make way for what can only be described as gumption. *Ah ha! It isn't drinking that's going to help me here, it's thinking!* I should have challenged Head Porter far more robustly. I should have made a point of detailing my successes and achievements. Why didn't I do that? I think it was the shock of it all, probably. Still. I expected better of myself.

Just then, the door to the pub opens, letting in a shaft of light from the sunny streets beyond and what passes for fresh air in The City. I am surprised to see the portly, amiable figure of Porter ambling through it. He looks flushed and sweaty, his ample frame obviously protesting at the recent demands made of it. He looks around and spots me. Porter bundles over to my table and unceremoniously pulls up a chair.

"Here you are!" he says cheerfully. "I've already tried The Albatross and The Shipman, I'm knackered. I'll have a pint."

"Err, right" I reply, getting up to head to the bar. "A pint? Fine."

The barman is friendly but it is apparent he is now a little suspicious of having two overly dressed patrons now occupying his establishment. Our crested jackets and College ties identify us as servants to the academic world, obviously we are not his usual type of customer.

Porter drinks a third of his pint instantly and wipes froth from his mouth before offering me a sympathetic smile.

"What are you doing here?" I ask, as politely as I can.

"What am I doing here? What are *you* doing here?!" comes his reply. My mouth opens, but no sensible words come out, so I close it again, giving the impression of an ineffectual fish of some description. "I heard about what happened with Head Porter, I guessed you would be wanting a drink. See, I was right!"

"Good news travels fast, obviously" I retort, a little more bitterly than I intended.

"Oh, you know what it's like, these things get out."

"How?!"

"Head Porter blabs just about everything, can't keep his mouth shut for more than a few minutes, then before you know it everyone knows! Apparently, he said you were crap and you told him to stick his job."

I let out an involuntary laugh.

"Well, that's a bit more dramatic than what actually happened. And I haven't actually resigned, or anything, but there was – shall we say – a full and frank exchange of opinions."

Porter nods knowingly and flicks some imaginary specks of dust from his sleeve.

"Look, you don't want to pay too much attention to what Head Porter says," Porter tells me. "And it's not true that nobody likes you. I like you. Most of the lads think you are doing a pretty good job. It's not you they have a problem with. It's how you got the job."

"Well, I filled in the application form, went for the interview. The usual stuff."

Porter shakes his head.

"No, no. Not about that. You already know, the previous Deputy Head Porter did not get on with Head Porter at all. He was an experienced Porter and had worked his whole life in College so he knew how things ticked. He retired just before you joined us, or he would be telling you this himself."

"Right, fine." I turn my attention back to my wine.

"You don't know the half of it, the things that went on before you came. Even if one of us had applied, we would never have been given the job. He wanted someone from the outside, who wasn't aware of the history of the Lodge. Someone he could manipulate and who would do as they were told."

"He picked the wrong person, then" I reply. "That's not me at all. Anyway, how could the Bursars allow this to happen? Didn't they want someone from a College background?"

"Well, that's just the point!" Porter exclaims "He held the interviews for your job during the summer shut down period, when The Bursars,

The Dean and The Master were all off on holiday! Who interviewed you for the job?"

I cast my mind back. *Yeah, that makes sense. I started in late September so my interview must have been in early August to allow me to give a month's notice from my previous job… it must have been in the two week August shut down…*

"I was interviewed by Head Porter and the lady from HR,"

Porter slaps the table jubilantly, making me jump.

"Aha! Exactly. You wouldn't know this, but for a role as senior as Deputy Head Porter, there should be at least one member of The Fellowship present at the interview – definitely one of the Bursars and probably someone else as well, most likely The Dean. We all think Head Porter timed the interviews deliberately so that he alone would be able to choose his Deputy. There were some really strong candidates, as well. He let us look through the application forms. I have to say, we were all shocked when we found out he had employed you. We all told him you were too young. And, obviously, you didn't know anything about College life. When we knew you had got the job, it confirmed our suspicions that he had fixed it. The first day you walked in, no offense, all slim and pretty and looking like you do, it just seemed obvious he thought he was going to push you around and try and shag you."

Well, it's nice to be reminded of my auspicious appointment. Except, before hand, I thought I got the job simply because I was the worst possible choice. Now, it seems, I got the job because Head Porter thought I was easy as well. I need another drink.

"Another one?" I ask Porter, gesturing to his empty glass. He must sense my consternation as he reaches for my hand as I get up to go to the bar.

"You have to understand, we didn't know you then. I'm not saying you can't do the job, because you can. You've really been a breath of fresh air in that Lodge. And you're right – he did pick the wrong person. He can't push you around and he knows it. That's what today was all about."

I smile gratefully at Porter. After all, he didn't have to come and find me and tell me all this. It was a kind thing to do. And, he said I was pretty! A small thing, perhaps, but I am easily pleased.

"I'll get you a pint," I say to Porter. "And I'm having another, too, because if that was supposed to make me feel any better, you failed miserably!"

"I haven't finished, yet!" Porter replies, giving me what I assume is a 'knowing look'.

While I wait for our drinks to be served, I think about what Porter has said. Clearly, there is a lot I don't know about Head Porter and the evident bad feeling in the Lodge. I find his apparent reasons for employing me interesting. I hope I have proved myself to be more than he thought I was, if not to him then to The Fellowship and my Porters. Needless to say, my opinion of Head Porter has diminished to almost nothing. To think I worked so hard to overcome the predispositions and sexism of Old College, only to discover that was the very reason I was employed in the first place! I wasn't there to challenge prejudice, I was supposed to embody it! No wonder Head Porter is so riled. He wanted a good little girl who would shut up and do as she is told. What he got, was me. I suppose I would be pretty pissed off, in his position.

I deliver a fresh pint of whatever passes for the best ale in this establishment in front of a very grateful Porter. I settle down with my third glass of wine and an entirely different view of the situation in hand. Although the wine must take some credit, my improved perspective owes much to Porter's revelations. And he is not finished yet.

"Right then," I take back a generous mouthful of what now seems like bloody good wine and attempt to summarise. "I got this job because Head Porter thought he could either bully me, or shag me, or both. He could then go on running the Lodge in whatever way he saw fit, without any challenge from me. He achieved this by fixing the interview dates so that he could pick the person he thought would be easiest to push around. Things haven't quite worked out like that, so now he is taking it out on me and is trying to assert some authority. I suppose after today's performance he hopes I will fear for my job and become subservient."

"It's not just that," Porter continues, having enthusiastically begun his second pint. "He feels threatened. You see, once we all found out he had given you the job, some of the Porters, myself included, went and told The Master and The Dean what was going on. About him fixing it and that. So there were some meetings set up, in secret, with some of the senior members of The Fellowship and some of the Porters. Head Porter would have eventually found out about this because you can't keep anything secret in this place. Porters like to gossip and word would have reached him before long. Anyway, it was too late to do anything because you had already accepted the position so The Fellowship had no choice but to go along with it. But they were pretty annoyed about the way it had all been carried out and I think the idea was to prove that he had made a bad decision and employed the wrong person to meet his own ends."

"Ah!" I interrupt "That might explain some of the strange errands and tasks I was given, early on?"

"Yes! I think they were trying to prove you weren't up to the job. Thing is, you've actually turned out to be quite good at it and I know a lot of The Fellows really quite like you…"

"Which is a good thing…?"

"Well, sort of, but it would have been better if you were rubbish because then they would have been able to drag Head Porter over the coals for employing a young girl with no experience."

I think about it for a moment.

"I'm not that young," is all I can think of to say.

"Besides," Porter continues "He has already rubbed quite a few of them up the wrong way. Like I said, you don't know the half of it. There's a few in The Fellowship that can't stand him. They are looking at any excuse to get him out."

"Really?" my curiosity is piqued "Who?"

Porter shakes his head and chuckles.

"I'm not going into that," he replies diplomatically. "But what I can tell you, there's some Porters that feel the same way."

There is an uneasy silence between us, where what is left unsaid says more than can ever be expressed in words. Porter finally breaks the stalemate.

"There are quite a few people at Old College that would rather you were Head Porter," Porter says finally. I stare into my glass. I haven't even completed one academic year, yet. In my heart, I know I am not ready to be Head Porter, if that could even be possible.

"I just want what's best for the Lodge," I eventually manage to reply.

"Have a think about what I've said," Porter is getting up to leave. "Don't let him get to you and don't believe what he tells you. Come back tomorrow."

I nod and smile. Against my better judgement, I get up and hug Porter. I watch him leave and I finish my wine. As I make my way through the streets of The City, I am at least grateful that there is never a dull moment where Old College is concerned.

I find it interesting that, while there are obviously some members of The Fellowship who seem very keen to keep him sweet, other members want him out. Just what is it about Head Porter that provokes such consternation? Why does a humble College servant hold such sway at Old College? Obviously, I have to find a way to find this out.

Oxymorons

I RETURN TO THE PORTERS' Lodge the next day with so many emotions running through my veins I do not even know what I feel. So much so, I must use the most hated oxymoron of 'felling numb'. This is clearly emanating through my every pore as Deputy Head Of Catering grabs my arm as I career through the Lodge.

"Are you alright?" she asks, her pretty, colourfully made-up face etched with concern.

"…Yeah" I reply, as brightly as I can. Which isn't very brightly.

"You were in that meeting a long time yesterday, did he give you a hard time?"

I see what Porter means about word getting around.

"A bit," I shrug my shoulders, as if to shake off the weight of the world I feel sitting there.

"Oh, I shouldn't take it to heart," she coos soothingly. I swallow hard and walk her through to the kitchen, where I can make some much-needed tea.

"He said… some things…"

"Pay no attention," she says quickly "He does this sort of thing all the time. I'm surprised it hasn't happened sooner."

"What?"

"Oh, it's just his way of showing you who's boss. All The Porters have had it at some point. Some more often than others. The man has no people skills. We were all wondering when he was going to give you the hairdryer treatment."

I stop and look at Deputy Head Of Catering. She is being deadly serious.

"What? Really?" I ask, a little non-plussed.

"Yes, it's just him. I hope you gave as good as you got!"

"I told him to find a new Deputy Head Porter," is my glum reply.

"Don't worry about it. The weekend is coming up, try and relax. Things will be back to normal when you come back."

Deputy Head Of Catering leaves me to my tea-making reverie and I turn her words over in my head and try to make sense of it all. The worst of it is the loneliness of it all. I have not been at Old College long enough to forge any really close, trusting friendships. There is no one in this surreal (and, it seems, sadistic!) world I can share my concerns with. No matter. It will probably all be alright. And, if not, I always have my 'security professional' qualification to fall back on! Indeed.

After my days off, I return to the Lodge to find a beautiful, brand new waistcoat hanging on my locker. It is lined with the same elaborate silk as my suit. The crest of Old College beams magnificently from the left breast. I also find a sealed envelope in my in-tray. Within is a lovely surprise. It is a letter from Senior Bursar informing me that I am in receipt of a very small (but very gratefully received) pay rise. Unexpected to say the least.

Hey ho, here we go. I obviously have misjudged my understanding of the intricate workings of Old College. Stick, carrot... looks like I am due more stick than I am carrot. To draw a rather saucy simile, it appears I will have to bend over and take the stick like a good girl. However, my buttocks will be clenched so tightly that that stick will be broken asunder if it hits me too hard.

Peacefully Sleeping?

I AM IN THAT WONDERFULLY pleasant state, somewhere between sleep and awakening, where everything and nothing seems possible and the mind is not troubled by anything more than simply being. I become vaguely aware of the theme tune to *Minder* playing somewhere in the middle distance. Why is the theme tune to *Minder* playing? That's strange. Then, I realise. That's my ring-tone. That must mean that my phone is ringing. Bugger!

I notice that my bedside clock is telling me that it is five twenty five as I scramble and fight my way free of the duvet. Half asleep and feeling slightly sick, I force myself upright and out into the hallway where my phone is on charge. I answer it.

"Deputy Head Porter, are you awake?" It is Junior Bursar.

"I am now, Sir," I reply, not half as sarcastically as I should.

"You must come into College immediately. I am afraid I have some very bad news. Professor K is dead. Please get here as quickly as you can."

I do not have an opportunity to reply, as Junior Bursar ends the call abruptly. Although there was nothing in his voice to suggest so, I get the feeling he is very upset.

The full weight of Junior Bursar's words don't really hit me until I am in the shower, hastily getting ready for work. *Professor K is dead!* I let out a little, animalistic whine as the concept washes over me. He was very old and he did come over quite poorly the other day. He seemed fine when I took him his breakfast but… I guess you just can't tell. He was my friend. My friend has died. An emptiness begins to creep its way across the bottom of my stomach and slowly crawls upwards. By the time I am at the sink, brushing my teeth, it reaches my heart, imploding on impact, forcing great sobs from my throat and tears from my eyes.

I have to do my duty, as a College servant. My duty to Old College and my duty to dear old Professor K. This is all I can focus on right now and it is all that prevents me from freezing up completely with shock and grief. The drive to Old College passes me by almost unnoticed and when I pull up in my parking space I have little recollection of how I got there. The thing to do is focus on the necessary. I have never had to deal with a death in College before, but I suspect there will be work to be done. Arrangements to be made. Tasks to be carried out. Practicalities to consider. This is a good thing.

I make my way to the Porters' Lodge. It seems like the sensible thing to do. Night Porter is still on shift, waiting for the morning man to relieve him. The Night Porters always look a little sombre anyway at this time of the morning, but the recent news is obviously weighing heavily on him.

"You've, heard, I take it?" Night Porter asks gravely. I nod.

"When did he die?" I ask.

"Sometime in the night, ma'am. I found him a couple of hours ago." Night Porter takes a deep breath as he steadies himself to continue. "About quarter past four, I noticed his lights were still on when I was conducting my patrols. I thought, what with him being ill recently and that, I'd better take a look. I found him in bed. Looks like he went peacefully in his sleep."

That's a phrase that keeps cropping up.

"Thank you, Night Porter" I reply. "Have you seen Junior Bursar this morning?"

"Yes, ma'am, I called him right after I found the Professor. I think he's in his rooms."

"Okay, thanks. Have we notified Nurse or called an ambulance?"

"Junior Bursar told me to leave everything to him, ma'am" Night Porter says this as if he is unhappy with this arrangement. "I haven't done anything else."

"Right. I'll go and see Junior Bursar," I say "Are you alright? I mean, it can be quite a shock finding a dead body."

"I'm alright," replies Night Porter, quietly.

"As soon as the morning man gets in you're to go straight home, okay? You've had quite a night of it."

"Yes ma'am, thank you."

What follows next is a bit of a blur, to be honest. I find Junior Bursar in his rooms, accompanied by Nurse. The atmosphere is sad, but business-like. This is a sensible and healthy approach to the early stages of bereavement, I find. Nurse is certain that Professor K didn't suffer and passed away peacefully in his sleep. This is, at least, of some comfort. *Not all sleep is as peaceful as it seems…*

I have several duties to attend to during the course of this unhappy day. I grimly hoist the College flag to half-mast; my fear of heights is noticeably absent today, the greater purpose of this act overtaking the normal human emotion and phobia. The lack of wind means that the flag doesn't flutter majestically but instead hangs sad, limp and still. I find this small detail particularly upsetting, I don't know why.

The everyday comings and goings of the Lodge are punctuated by the arrivals of various persons in black. Some officials, some mourners, some I have no idea who they are. It is always the ordinary and everyday things that seem so pertinent after a death. The post is still delivered and then collected. Keys are still lost and found. Tourists and visitors still pose happily, cheesy grins and jaunty stances, by Old College landmarks. That's the thing about life. It goes *on*.

Life Goes On

AND SO, INDEED, LIFE DOES continue. Of course, there is a melancholy air about Old College in the days following the death of Professor K, but this subsides to the general feeling that he was an old man, he had a good life and these things happen. And of course, this is true. Something is niggling me, though. Call it the old policing instinct, call it paranoia, call it what you like. The more I think about it, the more I think the Professor was trying to tell me something. Something quite important. I think the events from all those years ago upset him. It appears to me that he was suspicious of the deaths of those Fellows, that there was much more to it. There must have been a reason, aside from his habit of talking in riddles, that he didn't tell me straight out what he was thinking. I wonder if he was scared of something.

Head Porter had the good grace to allow me to attend Professor K's funeral, which is being held in a small but prestigious chapel in The City. It is within walking distance of Old College, so I don my bowler hat and smart black woollen coat and make my way through the streets. It is a funny feeling, being a College Porter outside of a College. Of course, The City has many Colleges littering its ancient streets so you do occasionally come across the odd bowler-hatted gentleman wandering around, but usually I feel quite conspicuous when out and about. College business doesn't often take me outside of its walls but when it does I must say that I do feel rather proud to be so obviously a Porter from Old College.

I have picked up on the fact that there is a bit of friendly (and, on occasion, not so friendly) inter-College rivalry in The City. This usually manifests itself in sporting events, the boat races in particular are especially highly contested. I am not aware of any inter-College Porter rivalry, but that may just be my naivety. I would quite relish a bit of Porter rivalry, actually. I could just see my chaps cornering the chaps from Hawkins College round the back of the bike sheds for a bit of fisticuffs. How well they'd fare, I have no idea, but it would be bloody good fun, I imagine.

But anyway. I'm on the way to a funeral and I really should be a little more sombre. Although, I have a feeling Professor K wouldn't mind a bit of frivolity on today of all days. I think of those twinkly eyes and I cannot help but smile, in spite of the tears in my own eyes.

As I enter the chapel, a tall elderly gentleman reaches out and grabs my arm. A little surprised, I turn to face him.

"Excuse me," he says politely "But are you Deputy Head Porter from Old College?"

"I am," I reply.

"It's a pleasure to meet you. I am the old deputy head porter!" It's the Old Boy! I suppose it is completely reasonable that he is here, he must have known Professor K for many years.

"It's great to meet you!" I exclaim "I've heard so much about you!" the Old Boy lets out a deep, throaty laugh that echoes rather embarrassingly around the old gothic building.

"When we've said our goodbyes to the Professor you must fill me in on all the College gossip!" the Old Boy says excitedly. "I really miss hearing about what all the students and Fellows are up to."

I agree to a quick cup of tea and a slice of cake (it was the promise of cake that eventually convinced me) after the service for a chat. I'm sure Head Porter won't mind if I'm gone a tiny bit longer than expected. Well, okay, he probably will, but I really don't care either way.

There is a respectable turn out for Professor K's farewell; mainly academics and Old College alumni from what I can gather. The service itself is a little dry, I feel, but respects are paid in a beautiful manner nonetheless. As we all shuffle out onto the vibrant City streets, the Old Boy catches my eye and gives a little wave to indicate for me to follow him.

As it happens, the Old Boy is taking me to one of The City's oldest and most famous teashops – The Tin Teapot. It is a wonderful, higgledy-piggledy little place with low ceilings and oak beams. It has been wonderfully maintained over the centuries, although some of the old City stalwarts will happily tell you that it was looking a bit tatty about twenty years ago. And, of course, it is nowhere near as good as it used to be when they were young.

We order a pot of tea and a couple of huge Danish pastries. I take an enthusiastic bite into the flaky loveliness, which I instantly regret, as the flaky loveliness is soon getting all over my coat and trousers. I brush myself down, but only really succeed in getting myself rather sticky. The Old Boy is patiently waiting for me to complete this miniature pantomime while he sips at his tea.

"Sorry," I offer. "I always get food down me. My mother says it's because I eat too quickly."

"You like your food, do you?"

"Oh, yes."

"You must be enjoying all the food at Old College, then"

"Yes, it's fantastic!"

"What about everything else at Old College? Are you enjoying that?" This seems like a bit of a loaded question from the Old Boy.

"Ye-es, I think so, it all seems to be going quite well," I reply carefully. Old Boy leans in and lowers his voice.

"What about Head Porter?" he almost whispers "How are you getting along with him?"

It seems my predecessor really is keen on a bit of gossip. I had better tread carefully, here.

"Fine, I think. He seems… okay." Old Boy gives me a 'knowing' look and a thoughtful nod.

"You don't have to be politically correct with me, mate" he says, obviously attempting to open up a channel of communication. "I worked with him for bloody years. I know what he can be like."

I let out a little relieved sigh. Well, at least it's not just me. I weaken a little. It would be nice to be able to talk openly about the less attractive elements of my job. Those elements being, in essence, Head Porter.

"Well – he can be a bit difficult to get on with, sometimes" I say. "I never really know quite what he expects from me. Or what he's thinking. If he's thinking anything at all. Do you know what I mean?"

"Oh, I know exactly what you mean," Old Boy is nodding vigorously in agreement now. "He likes to play his cards very close to his chest, that one."

"He's hardly ever around, either" I continue, emboldened by tea and pastry. "Most of the time, I have no idea what I'm doing and he's never there to point me in the right direction. The Porters have been pretty good, actually. But then you'll get some incident, or bizarre request, or whatever, and Head Porter's nowhere to be seen!"

"Yep, he was just the same when I was in your position. Left all the grafting to me, then moaned about me doing it wrong."

"How does he get away with it?" I ask. "I mean, with The Fellowship? Surely they notice these things."

"Ah, well, yes – The Fellowship do notice a lot of things," Old Boy's tone is once again lowered. The walls of The Tin Teapot must have ears, I reckon. "A lot more than you might give them credit for. They might seem a bit preoccupied at times, and definitely a bit eccentric, but they ain't stupid."

"Well, obviously they're not *stupid*," I agree "They're some of the finest minds in the country. So why do they put up with someone like him as their Head Porter? I mean, Old College is one of the most famous Colleges in the world! And they've got him as a front man? I just don't get it."

"Would you like to know why?" Old Boy is clearly enjoying himself. I can't work out if it is because he has found a kindred spirit after all these years – a fellow 'victim' of Head Porter; or if he is simply enjoying the old-woman-over-the-garden-gate nature of our conversation. Whatever. Of course I want to know why.

"Go on, then" I say "Tell me why."

Old Boy rearranges himself in his chair and pours himself a top up of tea. Clearly this is going to be so good he needs to *prepare* himself.

"Firstly, they haven't got a clue what goes on in the Lodge. And neither does anyone else, really. Head Porter likes to keep everyone in the dark about what he actually does, day to day. Information is power, you see. As it happens, Head Porter came to be in possession of some very… private… information, relating to the College." Old Boy pauses. I am sure this is for dramatic effect. To be fair, I am intrigued. "Let's just say, he knows where the bodies are buried. So to speak." *A-Ha!*

"Bodies?" I think I know where this is going. "Is this about when they dug up the Porters' Lodge?" Old Boys eyes widen in what looks very much like disbelief.

"Oh? So you know about that as well, do you?" *As well?!*

"As well as what?" I ask

"Didn't take you long to find out all the dirt, did it?"

"Look, all I know is that when the Porters' Lodge was rebuilt, there was some kerfuffle, then two Fellows died suspiciously quickly afterwards. That's all I know."

"Well, knowing that alone is dangerous enough."

I am losing my patience a little bit. Why can't anyone just come out straight with what they are trying to say? I had put it down to being a bit of an academic thing, but even the Old Boy's at it now.

"Just. Tell me. What's going on. Please" I feel my request is firm, but polite.

"Let's just say…" the Old Boy begins. *Here we go again* "Let's just say that people who have had that particular piece of information in the past have come to a bit of a sticky end."

"Right, well, shall I tell you what this sounds like to me?" I am resorting to throwing wild conspiracy theories at him and see what comes out. "This sounds like Old College somehow bumped off those two Fellows years ago to keep them quiet. From what you're saying, other people may have found out about this somewhere along the line. Are you suggesting they got bumped off too?"

Old Boy makes a deliberately poor attempt at looking nonchalant which can only lead me to believe that this is exactly what he is suggesting. I know I keep saying that I have learnt not to be surprised by anything about Old College these days, but this does seem a little excessive. Let's go along with it for now.

"So what has this got to do with Head Porter?"

"He's a sneaky one, Head Porter," replies Old Boy, slowly. "Always watching, listening to things he shouldn't be. Know what I mean?"

"Well, he's not dead, is he?" I point out. "In fact, he has the cushiest number around! Comes and goes as he pleases, gets away with doing a half-arsed job all the time…" *O-oh. Right. That's why.* "Why don't they just kill him? If it was me, I'd have just bumped him off like the others."

"They need him to run the Lodge!" Old Boy obviously feels we are straying somewhat from the original point he was making. "Look, what I'm saying to you is – the information that you have could be dangerous. Don't let on to anyone that you know about it, alright? I kept it quiet, I can tell you that."

"I see your point." And indeed I do. Probably best if I keep this to myself. I notice the time. "This has been great but I really should be getting back to the Lodge,"

"Yes, you don't want to be giving Head Porter an excuse to have a go."

"Well, quite." I stand up and offer my hand to Old Boy, who clasps it warmly in his own large, shovel-like hands. "Thank you, and all the best!"

Walking back to Old College, my mind is racing. Of course, I'm not sure how much of what Old Boy said is true and how much is a result of College gossip, rumour and myth. But it does have echoes of what Professor K had been trying to tell me before he died. Before he died… peacefully in his sleep. Hmmm. Perhaps Professor K knew more than was good for him.

A Friend Of The Dean

THERE IS A CRISP CHILL in the air as I make my way, at some considerable speed it must be said, to The Dean's rooms. I have been summoned. I am silently racking my brains for some recollection of a minor misdemeanour or faux pas I may have committed recently, to warrant being called at such haste to the formidable man's rooms. I cannot think of one, but that does not necessarily mean that I haven't done something of an unsatisfactory nature.

I hurry up the staircase towards the surprisingly small and unassuming wooden door with a carefully painted sign bearing the legend: 'The Dean'. In my rush I almost trip over a Bedder, who is diligently scrubbing a skirting board. She gives me a ferocious look as I mumble an apology and continue my ascent up the rickety staircase.

I reach The Dean's door somewhat flustered. I am probably about to be shouted at for no discernable reason and I have just about given a Bedder a bit of a kicking. This is not an auspicious start to my day. I take a deep breath and bravely knock on The Dean's door.

"Who is it? What do you want?" comes the booming reply from behind the door.

"It's me, Sir. Deputy Head Porter," I reply, wincing. "You asked me to come and see you right away?"

A pause.

"Oh! Yes! Of course..." There is some commotion, then The Dean throws open his door and beams at me magnificently whilst striking a gallant pose in today's mis-matched outfit of a pink jumper, purple trousers and a yellow shirt. "Do come on in, Deputy Head Porter!" He is almost being charming. This is even more disconcerting. Why on earth is The Dean being nice to me? Well, I had better go in.

I follow The Dean into his rooms, which are in their usual repose of being grandly chaotic. Huge books are scattered across every surface; some open, some propping up other books, some being used as coasters. His desk looks like a small war is being fought on it.

I do like his fish tank. It should be a little corner of calm in this otherwise anomalous environment, but quite frankly even the fish look rather annoyed.

"Thank you for coming so quickly, Deputy Head Porter, I appreciate your time is precious."

Thank you?! I think to myself. *My time is precious?! He's being far too nice. He wants something.*

"It is my pleasure, Sir. What can I do for you on this fine day?"

"Well now you mention it, there is one little thing." The Dean licks his lips, which makes me think he is nervous. The Dean is never nervous. "You see, I have a very eminent guest arriving from America and it's all rather short notice I'm afraid. But he is incredibly important and will need rooms here for a few days, I hoped you would be able to arrange something suitable for such a respected gentleman?"

Oh, this isn't too bad. I'm sure I can sort something out with Head Of Housekeeping.

"I'm sure that will be fine, Sir. When is your friend arriving?"

"Ah, well. He has just telephoned me from the train station so I would say in about half an hour." *Half an hour?!*

"Sir, that is rather short notice…"

"I know, I know. Truth be told I thought he was coming on Wednesday but it appears I was wrong," I half expect The Dean to implode at the point of admitting he was wrong. "I know this is an unusually unreasonable request, Deputy Head Porter, but it is essential it is carried out. And I would like you to greet him personally, make him welcome, you know."

I sigh. I don't really have much choice, do I? I wonder who this friend is and quite why he is so important.

"Very well, Sir," I say as confidently as I can. "May I ask, who is the guest?"

"Oh, he is a very well respected man. We met at a conference in Dubai some years ago and have conversed in academic internet forums ever since. He is on his way to conduct business in London next week, but thought he would visit Old College beforehand. You will recognise him by his immaculate dress sense and his top hat. He is Professor VJ Duke."

"I look forward to meeting him, Sir. Now – I really should be getting on with the arrangements Sir. If you would excuse me?"

"Of course, Deputy Head Porter." The Dean seems relieved and delighted "I do thank you for this rather last minute request."

The moment The Dean's door closes behind me, I break into a panic and run as fast as I can to see Head Of Housekeeping. She will not be best impressed, I am sure. Having to find a suitable room and prepare it at such short notice is bound to be an unwelcome request. Indeed, she laughs in my face when I explain the circumstances, but takes pity on me and promises to arrange something as urgently as possible. I take a few moments to hurriedly straighten myself up and try to look appealing to our expected guest.

I do not have to wait long. I see the hat bobbing down the street towards the Porters' Lodge, resting elegantly upon the head of a striking looking gentleman, beautifully attired and carrying an enormous suitcase with such ease I almost think that it must be completely empty. I straighten my tie and put on my very best smile. As he walks through the door, I move to greet Professor VJ Duke.

"Good morning, Sir!" I announce, brightly. "You must be Professor VJ Duke. Welcome to Old College."

The Professor returns my smile with his own mega watt grin, characterised by a shiny set of perfect American teeth.

"Happy, happy morning!" His voice is wonderfully clear and deep and his eyes even more so. "I am P.VJ, it's a trip to meet you. I mean that in a good way, I hope you understand."

We shake hands and I reach out to take his bag. Porters would not usually carry the bags of guests, even important ones, (Porters are the keepers of keys, not the carriers of bags) but he is a friend of The Dean so I feel I should. The Professor looks uneasy for a second, but allows me to take his bag. To my surprise, it is incredibly heavy. He walked along the street, brandishing it as if it were paper and I can barely lift the thing. I drag it a few inches towards the desk, a token gesture, and assure him that a Porter will bring it to his room in due course.

"Would it be alright to show me to my rooms directly?" asks the Professor. "I have been traveling for quite some time and could benefit from some rest before I meet up with The Dean. This professor is a bit baggy about the eyes."

I pause. I smile. I do not even know what room is to be allocated to Professor VJ Duke and I am certain it won't be ready.

"Yes… Sir," I reply slowly, trying to give my mind time to think of something. "If you would like to follow me?" I surreptitiously instruct the Porter on duty to notify me the second the Professor's room becomes available, before leading my guest out of the Lodge.

I have no idea where I am going to take him, but Old College has any number of interesting diversions with which I hope to distract Professor VJ Duke. As we approach the bridge, I cannot resist any longer.

"May I say, I do like your hat, Sir," I say as politely as possible. My love of wearing a bowler is well documented, but I must make it clear also that I simply adore a gentleman in a fine hat.

"Many thanks, Deputy Head Porter!" Professor VJ Duke replies. "The professor is fond of your hat as well. Do you like wearing a hat?"

"I do, Sir. The bowler is my favourite, but I should love to be able to carry off a top hat, like yours. I fear that I am not tall enough, though."

"Height doesn't matter!" the Professor says. "A top hat actually adds to one's stature, you know. You should get one. But one thing about top hats…if you wear one, you may be in danger of becoming professorish. Of course, you'd need the white suit, too."

"I cannot help but agree with you, Sir!" I exclaim. What a fascinating chap this friend of The Dean's is. I walk as slowly as I can, partly because I have no ultimate destination in mind and partly because I want to talk further with the Professor. "I must say, you seem to be a very interesting gentleman, Sir. Won't you tell me a little about yourself?"

"Well, this Professor is highly secretive about matters like that. You see, there are some dastardly fellows who would give their left thumbs to catch up with me. It's all very hush-hush—and quite dadblame dangerous."

"Well!" is all that I can think to say. I can see why The Dean likes Professor VJ Duke so much, but I cannot for the life of me fathom out what the Professor would see in The Dean. Maybe it is his celebrated whiskey collection? As I am pondering this, I feel a faint rumble in my pocket. It is my College phone. I excuse myself briefly while I take the call. It is the call I have been waiting for.

Professor VJ Duke's room is ready and it is one of the finer rooms in Old Court. I turn to the Professor and apologise;

"I am sorry, Sir, with all our chattering and wandering, I quite forgot that I was supposed to be taking you to your rooms."

"You know, it totally skipped my mind as well," says the Professor. But I am sure he is only being polite.

"I will take you there at once."

Old Court is a beautiful part of College and I am grateful to Head Of Housekeeping for ensuring her team did such a wonderful job in the presentation of the Professor's room. There are even fresh flowers in a little vase by the bed. I recognise them as having come from by the riverbank. I do hope Head Gardener doesn't see them, he is very particular about his flowers being picked.

"What a stellar room!" says the Professor. "I shall be very comfortable here, I'm sure…"

But then we both stop in our tracks. I am horrified to see, there, nestled amongst the pillows, my arch nemesis – The Master's Cat! The malevolence in his spiteful green eyes is evident. He has done this on purpose. He mews and hisses at us as he squirms and wriggles on the bed, marking his territory.

"Oh no… I am sorry, Sir," I apologise again to the Professor. "This is The Master's Cat, he is a damned nuisance. I can't imagine how he got in here… I shall get rid of him."

Nervously, I approach the demon Cat as he watches me intently from his cosy vantage point. As I draw nearer to the bed, he flattens his ears against his head and bares his pointy white teeth, hissing like a furry snake. I see him extending and retracting his impressive claws, in readiness to tear me to ribbons, no doubt.

"Umm…" I try to think of something to say to the blasted creature, but I am quite unnerved by his vicious stare. Professor VJ Duke is watching me with some amusement, I notice. He has the look in his eyes of a man with a plan.

"Deputy Head Porter, you should leave this to me!" The Professor removes his hat and places it carefully on the dresser. He adjusts his jacket and brushes me gently aside as he approaches the beast, quite unafraid. To my amazement, The Master's Cat remains silent; the malevolence has drained from his now watery eyes and I would say the creature was afraid.

Professor VJ Duke leans down towards The Master's Cat and places his lips close to the feline's ears. I do not hear what he says, his voice is far too soft and I suspect he is speaking in a language I wouldn't understand anyway. Whatever he says, though, has the desired effect. The Master's Cat squeals in terror and streaks like hairy lightening off the bed, out of the door and out into the College beyond. Professor VJ Duke turns and smiles broadly to me.

"Sir! How did you..?"

"Simple! When you know how."

I return the Professor's smile and stand for a few moments in awe and, I admit, a little smitten.

"I learned the trick in Dubai. Now, Deputy Head Porter, you must excuse me while I get some rest before I pay my dear friend The Dean a visit."

"Oh! Quite. Yes, Sir," I really did forget myself for a moment there. "I hope you enjoy your stay...and I do hope our paths cross again."

"Absolutely! The professor would be quite disappointed if he didn't get to see you again." Professor VJ Duke smiles, and gives me a friendly wink. "Have a stellar, stellar—and professorish—day."

Tea & Sympathy

I'M NOT SURE HOW MUCH of the Old Boy's 'revelations' I actually believe, to be honest. It does all sound a little… well, preposterous, really. Dammit, I wish Professor K was still around so I could ask him. Then again, getting an unequivocal answer from Professor K was like prising a Fellow away from his dinner; nigh on impossible.

It was somewhat comforting to know that the Old Boy had a similarly tempestuous relationship with Head Porter. It's not just me. I feel a little pang of sympathy for my superior, actually. He is not a bad chap, all told, and if there is any truth in what the Old Boy said he must be quite anxious at being party to such sensitive information. Although, my jury is still out on the plausibility of that particular scenario.

I am making my way across the bridge, enjoying the sharp spring air and admiring the reflected twinkles of a late morning sun on the waters below, when I catch sight of Head Porter lingering further along the riverbank. He cuts a slightly sad figure amongst the cheery daffodils, waving their little yellow heads in the breeze. I wonder what he is up to.

Head Porter seems completely oblivious to my presence as I approach, his mind quite clearly elsewhere.

"Hello, Head Porter" my voice seems to bring him abruptly from his reverie.

"Oh! Hello, Deputy Head Porter," his voice is generously furnished with its usual brusque tone but his attention is somewhat wandering.

"Are you alright?" I ask "You seem a little… odd."

Head Porter regards me strangely, as if he is seeing me for the first time and I am not quite what he expected.

"Head Porter?"

"I'm fine, I'm fine" he replies, a little more like his usual self. "I'm just a bit... tired. I haven't been sleeping well. I seem to be having some very odd dreams lately." *Something on your mind, Head Porter?*

"I'm sorry to hear that," I offer, sympathetically. "How about a nice cup of tea? That usually brings me round." Head Porter appears to give this an inordinate amount of consideration.

"Do you know, I think that sounds like a good idea, Deputy Head Porter," he replies, brightening a little. "You put the kettle on and I'll fetch the biscuits. Alright?"

"Right!"

Well, this *is* a turn up for the books, I think to myself as I accompany Head Porter back to the Porters' Lodge. Biscuits! Biscuits have not been mentioned for quite some time. Not since the unfortunate episode of Senior Bursar's biscuits, certainly. And the less said about that the better.

In the little kitchenette at the rear of the Lodge, I happily clatter about with mugs and teaspoons (if there is a more delightful sound than the preparation of tea, I have yet to hear it) while Head Porter retrieves the biscuit tin from its high shelf with the utmost deliberation and ceremony. I do feel like the preparation and arrangement of tea things is a little ceremonial. When I visited China some years ago, I was delighted and intrigued by the tea ceremonies and felt very at home with a culture as enthusiastic about tea as I am.

Tea - English tea certainly - is often depicted as a delicate and dainty refreshment to be sipped elegantly from hand painted china cups which repose upon gilt edged china saucers. This is all very well, but I like my tea thick and dark and plentiful and as such china simply will not do. A sturdy mug is my preferred vessel of imbibition, which is just as well as the Porters' Lodge does not have much in the way of fine china.

Head Porter and I sit on stools, squashed together whilst leaning on the small counter. He generously nudges the biscuit tin in my direction.

"Go on" he says "I know you like the chocolate ones." I beam broadly and take a hearty handful of chocolate biscuits from the tin. This isn't as greedy as it sounds, as my hands are very small.

I am considering asking Head Porter about what the Old Boy said. If it is indeed true, Head Porter must be very weighed down and anxious by it. As well, he may know something of what Professor K had been hinting at. And he looks so troubled today, maybe he has something he wants to get off his chest? My mind made up, I decide to ask him.

Our eyes meet and I open my mouth to say the carefully planned words I have just this minute thought of. But then –

"'Scuse me, Head Porter, ma'am!" It is Porter, in something of a fluster. His fat red cheeks (closely followed by the rest of him) appear round the door of the kitchenette.

"What's the matter, Porter?" I ask.

"Come through to the front quickly. Junior Bursar has an announcement."

Both Head Porter and I sigh in unison. We unhappily abandon our tea and biscuits and follow Porter through to the front, with some trepidation.

Junior Bursar's Announcement

HEAD PORTER AND I ARRIVE at the front desk of the Porters' Lodge to be greeted by a smiling Junior Bursar. This does not bode well, I fear. A grumpy or enraged Junior Bursar is more along the usual line of things. A smiling Junior Bursar is something of which to be cautious. But he does seem to be genuinely delighted about something and so my interest is piqued.

"Good day, Sir" Head Porter greets him, he himself clearly unnerved by Junior Bursar's unfamiliar demeanour. "To what do we owe this pleasure?"

"Good to see you Head Porter! Thank you for coming so quickly," replies Junior Bursar. Head Porter slings me the briefest of looks, a wryly-raised eyebrow taking the place of a thousand words.

"Not at all, Sir!" Head Porter returns Junior Bursar's amiable grin. Amiable grins do not suit Head Porter at all, but it's good to see him make the effort. "Is there something we can do for you?"

"All I require from you and your men... ahem. Your people, Head Porter, is a keen pair of ears and an understanding disposition. Do you see?"

"Yes, Sir," Head Porter replies carefully. "Porter! Come over here, will you, and... listen keenly."

Porter, who has been ear-wigging the conversation anyway, scoots over to join us and makes a valiant effort to appear to be both keen and understanding. I myself strike the keenest pose I can muster. Which is pretty keen, I can tell you.

"Now then, Porters," begins Junior Bursar, grandly. "I have an important announcement to make. The Fellowship have just received the

145

same announcement and, although understandably distressed, have taken the news quite magnanimously. I don't expect College servants to be made of quite such stern stuff, but I do hope you will do your best." He pauses, for what he probably thinks is effect, but rather makes him appear to have forgotten what he was saying. I look to Head Porter. He is as perplexed as I am. Junior Bursar continues

"The time has come, Porters, for me to pass on the torch of Junior Bursary. The time for me to look back on a life of labours and service to Old College and a time for me to look towards the twilight of my years..."

"Labours and service?!" Porter rasps to me under his breath, incredulous "The man has barely done a stroke his whole life!" I struggle to restrain a small giggle.

"Ssshh!" Head Porter scolds. Junior Bursar is not put off his stride; I feel he may have been rehearsing this speech for some time.

"After so many years at Old College, the time has come for me to take leave of this place and enjoy the autumn of my existence in the embrace of my long adored mistress and muse..."

Three sets of eyebrows, mine included, hit the roof

"I refer, of course, to my beloved Tuscany, where to I shall be retiring at the end of the academic year!"

Well. As speeches go, it certainly had its moments. Head Porter looks to be stiff with shock, I don't think his brain has got past the bit about the embrace of a mistress. Porter appears fairly dispassionate, whilst Junior Bursar basks in the after glow of his performance, like a Shakespearian actor awaiting the applause of his audience. I feel I had better say something.

"That is marvellous news, Sir!" I say enthusiastically. Junior Bursar looks slightly crest fallen at this response. "I mean – not that you will be leaving us, rather that you have such a lovely, er, mistress to, um, retire to. What I mean is, we are very happy for you"

"But... but very sad for the College, of course," Head Porter comes to my rescue "How will we manage without you?"

"Well, quite, Head Porter!" says Junior Bursar, far happier with Head Porter's response. "But I am sure Senior Bursar will do an admirable job of keeping Old College on its toes following my departure."

"They won't be... replacing, you Sir?" asks Head Porter.

"I shouldn't expect so," is Junior Bursar's reply. "I think you will find me quite irreplaceable" another smile. "If you must know, The Master has decided to keep an open mind about finding a new Junior Bursar. He seems to think Senior Bursar will be quite able to maintain the status quo on his own. We shall soon see about that, I suppose."

There is a brief, bitter silence in the Lodge as these last words settle into the background.

"Well! Thank you for coming to tell us your news, Sir" Head Porter seems keen to usher Junior Bursar on his way (I imagine before he comes up with some errand or task for one of us) "We will take a moment to let this... startling news sink in."

"Yes, you do that, Head Porter" Junior Bursar allows himself to be guided towards the door by Head Porter "I expect to see you at my leaving party?" Head Porter, I can see, is quite taken aback by this. An invite to Junior Bursar's leaving do? This is quite something for a humble College servant. "I shall be needing someone to keep an eye on the coats and what not and I believe you are just the man for the job!"

I see Head Porter do a grand job of keeping his annoyance in check as he agrees, through gritted teeth, to act as cloakroom assistant.

When Junior Bursar is safely out of the way, I say to Head Porter

"I must say, I wasn't expecting that!"

Head Porter shakes his head.

"I think you'd better put the kettle on again, Deputy Head Porter".

The Open Window

JUNIOR BURSAR'S ANNOUNCEMENT CAME AS something as a surprise to me. It never occurred to me that anyone actually retired at Old College; I always just assumed that the only way Fellows ever left was in a box. Head Porter hasn't said much but I can tell he is a little fuddled about the matter. He certainly wasn't expecting this. Of course, once Fellows reach a certain age (or a certain state of mental confusion) their College duties diminish or cease altogether. But they certainly don't go away, they remain seemingly sempiternal within Old College until they are called to the great lecture theatre (or, more likely, Dining Hall) in the sky. Like Dr D and Professor K. In Dr D's case, even death itself wasn't enough to shift him from his seat by the fire. I am sure Junior Bursar must have his reasons and he is dreadfully fond of Tuscany, after all.

Tea and biscuits with Head Porter have been lovely but by the end of my shift I feel that a more substantial form of refreshment is required. Late afternoon gives way to evening with quiet dignity as I leave Old College and The City streets are more beautiful than ever, bathed in the amber warmth of the setting sun. This part of The City is dominated by imposing architecture, some of which is over eight hundred years old. Fabulously modern buildings intermingle with the ancient not so very far from here, but these streets belong to bygone ages. It is a pleasant route to an even more pleasing destination.

The Albatross boasts of being the oldest public house in The City and I am sure that this is probably the case. This claim has also made it one of the most famous and so is often filled with tourists, as well as the more

148

sociable locals. The prices are a little higher than other nearby pubs but I am prepared to splash out a little extra for the anonymity of drinking in a busy establishment. It is far easier to be alone in a crowd of strangers than to find solitude in a sparsely occupied bar. This I know from experience.

As it happens, there are not only strangers in The Albatross this evening. Cheerfully ordering a large Scotch at the bar is Head Gardener. The pub is filling up quickly so I hurry to his side in the hope of jumping the queue. I am happy enough to share a drink with this most friendly chap.

"Hallo, Deputy Head Porter!" Head Gardener greats me amiably. "Drink?" *Aha! My plan has worked.* I request a glass of Bordeaux, large of course. I cannot be sure if the news of Junior Bursar's retirement has yet reached the Gardeners, so I decide to avoid the subject for now. We take a table in the pub courtyard and each roll a cigarette. The evening is a little chilly to be sitting outside but if we wish to indulge in our filthy habit, we have no choice.

I lean back in my chair as I savour my first exhalation of tobacco and notice something strange.

"Hey, look up there," I say pointing upwards. "Someone's left a window open up there. That room is going to be freezing!"

Head Gardener follows my gaze and laughs.

"That window is always left open," he replies. "It has to be!"

"What do you mean?" I ask. "Why does it have to be left open?"

"Oh, don't you know?" he says with some surprise. "It's so the ghost can get out." I laugh at this.

"What ghost?"

"I can't believe you don't know," Head Gardener sips his whiskey and re-lights his roll up. "This pub has been owned by Caelestis College for, oooh, centuries now. Back in the old days, probably about three hundred years ago, the College wasn't the best of landlords. That window up there was hanging off its hinges and the landlady of the pub at the time was concerned, what with that being her little boy's bedroom. Rather than properly fix it, the College send round a chap with a ladder to nail the window shut. Well, that was all well and good and at least the little lad couldn't accidentally fall out the window. But then there was a terrible fire in the pub, destroyed most of it, it did. The poor little boy was trapped in his room and the fire was too fierce to try and get up the stairs to rescue him. They put a ladder up to his window but they couldn't budge it, on account of it being nailed shut. The lad died in that fire and all they could do was listen to his screams as he burned."

"That's horrible!" I squeal.

"Yes, it is" Head Gardener finishes his roll up and starts to construct another. "Since then, the window to that room has always been left open. So that the little one isn't trapped. If the window has ever been shut, they say it opens itself again. Or, there is such a dreadful presence felt in the whole building it is unbearable. The presence leaves as soon as the window is opened."

"Really?" I ask, sceptical "People really believe that?"

Head Gardener shrugs.

"I dunno," he says "But the window is always open, whatever the weather, whatever the hour of day. That much I can tell you."

I take a large mouthful of the (very good) Bordeaux and eye the window suspiciously. If true, this is indeed a very sad story. And for three hundred years The Albatross has ensured he would never be trapped again. Sadder still, the little boy evidently still has not escaped that room. I hope that one day he does.

Something Amiss

"DEPUTY HEAD PORTER! DEPUTY HEAD Porter!"

The abrupt sound of The Dean's voice causes me to jump in my seat and spill a little of my tea over my desk. I look up but it is a few seconds before the formidable figure of The Dean comes into view. Today's outfit is a good one – blue trousers, a stripy shirt (sleeves rolled up in a rakish manner) and a charming pink jumper slung elegantly over his shoulders. This style of jumper-wearing is popular in Old College. Why is it that highly educated people cannot fathom how to wear a jumper correctly? But anyway. I get to my feet to greet my esteemed visitor.

"Good morning Sir!" I beam.

"Do you know what I can't stand, Deputy Head Porter?" The Dean barks at me. I imagine there is an endless list in answer to his question, but by his tone I don't think he would appreciate this.

"What can't you stand, Sir?" I enquire with trepidation.

"Idiots!" he replies, emphatically. "Idiots, Deputy Head Porter. And I tell you what else. Fools!" Well, this seems reasonable enough, I suppose. "Do you realise how many idiots and fools I have had to deal with already today?"

"I cannot imagine, Sir".

"Too bloody many! I tell you, Deputy Head Porter, this is supposed to be an educational establishment but I find myself faced with incompetence at every turn."

It is difficult to judge The Dean's intentions, here. On the one hand, he could have just had a bad morning and has come to vent some frustration

151

in my general direction. On the other hand, I could be in an awful lot of trouble for one reason or another. The Dean rolls his eyes and shakes his head in a mock world-weary manner and perches himself on the edge of my desk. I think I'm in the clear on this one.

"So come on then, Sir. Where are all these idiots and fools? I'll go and sort them out for you" I feel this is above and beyond what is required of me but this is The Dean, after all.

"They're mainly part of the furniture, I'm afraid" replies The Dean, with humour. "If they could be sorted out, I'd sort the buggers out myself."

"I'm quite sure you would, Sir."

"Anyway, Deputy Head Porter, how are things with you?" I consider my response carefully.

"I am living the dream, Sir." The Dean looks mildly surprised for a second, then bursts into laughter when he recognises my deadpan sarcasm. He places a hand on my shoulder and says

"Oh! I thought you were being serious there for a moment! Haha!"

Well, The Dean is in a jolly mood today. This is unusual in itself, but even more so when he has clearly had a run in or two with person or persons unnamed.

"Things are pretty much as they should be, Sir" I continue "Nothing of note to report either way. So what can I do for you? Have you just come for a bit of a moan?"

"No, no, I do actually have a real reason for coming to see you. I don't suppose you have seen Senior Bursar, have you? I've been trying to track him down but there's no reply from his rooms and I can't seem to get hold of him."

I think carefully. Senior Bursar certainly arrived in College first thing this morning, he made his usual trip to his pigeon hole to check for any messages.

"I saw him earlier, Sir. Hang on, let me just check something" I lean over to my computer and click open my email. Yes, I thought so. "And he sent me an email about an hour ago, look" The Dean looks over my shoulder, then scratches his head.

"That is particularly strange, I've been to his rooms several times around that time, and rung him too."

"He's ignoring you, Sir" I tease The Dean.

"He had better well not be!" The Dean replies, but without malice. "Odd though, don't you think?"

"I don't know, Sir. Senior Bursar ignores me all the time."

"Yes, but I am The Dean Of College!"

"That is true, Sir." The Dean thinks for a moment then turns to me again.

"I wouldn't normally ask this, Deputy Head Porter, but can you get me into his rooms?" I hesitate. Of course I can, I can get into any room in Old College.

"I can, Sir, but it would be a little… irregular" I answer carefully.

"Well, I want you to open his rooms for me," The Dean says firmly "On my head be it, I'll make sure you don't get in any trouble. You are following my orders after all."

"I cannot very well refuse the orders of The Dean Of College now, can I?"

"Quite right. Bring your keys and follow me."

I accompany The Dean, at some pace, to Senior Bursar's rooms. They are at the top of a large staircase which has such widely spaced steps that my little legs always struggle to get up there at speed. The Dean is not so encumbered as he has longer legs than me, which means I have to scurry a little to keep up. By the time we get to the top, I am quite out of breath.

We reach Senior Bursar's door and I knock and call to him, just to be sure. There is no response.

"He must be out somewhere," I suggest.

"Just open the door" replies The Dean.

I find the correct key and it turns smoothly in the lock. I push the door open and The Dean enters before me. Unsure as to whether I should be following him in, I hover in the doorway awkwardly. Then,

"Oh my GOD!"

I hurry in to find The Dean in a state of shock and covering his face with a trembling hand. A quick look around the room and I soon see why…

A Shocking Event

THE DEAN IS PEEPING THROUGH his fingers at the prone and slightly charred body of Senior Bursar lying on the floor. In his blackened and gnarled hand is a partially melted kettle.

"It looks like he has been electrocuted by the kettle," says The Dean, rather unnecessarily.

"Oh, my goodness" is all I can bring myself to say. Then, "I'll call an ambulance."

"I'd say it's a bit late for that," says The Dean grimly.

"Well, we can't very well leave him here, Sir" I reply reasonably.

"One moment," The Dean says. He goes over to the wall socket and deftly yanks the plug of the kettle from the wall. He then carefully approaches the body of Senior Bursar and leans over to take a closer look. His face wrinkles into a frown.

"What is it, Sir?" I ask. No reply. The Dean straightens up and gingerly pokes the arm that isn't holding the kettle with his foot.

"He's stiff as a board!" exclaims The Dean.

"Rigor mortis as set in?"

"It would appear so. That's strange."

"Then he must have been dead for a few hours already," I meant to say this in my head but the words somehow managed to find their way out of my mouth. "I suppose that explains why he didn't answer the door or pick up your calls."

"Yes, but I thought you said he sent you an email only an hour ago?" The Dean points out. *Hmmm.*

"I'm no doctor," I reply "But I'm fairly certain that dead men don't send emails."

"Right! So, either he wasn't dead an hour ago and was just ignoring me, or…"

"Or someone else sent the email." An unpleasant silence falls upon the room, adding to the already macabre atmosphere. It is a silence that seems to grow in weight and presence until I feel that my ears could almost bleed. As The Dean and I simply stare at each other across the corpse of our former colleague, I feel I have to do something. "Sir, we must call an ambulance. And the Police."

The Dean moves swiftly towards me until he is standing very close. I realise that I am shaking ever so slightly and I feel a little sick. This is simply the after effects of the adrenalin my brain has dumped into my body following the shock discovery, this I know, but it is unsettling nonetheless. I look into the face of The Dean and he appears calm and controlled. At least one of us is.

"Now listen to me, Deputy Head Porter" he says in such a low voice I almost have to strain to hear. "You are not to say a word of this to anyone, do you understand? Not anyone at all. Not yet."

"But Sir…" I mean to make a protest of some kind but I am sorry to say that all strength has deserted me and I find myself quite unable to speak further.

"Don't worry, Deputy Head Porter," The Dean says gently "Of course I will make sure Senior Bursar is dealt with in the proper manner. But there is something unusual here and I mean to find out what it is. I will have Nurse come up and do the necessary. This will be dealt with inside of College, you understand?"

"I understand, Sir." Somehow, this doesn't surprise me.

"I want you to go home now, Deputy Head Porter, you've had quite a shock," *And he hasn't?!* "I will tell Head Porter I have sent you out on an errand for me. If you give me Senior Bursar's keys I will ensure that the room is secured. Return to work tomorrow and try not to worry. I will deal with this."

"Sir, if I may be so bold" I find my voice, somehow "I don't think this is the only strange incident involving the death of a Fellow. Professor K…"

"Hush, hush Deputy Head Porter," The Dean tries to sooth me but his method is ineffective. "We will speak more of this tomorrow. Now, you must get yourself out of the way and leave this to me."

I swallow down the rising nausea in my throat and nod my head. At the back of my mind, I am wondering why The Dean in so insistent that I leave College and keep out of the way. But at the forefront of my mind my instincts are urging me to get out - out of this room, away from the dead body and away from the sinister dramatics that seem to grip Old College.

And so I go. I hope The Dean knows what he is doing.

Curious

I COME IN THE NEXT morning to a very sombre Porters' Lodge. Head Porter is already at the front desk with a mug of steaming hot tea and a lugubrious expression. I bid him good morning and he solemnly offers me the tea.

"I have some bad news, Deputy Head Porter" he says "You'd better sit down." I obediently take a seat behind the front desk and try my best to maintain a blank expression.

"What is it, Head Porter?" I ask innocently.

"It's Senior Bursar. I'm afraid… he's dead." Head Porter takes a couple of deep breaths and composes himself. "A terrible accident involving a kettle. Dreadful business. The Dean found him."

"Oh dear, that is dreadful" I am giving the performance of my life. "When did this happen?"

"Yesterday sometime, whilst you were out looking at paintings for The Dean's office," Head Porter replies. *Looking at paintings? Couldn't The Dean come up with anything better than that?* "We don't know the full details yet, of course, but it appears he received an electric shock from the kettle in his rooms whilst making a hot drink. Very, very sad."

"Yes, very sad." I take a sip of tea and adopt a suitably mournful countenance. "In fact, you might say it's shocking, Head Porter." Head Porter eyes me with a look like granite.

"If that is a joke, Deputy Head Porter, it is in remarkably poor taste."

"No no, not a joke" I explain quickly "A bad choice of words, I admit. Certainly surprising, though."

157

"Surprising the bugger was making his own drink!" Porter joins us unexpectedly from the rear of the Lodge.

"Porter! That is uncalled for!" Head Porter chastises him sternly. Porter mumbles something incomprehensible and busies himself by sorting through the key cabinets. "Honestly, a man is dead. That calls for some decorum, surely?"

"It surely does, Head Porter" I agree.

"The Master has requested that the flag be flown at half mast, which is only right. Will you do the honours, Deputy Head Porter?" I rise to my feet.

"It would be my pleasure, Head Porter" I reply. "I'll go now."

Today, the journey through the elegant courtyards does not fill me with the sense of awe and admiration it usually inspires. Rather, it gives the feel of ever increasing panic and dread snapping at my heels and clawing at my ankles, trying to bring me to the ground with every step. This ancient and mystical place that once aroused delight and wonder now exudes an air of jeopardy and betrayal. Although recent events have been unpleasant to say the least, I must confess to feeling a little excitement in the pit of my stomach. The cabalistic nature of Old College appears to be revealing itself with fervent urgency.

As I near the Flag Tower, I see Head Of Housekeeping coming towards me. She appears rushed and harassed, as ever, but stops to speak to me.

"Morning, Deputy Head Porter" she says in her usual brisk manner "Terrible news about Senior Bursar, isn't it?"

"I know, it's awful" I reply "I'm just on my way to raise the flag at half mast."

"That is very fitting, yes" Head Of Housekeeping appears troubled and is fussing with the keys in her hand. She is quiet for a moment, then continues "I must say I can't help feeling dreadful about the whole thing."

"I don't see that there is anything you could have done about it," I say, surprised.

"I suppose not," she says "But obviously that kettle was supplied by the Housekeeping Department and I suppose it must have been faulty to have given him a shock like that."

"But all the appliances are rigorously checked by Maintenance, surely?" I ask.

"Of course they are!" Head Of Housekeeping shakes her head sadly. "The awful thing is, that kettle was brand new, only replaced his old one a couple of days ago."

"What was wrong with the old one?" I enquire, suddenly feeling the beginnings of suspicion scratching at the back of my mind.

"I'm not sure, I assume it was just broken," replies Head Of Housekeeping. "I received a note asking for a new one. I didn't really think twice about it - if Senior Bursar wants a new kettle, Senior Bursar gets a new kettle. It's as simple as that."

"Who sent you the note? If you don't mind me asking"

"I don't know, it was just left on my desk"

"Did you recognise the handwriting?"

"It was a print out. What's that got to do with anything?"

"Oh – don't mind me," I reply, attempting to lighten my tone "Asking questions is just a habit I picked up from my previous incarnation, you know. And, you know, it's such a waste of paper to print emails, don't you think?"

"It wasn't a printed email, just a little note" Head Of Housekeeping says stiffly. I'm picking up the sensation that she feels she is being questioned.

"That's just so typically old fashioned, isn't it?" I try to laugh it off "Delivering notes indeed! Well –"I had better get that flag up, you know."

"Yes, don't let me keep you. I am incredibly busy myself." Head Of Housekeeping bustles off in the opposite direction and I watch as she disappears into a cloister.

I brace myself to ascend the Flag Tower (my dislike of heights is well documented) and distract my thoughts of plunging to my death with those of Professor K and now Senior Bursar. I really think I should find a moment to speak with The Dean.

An Unlikely Coupling

ONCE AT THE TOP OF the Flag Tower, it is not quite as unsettling as I imagined it to be. Certainly, the first time I ascended this ancient structure I was absolutely terrified. I have always been far happier with both feet safely on *terra firma* but my occasional flag-hoisting duties seem to be taming the phobia. The only tricky thing now is to make sure the flag is at *exactly* half mast. And as today's flag flies in the honour of such an exacting gentleman as Senior Bursar, this is very important indeed.

I wrestle with the ropes a little until I am satisfied that the College standard is perfectly placed. I take a moment to admire my handiwork and also to take in the breath-takingly beautiful cityscape that surrounds me. Although, The City is quite unlike any other city I have ever known (well, maybe one other comes to mind…) in that the truly historic and the sublimely cutting-edge nestle together so comfortably. Well, perhaps not so comfortably; as I look around me I get the distinct impression that some of the older structures of The City are decidedly displeased with their more youthful neighbours. I sometimes think that Old College feels exactly the same way about me.

My mind is just starting to wander in the direction of what might be served for lunch, when I become aware of footsteps coming up the stone spiral staircase of the Flag Tower. I am suddenly a little nervous – I am certainly not expecting company up here. The incidents of recent unpleasantness flash through my mind as I become increasingly aware that the Flag Tower is quite a dangerous place to be.

There is really no cause for concern, though, as I am relieved (if a little surprised) to see that it is The Dean who emerges though the little wooden door to the staircase.

"Good morning, Sir!" I greet him cheerfully.

"Deputy Head Porter, good morning" replies The Dean. "How are you today? Not too traumatised by yesterday's occurrence, I hope?"

"I'm fine, thank you Sir" I answer "Although I am rather suspicious about the whole situation."

"Indeed! A less cynical man than myself might well be prepared to accept that what happened to Senior Bursar was nothing more than a tragic accident," The Dean takes a breath "But, as I am sure you know, Deputy Head Porter, I am a very cynical man indeed and also particularly suspicious. Especially in events where dead men appear to be sending emails."

"Well, quite, Sir"

"Which leads me to believe that someone wanted us to think Senior Bursar was still alive when in fact he was very much dead."

"Yes, Sir, but who?"

"That is what I intend us to find out, Deputy Head Porter"

"Us, Sir?" I am a little taken aback. I hadn't expected The Dean to be quite so keen to join forces with me. Of course, he does not yet know the full extent of my suspicions about the death of Professor K.

"Yes, Deputy Head Porter" The Dean continues, really getting a feel for the idea now. "We can be like Holmes and Watson."

"Which one are you, Sir?" I ask jovially.

"Well, I suppose I should be Holmes," he replies. Then thinks. Then, "But actually, as I am a Doctor, maybe I should be *Doctor* Watson..."

"I've got the right hat to be Watson," I point out, indicating my bowler "And I'm not nearly tall enough to be Holmes."

"Good point"

"Besides, Watson is a proper Doctor..." the look The Dean gives me at these words is priceless. And terrifying. "I mean, a medical Doctor. Not an academic Doctor... I mean... Couldn't I be Hercule Poirot instead?"

The Dean sighs.

"Bugger it, no. I'll be Holmes and you be Watson. Alright?"

"Alright Sir" I reply. "Sir?"

"Yes, Deputy Head Porter?"

"Shouldn't we be getting on with solving the case, then?"

"Oh! Right! Yes. Yes indeed" The Dean is rather wrapped up in the role-playing element of our adventure, I suspect. "And, actually, I think I have found some clues already."

"Brilliant, Sir" I say "I think I may have picked up one or two things as well."

"Good. Now follow me to my rooms were we can begin our investigation proper"

Is It A Trap?

I AM PLEASED TO NOTE that The Dean's rooms are today in a remarkably well-ordered fashion - quite the unusual state of affairs. It appears that he has had a bit of a clear out; the surfaces of much of the furniture are clearly visible and there is even room to sit on the settee, if you are not too hefty. Although, I also notice, that heftier guests now have use of a majestic-looking armchair that was previously buried by an enormous pile of books. The Dean has a quick look out into the hallway before locking us in to his rooms.

"Is it too early for a drink, do you think, Deputy Head Porter?" The Dean asks, hands thrust into the pockets of his rather jaunty tweed trousers.

"Considering the present circumstances, probably not" I reply. This appears to be the correct answer.

The Dean strolls over to his desk and retrieves a fine looking single malt from the bottom drawer. Then he frowns and starts searching all over his desk.

"Where in buggery is my tumbler?" he says to no one in particular. As I am the only other person in the room, I feel obliged to have a look for it. I have had to look for things in The Dean's rooms before and those previous occasions can only be described as challenging.

As The Dean swears politely under his breath I have a rummage around and it is not long before I come across the item, albeit otherwise employed. Sat next to the telephone I see a beautifully cut crystal tumbler, crammed full of pens, pencils, paperclips and other related paraphernalia. The Dean spots it almost immediately and more swearing is forthcoming as he tips the contents onto a previously clear space on the desk. Undeterred, he hooks the cuff of his jumper over his palm and gives the tumbler a hasty dusting.

Satisfied the glass is suitably clean, The Dean pours himself a sensible amount of the whiskey. He doesn't offer me any - which is fine because I wouldn't have been able to accept it anyway – but a bit of a shame because I am always a little shaky after any dealings with the Flag Tower. Anyway.

"Now then, Deputy Head Porter, there is certainly something not quite right occurring here, I'd wager" The Dean says in a low voice, obviously concerned about us being overheard. "This business with Senior Bursar is very suspect indeed. And Professor K's death never sat that comfortably with me, either."

"I agree, Sir" I reply. "I think Professor K was trying to tell me something before he died. It all kicked off when I asked him about something The Master told me late one night in the Crypt…"

"What was that?"

I open my mouth to continue, but I stop myself just in time. What was it the Old Boy had said about keeping this information to myself? This was dangerous information, he said. People who stumbled upon this particular little gem didn't usually get the opportunity to pass it on. There is a possibility that The Dean already knows all this, of course. But I doubt he would be so quick to involve me in his amateur sleuthing if this was the case. But… It could be a trap! To find out how much I know.

Oh, Lord, what I do say?! I am suddenly very aware of my precarious position and even more aware of the locked door behind me. *The window?* I'm on the second floor, it's not a good option.

"Well, Deputy Head Porter," The Dean fixes me with a dark stare and takes a couple of steps towards me, crystal tumbler still in his hand, the amber liquid being gently warmed by the heat of his palm. "What did The Master tell you in the Crypt?"

A sudden sweat like a sheet of ice on my back, I take a deep breath and compose myself as best I can. Conscious that whatever I say next could have quite alarming consequences, I reply in the best possible way I know how…

The Truth, The Whole Truth
And A Little White Lie

So I TELL HIM EVERYTHING. *Everything.* My conversation with The Master in the Crypt; the various puzzling exchanges with Professor K; The Order of the Lesser Dragon_– I even impart to him details of what the Old Boy told me after the funeral. Even as I am relaying this most bizarre and unlikely tale, I am doubting the wisdom of my chosen course of action. But there is nothing else for it.

Any suspicions I had about The Dean being somehow involved in this debacle disappear as quickly as the whiskey he is enthusiastically making his way through. I watch his face wrest with numerous expressions, many of which I do not recognise. This is to be expected, I suppose.

As I come to the end of my revelations (which, when said out loud, sound ridiculous even to me) The Dean re-fills his tumbler yet again and offers it to me.

"Here, you could probably do with this" he says "Sorry I've only got the one glass".

"That's quite alright, Sir," I reply as I take the glass from him. I would never, ever have normally accepted an alcoholic beverage on duty under any other circumstances. But, these are unusual times and unusual times call for unusual measures. Or, more specifically, *large* measures. Of whiskey.

The Deans puts his hands in his pockets (a sure sign that he is mulling something over) and paces a little. I sip the whiskey as I watch him stroll to the window. What is it about looking out of windows when considering a weighty matter? I have noticed this, people do it a lot. It is maybe something to do with an unconscious desire to look outside when what one really should be doing is looking within. But introspection can be difficult and displeasing; you just never know what you might see.

"You have been making interesting use of your time here at any rate, Deputy Head Porter" says The Dean, after some short contemplation.

I shrug. What can I say, really?

"Are you telling me that you think members of The Fellowship have been… doing away with each other since the unpleasant business with the Porters' Lodge fifty years ago?" *No, I think it has actually been going on far longer than that.*

"I am not quite sure what to think, to be honest, Sir" my reply is a little white lie. I am now fairly certain that this is exactly the case. And Professor K and Senior Bursar are the latest victims. Professor K clearly needed to be silenced but for what reason is Senior Bursar more preferable dead than alive?

"Well, I know what I think," continues The Dean "I think you and I should get to the bottom of this before anyone else ends up slaughtered. More importantly, before I end up slaughtered!"

"Well, absolutely, Sir."

"I'm going to go through some of the College records, see what I can dig up about chaps being dead and what not"

"What would you like me to do, Sir?"

"I'd bloody well keep my head down, if I were you Deputy Head Porter"

"Well, other than that, Sir"

"See you if you can get to the bottom of Senior Bursar's new kettle" The Dean thinks for a moment "I'm sure it's important."

As I make my way back to the Porters' Lodge it is all I can do to contain the little fizzes of excitement that are sparking away at in my tummy. With The Dean on board, I have no doubt that the mysteries of Old College will soon be revealed. Brilliant! That is, if we don't end up dead, of course.

Gateway To Nowhere

BACK IN THE PORTERS' LODGE, Head Porter appears somewhat unsettled. He is fussing around the front desk and shuffling piles of envelopes from one place to another. Distractedly mumbling to himself, there is clearly something up.

"Cup of tea, Head Porter?" I offer.

"Oh, hallo, there!" he replies, almost a little jumpy. "Yes, tea would be nice. Where have you been, by the way?"

"Just having a little chat with The Dean" I answer, then remember The Dean's unlikely excuse for my previous absence "About the new paintings for his rooms, you know."

Head Porter wrinkles his face the tiniest amount and looks at me carefully.

"What is it with these new paintings?" he asks. "I hadn't realised you were such an authority on the matter, Deputy Head Porter."

"I'm not, really. The Dean just thinks I... have a good eye, apparently."

Head Porter shrugs and seems reasonably happy with this, for the time being.

"Right, well, fair enough, I suppose" he says. "I think I'll have an extra sugar in my tea today, Deputy Head Porter, if you're making a brew."

"No problem, Head Porter. Are you quite alright? You look a bit pale."

Head Porter looks furtively around the Lodge. Satisfied that we are alone, he leans in towards me and adopts a conspiratorial tone.

"There's a key missing" he whispers, his voice slightly distorted by a barely perceptible tremble. "What key?" I ask.

"The key to the back gate of The Master's garden," Head Porter is almost squeaking now.

"I didn't realise there was a back gate to The Master's garden," I say, puzzled. I thought I had finally got a handle on the esoteric art of key management.

"It's in the far wall, backing onto the river" Head Porter replies. "It hasn't been used in years, of course, as essentially it doesn't lead anywhere"

"Bit of an odd place to have a gate, then, isn't it?"

"I think years ago The Masters could moor a punt there or something. It was an inconspicuous way of getting on and off the river I suppose. Besides, just because it's an odd place to have a gate doesn't mean there shouldn't be one there."

"Well, that makes sense" I reply "By Old College's standards, anyway. So, I take it the key wasn't signed out by anyone, then?"

"There's no record of it" he says "So goodness only knows how long it's been gone. I only noticed it by chance this morning whilst I was looking for something else."

"Who on Earth would want the key to a gate that leads nowhere?" I ask myself aloud.

"That's what worries me" Head Porter mumbles darkly.

A thought strikes me. Head Porter is rather unduly upset about such an inconsequential key. A gate that goes nowhere, locked or unlocked, is no security threat to College. What's the big panic? So I ask him.

"Surely this isn't something to be too concerned about, Head Porter" I point out. "Let's just get the lock changed. I'll get on to Head Of Maintenance..."

"No! No... don't do that," exclaims Head Porter, grabbing my arm firmly. I can feel the shaking of his hands through his grip. He notices my alarm and gently releases me, patting me amiably on the arm as he does so. "Haha —no, don't bother Head Of Maintenance with this. Why, I'll never live it down if he finds out I've lost a key! You know what he's like, the bugger."

I laugh along with Head Porter's uneasy chuckle, which does a poor job of concealing the startling panic in his eyes.

"Yes, he is a bugger, isn't he?" I play along. "But seriously, Head Porter, why are you so upset about this key?"

A strange coldness falls upon him and Head Porter looks for a moment as if he would tell me the truth. But he doesn't. He tells me this instead -

"I just hate losing keys, Deputy Head Porter" Head Porter's voice is dry and cracked. "Being a keeper of the keys, it's very embarrassing when one goes missing."

I nod my head to express my understanding and decide to let this one go, for now. No point in upsetting the chap further.

"Well, there's no need to be embarrassed," I reassure him as best I can "No one need find out about this. Let's keep it between us"

"Right."

"Now, to be on the safe side I'll go and take a look at this gate. See if anyone's tried tampering with it."

"Thank you, Deputy Head Porter" Head Porter says. I smile and turn to go but he again takes me by the arm, gently this time. "And… just be careful, won't you?"

"Head Porter?"

When he speaks next his voice is urgent, but not threatening, although desperate to convey a message that it not expressed in his words.

"Whatever it is The Dean is getting you mixed up in… just be careful. Sometimes that man just doesn't have a clue what he is doing."

These words bounce like echoes around my racing mind as I stroll across the bridge and towards the gardens of The Master's Lodge. No time to worry about it now. I am far too interested in discovering this intriguing gateway to nowhere.

A Friend Returns

ON A BRIGHT AND SHINY spring day such as today, there is surely no finer place to be than The Master's garden. I consider my great fortune at having a job which allows me unprecedented access to places of such unusual great beauty. And consider also, if you will, the very nature of the task that brings me to this charming spot – the enquiry of a long forgotten gate that doesn't go anywhere. The key to which someone, for reasons best known to themselves, has seen fit to remove secretly from the Porters' Lodge. I shake my head and indulge myself in a little chuckle. It certainly is a funny old world, within the walls of Old College. So funny, in fact, that it is almost enough to make a girl forget about the dead Fellows scattered carelessly about the place. Almost.

I am no horticulturalist, and so cannot properly identify the cheerful specimens currently occupying the beds and pots in The Master's garden. But let me tell you, there are some fabulous blooms on display. A few early bees are fastidiously busying themselves about a bush adorned with blueish purple trumpet-like flowers, while a flush of yellow tumbles from a solid-looking urn, the rounded heads putting me in mind of bulging fried eggs. My colleague and sometime drinking partner Head Gardener, really has done himself proud.

But I am not here to admire the view, I have business to attend to. I walk along the back wall of the garden and at first I am stumped. There is no sign of a gate, nor sign of a sensible place where one might be. Parts of the elderly wall are covered in a thick ivy, which appears to be the only thing holding it up in some places. Maybe the gate hides beneath the greenery? I roll up my sleeves and tentatively rustle around a little.

Unconvinced that this is the best way forward, I am considering another course of action when I am abruptly disturbed.

"Goodness me! I think you could be bothering that wall, you know."

Leaping figuratively out my skin and actually about a foot in the air, my shock and surprise turn to delight when I see the familiar figure standing behind me. The top hat worn at a jaunty angle atop a face full of genius and mischief, a dramatic pose struck and all wrapped up in a suit so sharp you could cut cheese with it – it can only be one man.

"Professor VJ Duke!" I exclaim with glee. "What on Earth are you doing here?"

"I'm just strolling about, you know. I do that from time to time. What are you up to?" replies the Professor, stepping forward to examine the wall with me.

"Oh, I'm looking for a gate" I answer. "There's an old gate somewhere along this wall."

"I really don't think I should believe that." Professor VJ Duke seems to think this is funny. "Where do you suppose the gate would lead?"

"Oh, I don't know. It can't lead anywhere, except straight into the water. It's some old access point from the river or something. It's an Old College thing."

"Well, the professor shall help. Perhaps there'll be a treasure behind the gate" and with the dexterity and elegance of a magician, the Professor flicks up his sleeves and gamely rustles around beneath the ivy.

"Anyway, Professor," I continue. "What are you really doing here? I can't believe you're just strolling about so far from home."

"Well, the last time The Dean and I spoke he said something about a mystery going on here. And this professor was passing through, so I thought I should help a bit. Who knows? There could be some fighting." Professor Duke begins to sing and hum happily as he tears away at the greenery, theatrically tossing it aside and, occasionally, over the wall entirely.

"Good noodles and a sweet-sauce! Here's your gate, for sure, Deputy Head Porter!" and he presents it with a flourish. It is still mostly hidden, but he has uncovered enough for me to see that it is, undeniably, a gate.

"Thanks Professor, well done" I say. But this isn't really that helpful. Whoever took the key to the gate either hasn't tried to use it yet or couldn't find the gate. No one has been near this for decades.

"Well! Let's see what lays behind it. Perhaps a dragon—or treasure!" Professor VJ Duke says with some excitement.

"I haven't got the key, it's gone missing" I reply glumly. "Anyway, it doesn't go anywhere."

"Rats and a heifer. Well, it's just as well. I'm not in the battle mood, and one must be to go through there, I'm sure," the Professor says ruefully. "Well, how about we go and see The Dean?"

As I lead the Professor across the courtyards to The Dean's staircase, he chats happily to me about his many adventures and travels. Although I have been unable to quite put my finger on what this Professor's area of speciality might be, he certainly has an interesting and varied time of it, with his 'research'.

On returning to The Dean's rooms, I find him in a much happier composure than when I left him. The whiskey bottle is nowhere to be seen and the beginnings of disorder are creeping back in from the edges of the room. It is strange how he tidies when he is unsettled. But anyway. The Dean looks up with some surprise to see me accompanying Professor Duke. A broad grin breaks across his face and he gets up to shake his friend warmly by the hand.

"P. VJ!" he exclaims "So good of you to come at such short notice! It is marvellous to see you, dear boy"

"Greetings, and so many of them, we better not begin saying them! Great to see you. I can't stay too long, but I'll give you any help I can. Professorish help, that is."

"Right!" The Dean rubs his hands together. "Deputy Head Porter, I've given P. VJ here the run down on our situation here in College. I can tell you, I've been doing a bit of digging and there have been a fair few instances over the years of Fellows expiring in the same manner as our dear Professor K – peacefully in their sleep. No suspicious circumstances attributed to any of them – even the younger Fellows. Paperwork all completed by College doctors then the chaps are popped in the hole as quick as you like."

"Aha! Fellows popped off and then all the details popped in the hole. No time for investigations, I suppose? Or for the authorities to look into the matter?" Professor Duke says, stroking his chin.

"Colleges ARE the authorities in this town," The Dean replies grimly. "They are more powerful than you'll ever know."

"But Senior Bursar didn't go very peacefully," I point out "Any mention of untimely accidents or things of that nature?"

"That's a good point," says The Dean "And no – nothing like Senior Bursar's demise."

"Senior Bursar's death seems a bit risky to me," the Professor muses "It's a bit of a noisy, messy death compared to Professor K's. Especially if you consider that 'peacefully in their sleep' seems to be the fashionable way to do away with people around here. Something's up".

"Then there's the thing about Senior Bursar having his kettle replaced just days before he was electrocuted," I say "And now the missing key. A key that is of absolutely no use to anyone."

"Keys, kettle and Professor K – do you suppose there's a clue in there?" suggests The Dean, more joking that not I'm sure.

"I think there could be. But...K – it's the chemical symbol for potassium?" Professor Duke is thinking fast. "Potassium cyanide – a poison! Professor K was a chemist, was he not?"

"That's right!" The Dean cries excitedly.

"Let's not get ahead of ourselves," I interject, feeling the need to reign this in before everyone gets too excited. "I think the 'K' thing might just be a coincidence. Let's focus on the kettle and the key."

"You say the key is of no use to anyone?" asks the Professor.

"That's right," I reply. "You saw the gate in the garden wall."

"But what if the uselessness of the key is exactly what makes it so useful!"

"What do you mean, Professor?" I ask.

"Perhaps that key is used so little, no one would notice if it went missing. Not for a while, anyway. But maybe there is a key that is very useful and is used often. And if it went missing, that would be discovered almost immediately. Maybe the useless key is sitting in the place of a useful key – hiding its absence by taking its place."

There is a brief silence while we consider this.

"That's a bloody good point" says The Dean, impressed. "But what key?"

Professor VJ Duke begins to fidget uncomfortably and checks his watch, irritated.

"My dears, I am already unforgivably late for my engagement" he says "I have to take my leave right away. The key, here, is the missing key. Find out which key is *really* missing. And the kettle – why would someone want to use a kettle as an instrument of death when poison has worked so well in the past? I hope I have been of some help. But I am a dull sort of fellow"

"Professor Duke, you have been a hero, as ever" The Dean gushes as he shakes his friend's hand once again. "Deputy Head Porter will see you out."

I take Professor VJ Duke to Sprockett Gate rather than arouse Head Porter's attention by taking him through the Porters' Lodge. As I hold open the huge and heavy wooden doors for him to take his leave, the Professor gives me a smile as big as the moon.

"It's been great to see you, Professor" I say, then a little sadly "It's a shame you can't stay longer."

"Oh dear! It is a pity, but I'll come back! Promise" he replies, his eyes twinkling "Besides, I'm sure you and The Dean will have this nonsense all figured out in no time, even without my help. You're a very smart lady."

"Oh, it's not just that...I..." But I can't think how to suitably end the sentence. "Travel safely, won't you Professor" is the best I can manage.

Professor VJ Duke tips his hat to me and smiles again as he strides merrily and hastily out into The City streets. I have a feeling I shall see him again. I only hope that time is not too far away.

Head Porter's Visitor

I AM BEGINNING TO SUSPECT that Head Porter is not fooled in the slightest by the (admittedly rather far fetched) story about me helping The Dean select artwork for his rooms. Head Porter has his moments of idiocy but this is a stretch too far, even for him.

I make a cup of tea whilst glumly envisioning the joyful task ahead of me, which shall involve sorting through an awful lot of keys. I feel that I am not as fond of keys as any good Porter should be; as fascinating as many of them are, they can become a little tedious over time. Like people. Anyway.

Head Porter joins me at the kettle and slides his elderly-looking tea mug along the counter towards me. I don't need to ask if he wants tea. It's always tea, with Head Porter. He looks at me and smiles in what he probably thinks is a friendly manner.

"And how is the great art hunt coming along?" Head Porter asks, genially.

"Yes. Yes." I reply, pathetically "It's doing really good, thanks."

"Only, I was starting to wonder if you were actually painting the buggering things yourself, the amount of time this seems to be taking up."

Sip tea. Think of something intelligent to say. Sip tea.

"I'm a rubbish painter. I'm more of a collage sort of a person."

Head Porter sighs and drops the jovial pretence. I am surprised to see what looks like concern creeping in at the corners of his face.

"I'm just a bit concerned about what The Dean's getting up to..."

"Oh, you know The Dean!" I cry "He's always getting up to something or other. It'll be something else next week…"

"I'm just worried about you," Head Porter speaks gently. I feel my thoughts stumble as I become immediately conscious of the warmth and sincerity in his voice. "Honestly. I just don't want…"

"There's no need to worry," I reply as convincingly as I can. "Really, it's nothing like that."

Well… hang on, nothing like what?"

We are interrupted, as we so often are, by Porter dashing through from the front desk. He comes, as ever, bearing news.

"Head Porter! There is a lady to see you. She's out the front."

"Thank you, Porter, I shall be there in a minute" Head Porter turns back to me "We'll talk about this later" he says vaguely.

I take a few minutes to wash and put away the tea things before heading to the front of the Porters' Lodge. There is no sign of Head Porter and his mystery lady visitor, but I spot Porter leaning against the front desk, intently watching something outside.

"Here, Ma'am, what do you reckon to this?" Porter whispers, nodding his head in the direction of the window looking out over the street. I join him at his vantage point and look out onto the busy City streets, awash with bicycles, tourists and a smattering of spring sunshine. Further up the street, on the opposite side of the road, there is a pub much beloved of Old College students. Standing by its white washed wall is the familiar bowler-hatted figure of Head Porter. With him is what appears to be (at this distance it is hard to be sure) an attractive young lady. Actually, a very angry attractive young lady. She has long red hair and a quirky patchwork coat, which comes down nearly to her ankles. I find myself wondering where she got the coat.

"I like her coat," I remark to an unimpressed Porter.

"Never mind the bloody coat," he says "What's Head Porter doing rowing with a woman in the street?"

"Good point," I reply. "Do you know who she is?"

"No idea at all."

"Well, whatever they're arguing about, it looks like he's losing."

Porter and I watch the short scene play out, until the dramatic exit stage left of the angry woman denotes the final curtain has fallen. A deflated-looking Head Porter shuffles back towards the Lodge, sullenly hanging his head. So sad is it to see a bowler hat tipped so mournfully towards the ground, I feel the urge to rush out and hug the man. But that would hardly be appropriate and I don't think Head Porter would like it much anyway.

I move away from the front row seats and urge Porter to do the same. Somehow I don't think Head Porter will be delighted to discover that he had an audience. We both attempt to act as normally as possible (surely the hardest thing pull off, even for seasoned actors) as he enters the Lodge with a weary shove of the door. Head still bowed, he avoids us both completely on his very direct journey to his office. The door is shut behind him with a little more force than is strictly necessary. Porter and I exchange worried glances.

"Should I go and talk to him?" I suggest.

"Rather you than me."

I consider my options. I decide quickly that approaching a grumpy Head Porter should not be something to attempt on an empty stomach and the whole thing should be reconsidered after lunch.

Eating Is Cheating

LUNCH IS AN INTENTIONALLY SOLITARY affair for me today, as I need to clear my head a little and focus on what is important. What is important right now is food. I haven't been eating as well as I should since the onset of polite slaughter at Old College and I feel that now is the time to redress the balance. An under-nourished mind is good to neither man nor beast. Or, I suspect, Deputy Head Porters.

I ensconce myself strategically at one of the middle tables, a chair or so away from two larger groups of chattering students. Tucked away here, there is little chance I will be joined by sociable colleagues due to the proximity of excitable youths.

Concentrating my attentions until the clattering racket of the chattering Dinning Hall fades to a distant tinkle, I pause for a moment to enjoy the sight and smell of the full plate before me. What awaits to be devoured is merely a lasagne, like any other. But the Catering staff are generous chaps and I have an impressive portion of a perfectly balanced pasta and sauce tower to enjoy. The crispy layer of bronzed cheese on top crowns it beautifully.

I am a little ashamed to tell you that I have accompanied my lasagne with a healthy-sized stack of chips, as well as an actually healthy pile of gently steamed broccoli. The broccoli can be a bit of a gamble; on some occasions it is practically raw and on others it is reduced to a pallid green mush. Today, though, it looks just right.

Finally, with my senses of sight and smell sated, it is time to indulge the greatest of the five – taste! Taking the knife and fork in my hands as if they were ceremonial weapons of some description, I begin my attack on my lunch with gusto.

Barely three forkfuls in and I am more than a little surprised to be interrupted by a sheepish Head Porter. I hadn't expected to see him so soon after his public altercation with the mystery lady. He never usually comes to lunch when he is in a huff. I can only assume he has either cheered up or become very hungry.

"I didn't expect to see you at lunch, Head Porter" I say, all wide-eyed innocence.

"Why ever not?" he asks, putting down a plate similar to mine but without any greenery. I am alarmed at how crass lasagne and chips appears without the accompaniment of some civilising broccoli.

"You seemed a bit... grumpy before. You never come to lunch when you're grumpy."

"A man can be grumpy and hungry, can't he?" Head Porter replies curtly.

"Certainly," I agree "In fact, I'd say it is almost impossible not to be grumpy when hungry."

Head Porter quickly glances around and lowers his voice.

"Are you going to tell me what you and The Dean are up to?" It is a matter of fact request.

"Are you going to tell me about your visitor?" I counter.

"That... isn't important right now," Head Porter falters. "But I'm fairly sure that whatever you've got yourself involved in is important. Am I right?"

It is rare that anything succeeds in causing me to stop eating, but Head Porter manages it well enough with his direct tone and a well-judged stare. I gently place down my cutlery and finish off my mouthful. If the Old Boy was right, Head Porter has a bit of an inside track on the more sinister side of Old College anyway. The trick will be to find out what he knows first, before I tell him anything. But I really do not relish having this particular conversation right here in the Dining Hall. These wood panelled walls may very well have ears.

"Listen, it's complicated," I explain. "I can't really think about it while I'm trying to eat my lunch"

"You mean you can't eat and think?" Head Porter is unimpressed. A much-used phrase from my younger days springs to mind,

"Eating's cheating," I say "Drinking's thinking. Why don't we go for a large one after work and have a chat then?"

Head Porter looks taken aback at this suggestion. I am a little startled myself – I never really ever pictured myself inviting Head Porter out for a drink. But it's done now.

"Alright then, Deputy Head Porter" he replies, sounding like he quite likes the idea. "It's a date!"

The horror of these last three words seep slowly into my head and nearly put me off my lunch entirely. Still, it seems to have cheered Head Porter up no end so I let it pass for now and consol myself with thoughts of what to have for pudding.

Drinking Is Thinking

It is nearly nine o'clock in The Albatross and Head Porter and I are just about to have one drink too many. What started out as an informal chat about work has delightfully mutated in something approximating a Fairly Good Night.

From what little I know of Head Porter, he doesn't strike me as a man much given to drinking. Or going out. Or existing much at all, outside of Old College. I thought, at first, that I was in for a bit of a tedious night as my unlikely companion seemed so uncomfortable and out of place. And, although relations between us have become somewhat warmer recently, we are hardly the best of friends.

Now, though, as he leans on the bar like a seasoned patron, giving me a Fonz-esque thumbs up, I almost want to give the man a kiss. Another glass of wine and I probably will. *Oh dear…*

Head Porter wobbles jauntily back to our tables, merrily sloshing our drinks (wine for me, a pint of something murky-looking for him) as he does so. He sits down heavily in the chair opposite mine and grins inanely, eyes shining with equal measure of joy and ale.

"What are you looking like that for?" I ask, taking a slurp of wine.

"I'm just… having a wonderful time!" replies Head Porter. *Ah. He is a 'happy drunk'. Excellent.* "It's not often I get to go out with friends. We are friends, aren't we, Deputy Head Porter?"

Tricky one, this. But let's just go with it.

"Certainly we are," I reply carefully.

181

"It's just… oh, you know…" and Head Porter sighs a sigh that sounds like it has been waiting to be sighed for years. "I know I'm not the easiest person to get along with…" *and here comes the 'reflective drunk'…* "I'm not that much fun, or the most intelligent person, or the best looking chap in the world…"

Head Porter stares forlornly into his pint for a moment.

"Yes?" I try to chivvy him along a bit. He looks at me, confused.

"Yes… I'm not the greatest… hang on, where am I going with this again?"

"We were going to have a chat about work, I thought" I say, hoping that a change of subject will avert an awkward conversation. Head Porter brightens considerably.

"I must say, I'm really going to miss Junior Bursar, aren't you?" he slurs. "I mean, I know we haven't always seen eye to eye, but… but… better the devil you know, eh?"

"Yes, I shall miss him" I reply "But the old chap deserves to put his feet up after all these years, I suppose. But it makes me wonder what The Fellowship are going to do, what with him retiring and Senior Bursar dead. We will be Bursar-less!"

This last remark appears to have been the most amusing thing Head Porter has ever heard, as great bursts of cackling laughter burst forth from his reddened face. I watch, amused, as Head Porter tries to bring himself under control and resume our conversation. Eyes watering from his effusion, he finally manages it.

"I heard they are going to replace them with just one Bursar. A sort of… super Bursar!" Head Porter is lost again in a fit of mirth. This is getting a little tiresome now.

"Where did you hear that?" I ask.

"I heard Senior Tutor talking to Dr M about it. They are going to hold the interviews during the Summer Vac."

"What? When none of The Fellowship will be around? How does that work?" This seems worryingly similar to the method by which I was employed.

"Well, they'll have to hang around, won't they" Head Porter takes another sip of ale "They have to have a new Bursar before the start of the next academic year."

"Talking of Bursars" I begin, hoping to guide the conversation towards something useful "What do you make of Senior's Bursar's unlikely demise?"

This seems to sober Head Porter somewhat, or at least draw his scattered focus a little. The alcohol may have reddened his cheeks, but I can see the colour draining beneath the artificial flush.

"It's like someone is tying up loose ends," he utters unsteadily. "What with Professor K, but then, with him gone…" Head Porter trails off. I decide to take a chance.

"I know about what happened fifty years ago" I state. The air between us becomes like a sheet of ice for a moment. Then,

"How..?"

"Probably best I don't answer that."

"Yes. Quite."

Head Porter takes this tense pause as an opportunity to get some more ale inside him. It is probably a good idea. I follow suit with my wine and consider getting another. I think I shall be needing it…

One Too Many

"WHAT DO YOU KNOW?" HEAD Porter's voice is barely a whisper and his glassy eyes are panicky beneath the boozy sheen. I carefully place my considerably diminished wine glass on the table.

"Well," I begin, swallowing hard to try to suppress my own sense of dread "I know that there are some crazy rumours going about the place. As far as actual facts are concerned, I'm not so sure. But I think Professor K was."

Head Porter nods slowly, his eyes never leaving my face. I can feel him trying to read my expression, but through the fug of ale I would have thought this was nigh on impossible.

"I think we should talk about this somewhere more private," he suggests "I mean, I only live round the corner, we could..?" Head Porter trails off as if he suddenly becomes nervous at the idea of inviting me to his home. I am not exactly delighted at this prospect myself but I want to get to the bottom of this.

"Sure, good idea" I reply as casually as I can. He seems quite pleased. I finish the last of the wine and get up to leave, indicating to Head Porter to do the same.

We leave The Albatross together, slightly wobblier than when we entered. In Head Porter's case, significantly wobblier. He staggers a little on the pavement and reaches out his hand to steady himself on my shoulder. I have an excess of experience in dealing with the inebriated, a familiarity which has served me well since coming to Old College. I gently guide his arm around my shoulder in order that I can walk him safely along the street.

Head Porter giggles, mutters and chatters away fairly merrily on our short walk from the beautiful academic centre of The City, on through to the residential area. I think to myself that we must make a peculiar sight, passing by the affluent three storey Victorian town houses, elegantly lining the streets and built of pale, narrow bricks. Head Porter's bowler hat is askew upon his ruffled head and we are taking quite a meandering route along the road. We must look like the worst competitors in the best-dressed three-legged race of all time.

Leaving the Victorian grandeur behind, we arrive at Head Porter's neighbourhood before too long. The houses here look tired and shabby in places, but it is not an unpleasant area. Head Porter indicates his house, a neat and tidy mid terrace property with a meticulously painted front door. I notice it is almost the exact same shade of the blue that Old College boasts as its standard.

With remarkable dexterity for a man so debilitated by alcohol, Head Porter unlocks the door and invites me inside. The hallway is quite cramped and dimly lit by a single bare light bulb hanging from the ceiling. I can see that the carpet is of good quality but old and worn. Ahead I see the staircase and beyond that, what appears to be the kitchen. Head Porter flings open a door to the left and shows me through to what turns out to be the living room.

"Make yourself at home," he offers genially "Do you fancy another drink? I fancy another drink. I think I've got some sherry or something left over from Christmas, wait here while I go and have a look."

Head Porter bustles off towards the kitchen and I decide to have a look around as politely as possible. His house is modest but beautifully kept. I wouldn't go as far to say that it is sparse, but if I was hoping to learn more about him from his home I am to be disappointed.

The carpet is the same as that in the hallway. A little path has been worn from the door-way, to the settee and to the television (the old, bulky kind) while the carpet at the edges of the room remain quite plump and fresh. The settee is an elderly brown leather affair, well used but also well loved. A matching chair sits in the corner of the room, I would guess for use by visitors. It looks barely used and seems a little sad in the corner by itself. Other than a coffee table and a little bookshelf, there is very little else in the room at all.

I hear Head Porter calling out from the kitchen, it seems he has found something or other for us to drink. Just then, I notice a small photograph in an elaborate gold frame on the bookshelf. I move towards it to have a look. It is a picture of a smiling, red-haired little girl of about three years old.

"Here, Deputy Head Porter, I've found half a bottle of sweet sherry," I jump as Head Porter appears unexpectedly behind me. "Do you want a glass?"

"Yes please" I reply and take the glass he is offering me. The sherry is cloyingly sweet and makes me feel a little sick. This is definitely one drink too many, for me. My head swimming a little, I help myself to the corner chair. Head Porter drops unsteadily onto the settee.

"So then," Head Porter begins. "Professor K told you all about it, did he?"

"Yes" I lie.

"I thought so. I suppose he just couldn't live with the guilt anymore. Hardly surprising, really. Why do you think he chose to tell you, of all people?"

I take a slow sip of sherry to afford myself some thinking time. Guilt?

"I'm not sure," I reply "We did seem to hit it off. We were friends, really. Maybe he just trusted me."

"Perhaps, yes" Head Porter eyes his sherry glass suspiciously. "Does this taste okay to you, Deputy Head Porter? I think it might have gone off."

"I don't think sherry goes off, as such" I answer "But it is an odd taste, certainly."

"Hmmm" Head Porter seems to lose himself in thought for a moment. "Here, aren't you a bit worried for your own safety, Deputy Head Porter?"

"What do you mean?"

"If anyone knows that Professor K was unburdening himself to you, you could be in for the same treatment."

"So you're pretty certain that Professor K was killed, then?" I ask, very aware that I am only vaguely aware of what Head Porter is talking about.

"Well, of course!" declares Head Porter "It's obvious. He must have been poisoned, of course, like the others. Ironic, really, don't you think?"

"Ironic, yes" I murmur. But why is it ironic? Because he was a chemist? Is a chemist being poisoned ironic?

"I can understand them bumping him off, poor old Professor K" Head Porter continues without a hint of melancholy "But Senior Bursar I don't understand at all. He was the last person who would reveal the secret of The Vicious Circle, and yet here he is – dead!" *Hang on a minute – what?*

"The... Vicious Circle?" I venture.

"It could have been a genuine accident, I suppose..." Head Porter muses, obviously oblivious to my query. "No, no. It can't be. I know what those lot are like, he must have been killed off too."

"The Vicious Circle?" I try again.

"Professor K told you about The Vicious Circle, I take it?"

"He didn't get quite that far before... you know."

Head Porter sighs, and reluctantly pours himself another sherry. I decline his offer of a top up.

"I suppose I'd better explain..."

The Vicious Circle

Sitting in the back of taxi on the way home from Head Porter's house, my head is reeling. Reeling and thumping from an early onset hangover. What Head Porter told me is simply so unbelievable that it must be true. And Professor K was making perfect sense all along, I was just too ignorant to realise.

So, if I have this right in my head (which after all the wine and sherry is a grand achievement) The Vicious Circle is not only a sequence of events that stretch back to the very foundation of Old College, but also simultaneously are a forever-shifting group of people from the elite of The Fellowship.

The tucked-away book in the Old Library held the first clue, had I been bright enough to spot it. The sacrificial peasants buried ceremonially in the foundations of Old College were indeed the bones dug up when the Porters' Lodge was rebuilt. This much Professor K had all but confirmed to me. What I didn't realise, however, was that two of the bodies cast into the ground were members of The Order of the Lesser Dragon, the ancient secret society that founded Old College.

Legend has it that these two unfortunates thought that the arcane method of burying peasants under buildings for good luck was a bit beneath The Order of the Lesser Dragon, what with them being such highly educated men. Their stance was that it wasn't very lucky at all, especially for the peasants. Their insubordination cost them their lives and it seems to be a pattern that has repeated itself in the years since.

Historically, it seems, The Fellowship have not been averse to despatching with those among their number who do not tow the party line. This practice became remarkably more popular following the discovery of the bones beneath the Lodge. Head Porter says there may even have been a couple of students who came to an untimely end when they questioned the sudden deaths of their beloved tutors.

Following that little episode of slaughter, there began what became known as The Vicious Circle. Whoever questioned or attempted to investigate the unexplained deaths met with the same fate; a knee-jerk panicked reaction from The Fellowship, a group of academics so powerful they simply believed that the normal laws and morals of society don't apply to them. The more deaths that occurred, the more questions were asked. And so more deaths occurred. And so on. A Vicious Circle, if ever there was one.

But that isn't even the worst bit. Not by a long shot.

Clear & Present Danger

Naturally, I had asked Head Porter about how The Fellowship went about killing off so many of their number. I somehow cannot picture the cloisters of Old College drenched in the blood and guts of its members. For a start, the Bedders would have kicked up a dreadful fuss about having to clear up the mess.

"That'll be eighteen pounds sixty, miss"

The taxi driver rouses me abruptly from my thoughts and I am aware that we have reached my house. A little dazed, I pay the man and shuffle myself out of the car and through my front door. My house, I am sad to say, is not quite as tidy as Head Porter's, but then I have considerably more clutter to contend with. Must be a girl thing.

Although tempted to further dampen my chaotic mind with yet more alcohol, I wisely choose to make a nice cup of tea instead. Dumping the tea bag in the sink, I shake my head in disbelief. *How could he?*

The hour is late and it is not particularly warm but I take my steaming mug of sanity out to the small terrace at the back of my house. I settle down on the back doorstep and watch for a while as the bats flit and arc around the trees, chattering in sonar. This is perhaps the most peace I will feel for quite some time.

So the *modus operandi* of The Fellowship was poison, perhaps unsurprisingly. And who better to prepare and administer such an instrument of death than a Professor of chemistry? Indeed. My dear departed Professor K was the avenging angel of The Vicious Circle for decades; expertly exterminating anyone who got too close to the truth.

Head Porter was unable to tell me quite how it was done, he isn't party to such information, but I do not feel that that really matters.

Head Porter believes that Professor K was struggling with his conscience and thought I would somehow be able to help him break the cycle. His general thinking is that someone realised what he was up to and killed him before he could reveal too much. Thinking back over our conversations, it all seems so obvious now. I curse myself for not realising all this at the time, I might have been able to save him. But how could I have known? How?

And why all the riddles and mysterious monologues? Maybe a combination of his own guilt and some kind of misplaced loyalty to The Vicious Circle, I don't know. But I could have saved him! Perhaps. Perhaps I could have saved him. Head Porter thinks he was scared to say too much in case he endangered me, too. But then again, he was killed *because* he was talking to me. Someone, somewhere knows this. And that someone is not shy of taking serious steps to ensure silence.

Head Porter ventured a theory that the poison was actually intended for me, not Professor K. It was, after all, me who ordered and collected the breakfast I took to him when he returned from hospital. No one knew it was for him. I was just trying to do a nice thing. Did I kill him? Although, we have no way of knowing how the poison was actually administered.

So many questions and so few answers. The problem with The Vicious Circle, Head Porter had said, is that you couldn't be sure who was a part of it. Certainly, it is a minority group within The Fellowship. He said that he was convinced Senior Bursar was involved, but now he is dead, too. An electrical 'accident', I suppose because there was no one readily available to arrange the more traditional method of poisoning.

If we follow the theory of those that ask the questions end up dead, The Dean and I are in a very precarious position indeed. It is too late now and I am too tired... to ponder this any further. I have no way of warning The Dean until tomorrow morning and my body is telling me to go to bed, even if my brain is suggesting other things. Like another drink. No. As my Grandmother always says, there is nothing that can't be solved by a nice cup of tea and a good night's sleep. I just hope she is right.

Distracted By Junior Bursar

A HEARTY FULL-ENGLISH HAS REVIVED Head Porter and I considerably. The healing powers of bacon have never let me down yet. The task that lies ahead fails to fill me with much joy, though. Head Porter, being Head Porter, has graciously delegated the 'missing key' task to my good self. For the foreseeable future I will be elbow deep in keys, keys, keys. Again. To strengthen my resolve, I make myself the finest cup of tea I can muster and start stockpiling biscuits. It is the only way I will ever get through this.

By mid-morning I start to think that I am actually going to die of old age before this task is completed. For the briefest of moments I rather feel that being murdered by The Fellowship might be a blessed relief. I am considering taking a break to replenish my tea and biscuit stock, when Junior Bursar creeps into the Lodge. I don't notice him until he is right behind me – I swear he must have been a ninja in a previous life.

"Good morning, Sir" I greet him, trying not to look startled. "You are very… stealthy… this morning."

Junior Bursar laughs

"Perhaps it is less that I am stealthy and more that you are unperceptive, Deputy Head Porter?" Hmm. He might have a point, here. My mind does tend to meander somewhat when faced with all these keys. "Anyway, what are you up to? Are you busy?"

"I'm just auditing the keys, you know, making sure they're all present and correct."

"That is quite a lengthy endeavour," replies Junior Bursar, sounding surprisingly sympathetic.

"It is rather, Sir, yes."

"And pretty dull too, I suspect?"

"I won't lie to you Sir, I've had more fun at the dentist."

"My dentist is quite amusing, actually" says Junior Bursar conversationally "He has all these little anecdotes about a young hygienist who used to work for him. Quite unbelievable, some of them."

"Really Sir?" I reply, not quite sure where this is going "You must give me his number. I'd like an anecdotal dentist."

"You like parties, don't you Deputy Head Porter?"

"I do, Sir" I reply cautiously. Junior Bursar does have this knack of suddenly springing conversations you have no desire to partake in, without you even knowing. Until it is too late, of course. He is also smiling, which is never a good sign.

"I thought as much. You know that I am retiring very soon, don't you Deputy Head Porter?"

"I do, Sir. A sad thing indeed."

"Indeed. Well, I would like you to help with the arrangements for my retirement party!"

This is the last thing I was expecting, to be honest. Events of this nature are ordinarily handled by Head Of Catering and his department. Porters don't generally do parties. Except, apparently now they do. Junior Bursar seems quite adamant on the matter.

I do not feel that I can say no, in fact, I know that I cannot say no. You don't say no to Junior Bursar. So my agreement is met with an even broader smile. I do worry that the man's face might crack open with all this unusual activity.

"Marvellous, Deputy Head Porter!" he exclaims. "Perhaps you would join me in my rooms to go over a few initial details?"

"What, now?" I ask.

"Yes, now."

"Head Porter was very clear that the key audit was a matter of priority, Sir."

"Why? They're not going anywhere, are they?" *They might!* "Leave this until later, Deputy Head Porter. I want to discuss my party. This is a matter that must be attended to immediately!"

And so, helplessly, I trot after Junior Bursar, who is inexplicably determined to employ me as a party planner. Still. It's got to be more fun than messing about with keys.

Not A Wizard. Probably

JUNIOR BURSAR HAS, IN MY humble opinion, the best rooms in Old College. Situated half way up the flag tower, they not only afford excellent views of both Old Court and the streets beyond the College, but also feel swathed in enchantment. Whether it is the smoothly curved stone walls or the very presence of Junior Bursar himself it is difficult to tell, but I feel like I am inside a wizard's tower.

I suppose Junior Bursar has something of a wizard-like element to him. I got the impression early on that the Porters were a little nervous of upsetting him, as if he had some kind of hitherto unknown mystical power. He can certainly be difficult at times but the only thing mystical about him is how he has managed to survive for so many decades at Old College without going completely insane. Or maybe he has, who knows? He may just be very good at hiding it.

The Junior Bursar I have before me now seems to be a very different creature to the one I have come to know and… well, not quite love but have certainly developed an unlikely affection for. The smile he offers me now is not just on his lips but permeates his whole face and even twinkles in his eyes. He radiates a sense of genial wellbeing. I suspect it has something to do with his impending retirement. And he is obviously very much looking forward to his party.

"Now, Deputy Head Porter" he begins affably "Of course Catering will be organising the food and drinks but I rather hoped you would be able to assist me in the area of entertainment!" I hope he doesn't mean me, personally, as the entertainment.

"What sort of thing were you thinking of, Sir?" I ask.

"Well, we will need a band, certainly" he eagerly replies "Something upbeat, dancing music, you know? And I saw once at a party where the host had hired a magician to mingle among the guests performing tricks, it was just super."

"You want a magician?" I try not to sound too surprised.

"What do you think, Deputy Head Porter? I think I would like one. Do you think it would be too much?"

"Not at all, Sir. It's your party, you have what you want." This seems to please Junior Bursar very much. His affiliation with wizardry is clearly more potent than I first thought.

"I shall tell you what else I would like," I detect a slight edge in his voice, now.

"Go on, Sir"

"I would like to know with whom Head Porter was arguing with in the street the other day?"

"I'm not sure I recall the incident to which you refer, Sir" I lie. Junior Bursar clearly does not believe me.

"Is that so? Well, well. Perhaps you should make a point of being better informed about such things, Deputy Head Porter."

"I will do that, Sir."

"Please make sure that you do" these words are delivered so sincerely I find myself searching Junior Bursar's face for signs of his intention. I see nothing but the genuine smile. "Balloons!" He says suddenly.

"Balloons?"

"I should very much like there to be balloons. I suppose The Master will allow balloons in the Wide Gallery, will he not?"

"I should think so Sir. Is that where the party will be held, in the Wide Gallery?"

"Indeed!"

The Wide Gallery is a very grand room in The Master's Lodge and, in my mind, completely unsuitable for dancing music and balloons. Which will make the whole event altogether much more fun, I have no doubt.

I leave Junior Bursar's rooms in absolutely no doubt that the retirement party preparations are to be my very uppermost priority. Junior Bursar will be requiring regular and detailed updates on every aspect of my endeavours. *But the missing key! I have to find out which is the missing key!* Now, why do I get the impression I am being deliberately distracted?

Trouble On The River

MY HEAD FULL OF MAGICIANS and balloons, I return to the Porters' Lodge, which appears to have descended into pandemonium during my short time with Junior Bursar. Porter is at the front desk comforting a very distressed young female student, who on closer inspection appears to be soaking wet. Head Porter is remonstrating loudly with two male students, who are boisterously threatening all kinds of things to persons unknown.

I don't feel that I have the patience for tearful young ladies, so I sidestep that particular obstacle and head straight for Head Porter and the shouting chaps. A situation that far better suits my mood.

"What's all this about, then?" I ask Head Porter, ignoring for a moment the inventive and colourful language being offered by our student friends, one of whom I recognise from a previous encounter.

"They've had some run in with a group from Hawkins College," explains Head Porter, exasperated. "They were punting and Penelope ended up in the river."

"The buggers rammed our punt deliberately! They *intended* to sink our punt…"

"Hey, don't I know you?" I ask the red faced young man. "It's Hershel, isn't it? I think we've crossed paths before. I ended up searching your room, as I recall." Hershel calms down remarkably.

"I apologise for our outburst," he says, much more reasonably. "But they really went for us on the river and Penelope was terrified…"

"Okay, okay," I reply. "I can understand you're upset but you can't go around shouting threats and things like that. We'll speak to the Hawkins' Porters and see what they say. Do you know who they were?"

"No, but there were five of them. Three chaps and two girls."

"Right. Take Penelope back to her rooms and get her cleaned up. I can't be having her causing a scene in the Lodge."

Hershel escorts his friends out of the Lodge and some degree of order is restored.

"Do we really have to go and speak to them at Hawkins College?" Head Porter whines. "I can't bloody stand their Head Porter. He's so smug."

"I know," I say "But we should probably nip this one in the bud. Hershel can be quite excitable."

"Hmm. Where were you anyway? I thought you were checking the keys?"

"I was dragged away by Junior Bursar to discuss his party arrangements, apparently."

Head Porter raises his eyebrows.

"Oh? Apparently?"

"He seemed more interested in your rather public row from the other day, though."

Head Porter looks a little uncomfortable.

"Oh. That…" he says.

"Yes, that" I continue "Don't worry, I pleaded ignorance."

"Thanks"

"But I did think you were going to tell me about this mystery lady?"

Head Porter sighs and is clearly irritated.

"It's not really any of your business, Deputy Head Porter,"

"Oh, I know that," I laugh "But I'm going to badger you about it anyway. Besides, I might be able to help. I'm quite good with affairs of the heart."

"For goodness sake" Head Porter is trying to sound annoyed but he isn't really. I can tell. "Come on, we'd best go and sort this out with Hawkins College."

"You're suddenly keen to get over there"

"Well, like you say, let's nip it in the bud."

"I could pop over there if you like?"

"You're not going over there on your own. I know what you're like. You deliberately wind up their Porters."

"It's good sport, Head Porter."

"Get your hat. We're going to Hawkins College."

A Trip To Hawkins College

ON THE SHORT JOURNEY TO our esteemed neighbours at Hawkins College, I decide to tackle Head Porter about his mystery woman, once and for all. He has not been forthcoming with details about the rather public row he had with her in the street the other day and this has annoyed me. Setting aside for one moment the inference that it is none of my business, I feel it is my duty as a dedicated Deputy to get to the bottom of it nonetheless.

"So this lady, then," I begin, casually "Who is she?"

Head Porter sighs, but he knows he is not going to avoid the question any longer.

"She is someone I have known for a very long time," he replies.

"A lover?"

"Hardly!"

"An ex-lover then? Come on, I only want to help."

Head Porter looks as if he might answer, but his eye is caught by a bowler-hatted gentleman who is watching us with some interest.

"There he is," Head Porter almost spits the words out. "Hawkins Head Porter. He must be expecting us."

Hawkins College is our nearest neighbour and there has been a long-standing friendly rivalry between the Colleges for centuries. Although it pains me to say so, Hawkins is, on the face of it, a far more impressive-looking College. Founded in the early 1400s as a sister to Eton, it took a string of King Henrys until the 1500s to finally complete the building. The Chapel is world famous and is widely regarded as one of the very best examples of late English Gothic architecture.

The towering spires and magnificent buttresses punctuate The City skyline and almost make our College seem a little tatty and understated. Hawkins is a College of supreme wealth and recent details of its wine expenditure has been the subject of much tittle-tattle in the local press.

Hawkins Head Porter is waiting for us by the main gates, obviously uneasy about letting us cross the threshold. It could be that he is being deliberately difficult, as is his way, although Porters are notoriously territorial and much happier when College boundaries are clearly defined. He is an ex-military man, with a perfect stance and an immaculate little moustache. His boots are so highly polished that you can see infinity in them and the way they reflect the early afternoon sun is positively blinding. I can feel the tension radiating from Head Porter.

"I wondered when you two might show up," Hawkins Head Porter's greeting is as friendly as can be expected. "I expect you've come to apologise about the incident on the river this morning?"

I lightly touch Head Porter's elbow as a silent reminder to remain calm. It is not that effective.

"What on earth have we got to apologise for?" Head Porter responds, his voice an octave higher with indignation. His counterpart is clearly delighted that his deliberate attempt to enrage has gone down so well. He expresses this delight by way of gleeful chuckling, which Head Porter finds even more irritating.

"Stop winding him up," I say politely but firmly to Hawkins Head Porter. "You should both behave a little more like gentlemen."

"He wouldn't know a gentleman if one jumped up and bit him on the bum!" he says, jabbing a finger at Head Porter.

"Gentlemen do not bite people on the bum!" Head Porter retorts, which is a fair enough point, to be honest.

"Listen!" I am losing patience a little, now. "We all know that students get up to all sorts and sometimes things go a little too far. All we're asking is that you keep an eye out for any troublemakers and keep a lid on them and we'll do the same with our lot. It's Exam Term and there's enough to worry about without our young charges getting into some ridiculous turf war over punts."

"Turf war? On a river?" says Hawkins Head Porter sarcastically "I really didn't think it would be possible for you to be as stupid as you look but you've gone and proved me wrong, Deputy Head Porter!"

As much as I feel like punching him in the face, I resist the urge for violence and smile benignly at Hawkins Head Porter. My own Head Porter feels somewhat differently, however, and launches himself at his counterpart, pinning him against the ornate iron gates. My complete surprise at his actions (and the fact it happens so quickly) prevents me from intervening until it is too late. Head Porter has his palms squarely on the shoulders of the equally surprised Hawkins Head Porter, preventing him from moving anywhere, whilst he expresses his displeasure with language that would make a sailor blush.

Coming to my senses, I pull Head Porter away and put a safe distance between him and the enemy at the gates.

"Come back here!" Hawkins Head Porter is shouting as I lead a reluctant Head Porter back down the street "Let's settle this like men!"

"Don't say a word to him!" I hiss. "Let's just get out of here."

"You're completely out of control! The Master will hear of this!" our friend from Hawkins College continues to bawl as we hurry away with as much dignity as we can muster.

"Goodness, man, I didn't know you had it in you!" I exclaim to Head Porter.

"Well, that man irritates me no end," he replies. "He always has."

"I shall make a note not to irritate you in future."

"Yes. Let this be a lesson to you."

We both spontaneously erupt with laughter right here in the middle of the street, much to the bemusement of passers-by.

"What if he goes to The Master?" asks Head Porter.

"Don't worry," I reply "We'll tell The Master that he started it."

"Good plan."

"Now then, Head Porter, about this girlfriend of yours…"

The mood changes swiftly at these words and I am aware of a chill in the air between us. Head Porter turns to me, a darkness falling across his face.

"She is not my girlfriend, Deputy Head Porter. If you must know, she is my daughter."

The Missing Key

"I DIDN'T EVEN KNOW YOU had a daughter!"

Head Porter manages to look indignant and uncomfortable both at the same time.

"That may well be because it isn't really any of your business, Deputy Head Porter" he replies stiffly. I decide not to push him further, for now. He *has* just been in a scuffle with his nemesis, Hawkins Head Porter, which is enough to make anyone feel rather unsteady. "Come on, we're going back to the Lodge."

We return to Old College in silence; him brooding (over the fight or his daughter, it's impossible to tell which) and me quietly delighted at having my honour defended so unexpectedly. I only hope we haven't worsened the situation between the students.

Back at the Lodge, things are busy and bustling and Porter gives us both a 'look' that suggests we have been away rather too long. By way of recompense I offer to make the tea, an offer which is grudgingly accepted. Head Porter has already disappeared into his office but I am sure he will want tea after such excitement, so make him a cup anyway.

As I gingerly enter his office to deliver the tea, Head Porter seems a little reserved. Without looking up from his paperwork, he says

"You should continue looking through the keys to find the missing one. If Junior Bursar catches you just tell him I have put some party preparation time aside for you tomorrow."

"Right you are, Head Porter" I reply. Then, because I feel it has to be said – "Thank you for earlier, at Hawkins College."

Head Porter looks up and forces a thin smile through the stony visage of whatever it is that is troubling him.

"I'm not going to let someone talk to my friend like that, particularly not that bugger. Besides, we have to look out for each other Deputy Head Porter. We are both in a somewhat precarious position, what with us chasing this murderer. We need to stick together."

"I'm with you all the way, Head Porter" I reply, smiling. I give a thumbs up signal for good measure.

Head Porter turns his attention back to the papers on his desk and I withdraw quietly to immerse myself in keys.

The essential but mind-numbing task of checking the keys takes me well into the evening. To further compensate for abandoning Porter this afternoon, I send him home early. Head Porter leaves soon after and I am left alone with the Lodge and the keys. After some time, the repetitive nature of this chore has an almost hypnotic effect and I am completely oblivious when I am joined in the Lodge by the unusually stealth-like Dean.

"Good evening, Deputy Head Porter" his booming voice makes me jump out of my skin.

"Blimey, Sir, what are you doing sneaking around like that!" I gently scold him "Things are disconcerting enough around here without you sneaking up on me."

"I was not sneaking" The Dean replies curtly. "*You* weren't paying attention. I tell you, it would be wise to keep your wits about you at a time like this."

"I know, but it's these bloody keys, they're sending me into a coma."

"Have you found the missing one yet?"

"Not yet, but I've only got these last few to check."

"Brilliant! Now. On to something not so brilliant," The Dean pauses for dramatic effect, as it his way. "I've had a complaint about Head Porter and your good self. From Hawkins College. I don't suppose you would know anything about that?" I consider my response carefully.

"There was a degree of… unpleasantness earlier, I'll grant you that."

"From what I hear, the unpleasantness was you two!"

"That's not entirely fair, Sir. He started it."

The Dean sighs and rests his hands heavily in the pockets of his typically garish trousers.

"Ok, fine, just consider yourself severely reprimanded, alright?" This is very unlike The Dean. He usually takes an unnaturally gleeful approach to reprimands and admonitions. I feel I am getting away rather lightly.

"Is that it, is it Sir? No raised voice or threats of violence?" I ask.

"What were you expecting?" The Dean answers "A sound thrashing across the buttocks to help mend your erroneous ways? Would that really do any good?"

I consider this option.

"Moving on from that, I have an excellent idea"

"What's that, Deputy Head Porter?"

"Why don't you put the kettle on while I finish looking through these keys?" The Dean looks a bit put out at my suggestion, he is not a man given to making tea for College servants. But he heads wordlessly to the kitchen area regardless.

Within minutes I have come across something even more exciting than the prospect of being spanked by The Dean. Or rather, I don't come across something, which is even more important in this case.

"Sir!" I call to The Dean "Sir! Come and have a look at this!"

The Dean jogs through from the back brandishing quite possibly the worst cup of tea I have ever seen in my life. He has somehow managed to produce grey tea. But anyway.

"What is it?" he asks, spilling some of the foul-smelling liquid onto the Lodge carpet.

"Look at this," I point to a rusted and elderly-looking key hanging innocuously on its hook. "This is the key to the gate in The Master's Garden."

"Oh!" exclaims The Dean, delighted at this most important discovery. "But what key should be there?"

"That's the interesting bit," I reply "What you would expect to find on this particular hook is the spare key to Senior Bursar's rooms…"

Sleuthing For Beginners

THEY WOULD ALWAYS TELL ME in the Police never to assume anything as it only makes an '*ass*' of '*u*' and '*me*', but in this case I cannot help but lean towards the presumption that whoever took the spare key was more than likely Senior Bursar's killer. Or, at the very least, a cohort of the killer. Or, killer*s*, indeed. Honestly, the further along we get with this investigation the more distant a resolution seems. It's always the way, isn't it?

The Dean had immediately demanded to return to the scene of the crime, which is why I find myself standing now in the almost abandoned rooms of the late Senior Bursar. The lack of spare key posed no problems as I carry master keys to almost every door and window in Old College. Which is an interesting point in itself; if the killer needed to use the spare key, he or she cannot have had access to a set of master keys. That puts myself and Head Porter in the clear, but who else? I make a mental note to bring this up with Head Porter later.

From the corner of my eye I can see the scorch marks on the wall and carpet where Senior Bursar met his unusual demise. I try not to look at them, but my gaze seems to be dragged back towards that direction with alarming insistence. I am far from squeamish but it is an unhappy sight, more than anything. I am a little surprised that the room has not been redecorated to some extent by now. The College is usually very exacting about its buildings and grounds (if not its Fellows) looking immaculate and any hint of a blemish is usually swiftly corrected. About the only thing that is done swiftly, certainly.

Maybe the rooms are being left untouched for a period of mourning, or perhaps they will become something of a shrine to the late, great Senior Bursar – a man who completely redefined the wearing of tweed, in my eyes.

It is late and I am getting tired. The Dean is poking around ineffectually, picking up bits of paper then discarding them in frustration when they fail to reveal some vital clue, or whatever. I don't know what he expects to find.

"What are you looking for, Sir?" I ask politely.

"Clues, Deputy Head Porter, clues!" he replies, violently opening and closing drawers in the manner of a particularly angry detective. "Look for clues, will you!"

Look for clues. Right-o.

In my experience, clues tend not to manifest themselves as hidden messages or esoteric symbols and signs. No. Clues tend to be the most mundane and innocuous things, but seen in the context of the crime. But seeing as The Dean is adopting the approach most favoured by literary and other fictitious sleuths, I feel I should at least show a little enthusiasm. I rather think I should have a large magnifying glass to assist me in my task, accompanied perhaps by a pipe and a perfectly waxed moustache. Maybe a dirty raincoat for good measure.

As The Dean chatters away throughout the course of his search, I become slightly distracted by a sad-looking plant on Senior Bursar's desk. It appears to need a good watering and some TLC to revive it, but it's hanging on, just about. I feel a bit sorry for the plant and decide to re-home it in the Porters' Lodge. It has some miniature lemons growing on it, which are nice. They have a lovely fresh scent, which would be very welcome in the Lodge. Pulling off a few of the dead leaves I suddenly think of something.

"Sir!" I say to The Dean, interrupting an especially ferocious examination of a bookcase "We already have a couple of clues to consider. Why not think on them first?"

"Splendid idea, Deputy Head Porter!" he replies. "Now, show me that you've been paying attention and reiterate to me what clues they are."

"We have the missing key, of course, which we have nearly got to the bottom of," I begin "Then there is the email that was sent to me by Senior Bursar – or at least, from his account – after his death and we also have the typed request to Head Of Housekeeping for a new kettle. The kettle that ultimately became the instrument of his death."

"Very good, my dear girl, very good!" The Deans booms with delight. "I knew you weren't as daft as you look. So, obviously, I have a clear and deliberated course of action conceived in my mind, but I would like to hear your thoughts."

I look towards the desk where the forlorn lemon tree resides next to Senior Bursar's computer. I walk over and switch it on.

"I believe, Sir, that we should start here."

A College Affair

TRYING TO GET INSIDE THE mind of someone like the late Senior Bursar is not something I would usually attempt, but faced with the password protected log-in screen of his computer, this is something I find myself having to wrestle with. The Dean and I have already tried a couple of times, but to no avail.

"Did he have any pets?" I ask The Dean, suddenly struck by inspiration.

"Good thinking!" replies The Dean. "Yes, he had a cat named Telemachus. Ridiculous name for a cat. Is it named after a footballer, do you think?"

I type 'Telemachus' into the password box.

"He's a character from Greek mythology," I say to The Dean "He was the son of Odysseus and Penelope."

I hit 'enter'.

Bingo.

"He is also our ticket into Senior Bursar's digital world, Sir."

"In that case, it's a great name for a cat."

I have a click around the desktop and do not find anything unusual, although annoyingly his email account has already been deactivated. I check the recent documents. In the days leading up to Senior Bursar's death there are just a couple of spreadsheets and an unnamed text document. A*ha*!

"Have a look at this, Sir" I open the text document and a familiar missive leaps onto the screen.

"Good lord!" exclaims The Dean. "It's the note requesting a new kettle!"

"Indeed," I reply. "I wasn't really expecting to find this on here. It rather suggests that Senior Bursar did in fact write the note himself."

"Well, that's right" The Dean agrees. "I would have expected to find this on the murderer's computer."

Really? I wasn't expecting to find this document at all. The murderer certainly wouldn't have saved a copy of it. And even if Senior Bursar did write it himself, why would he keep a copy? Why didn't he just send an email of the request? Quite frankly, the very existence of this document is highly suspicious.

"This is all very odd, wouldn't you say, Deputy Head Porter?" says The Dean.

"Certainly is, Sir."

The hour is getting even later and my stomach is protesting wildly at not having been given a meal for many hours. Maybe it is fatigue, or perhaps the lack of sustenance, but the atmosphere in these rooms seems to become more oppressive with each passing moment. I think I just want to go home.

"I think we've done all we can here tonight, Sir" I say, stifling a yawn and shutting down the computer. "Also, I'm starving."

The Dean checks his watch.

"Oh bugger, I've missed Formal Hall" he curses. Nothing makes a Fellow angrier than having to arrange his own meals. "I shall have to get something in town. The Albatross will still be serving, don't you think?"

Before I can reply, we are interrupted by a familiar voice.

"Making dinner arrangements, are we?"

I swing round to see Junior Bursar standing by the door, hands clasped behind his back. The man can move like a ninja when he has a mind too; neither of us detected the slightest hint of his presence.

"Good evening, Sir" I offer, weakly.

"Yes, I'm sure it is" Junior Bursar replies, smiling the smile of one who is certain he has the upper hand. "What are you two doing in our dear departed Senior Bursar's rooms at this hour?"

Think. Think. What are we doing here... What can I say we are doing here that doesn't sound at all unscrupulous or suspect...

The words are forming in my mind and hastily making their way towards my mouth when the tense silence is broken by The Dean.

"We are having an affair, Junior Bursar" his delivery is blunt, to the point and utterly believable. Had he said any other words at all, I would be delighted at the result. I freeze, open-mouthed and breath held tightly as I wait for Junior Bursar's reaction. To reinforce the point, The Dean puts his arm around my shoulders. It feels more like a mugging than a hugging.

Junior Bursar just about manages to keep a straight face while the cognition of this information plays around that brilliant mind of his. His smile is no longer quite so certain, but it is rather wry.

"Is that so?" he asks, his eyes flicking between the two of us. I decide that it might be better if I do not say anything. But then, I consider the wisdom of allowing The Dean to do the talking. That could be calamitous, to say the least. As it transpires, neither of us are required to say a word as Junior Bursar continues with aplomb. "I must say, I am very surprised at the two of you. The Dean of College and a College Servant – well well!"

"I am very surprised as well, Sir" I say.

"I trust we can keep this between ourselves?" This isn't a request from The Dean, but rather an instruction.

There is an intense period of eye contact between the two Fellows, which is almost electric. After a short time, I would say that the winner of this stand off is The Dean. Junior Bursar looks suddenly awkward and fusses with his jacket. He finally speaks.

"Well, this is your business, of course, but I would suggest you find somewhere more suitable for your passionate liaisons. The rooms of a dead man hardly seem fitting for activities of this nature."

"You are right, of course," The Dean replies, keen to keep things civil. "My idea. I thought we wouldn't be disturbed."

"I was also hoping to rescue this," I say, indicating the wilted miniature lemon plant. "Seems a shame to leave it here all lonely when it could come and live in the Lodge."

"I suppose that would make sense," replies Junior Bursar. "I hope you are making excellent progress with my retirement party arrangements?"

"She has been slaving over it day and night, I assure you" The Deans reassures him.

"Good. Good." Junior Bursar takes a moment to inspect us both again, obviously unsure about something. "I think it's time we secured these rooms and left them in peace, don't you?"

I nod in agreement and collect the little lemon plant in my arms. It really does smell very nice indeed. The Dean maintains his grip around my shoulders and walks me towards the door in what he probably assumes is a gentlemanly manner.

"Good evening, Junior Bursar" he shakes his colleague's hand in the most convincing fashion. "I can assure you we will be more discrete in future. Come on, darling".

The Wrong Tea

EXPLAINING TO HEAD PORTER THE events of the previous evening is challenging, to say the least. He seems less interested in what we found on Senior Bursar's computer than in the other rather tricky matter of The Dean and I now being embroiled in a fictional love affair, the subtle nuances of which Head Porter struggles to grasp.

"So, are you *really* having an affair with The Dean?" he asks, troubled.

"Of course not" I reply "It was simply a diversion tactic to throw Junior Bursar off the scent."

"But why an affair? That could get you into a lot of trouble."

"Probably not as much trouble as searching Senior Bursar's rooms and snooping on his computer."

I try to explain that it was all The Dean's idea and that I was unable to bring into play my genius plot of rescuing the miniature lemon plant. Head Porter seems stuck on the facade of the inappropriate relationship and has missed the point entirely that our secret investigation could have been uncovered there and then. Although it is not unusual for him to grasp the wrong end of the stick on occasion, I sense that there is something on his mind.

"Penny for your thoughts?" I suggest to Head Porter. He seems perturbed.

"I haven't got any," he replies brusquely "And even if I had, they'd cost you a damn sight more than a penny." *Goodness, he is touchy this morning.*

I decide to stick to the safer subject of tea. Of course he wants a cup of tea. I shall go and make the tea *immediately.*

I am annoyed to discover that the Porters' Lodge is completely bereft of English Breakfast tea – not only my personal favourite but also the most appropriate beverage for this early part of the day. I must have a word with Head Of Catering to replenish our supplies. We have Earl Grey tea, of course, but that is hardly a suitable tea for first thing in the morning. Perhaps Darjeeling will do? I suppose it will have to. Hardly a fitting substitute for a fine Assam, though.

Head Porter is apologetic when I present him with his tea (not half as apologetic as I am, though, for being forced to serve Darjeeling). I was right – he does have something on his mind. Although he is reticent to share, he concedes that he is distracted by a lunch meeting he has planned for later.

"But lunch meetings are great!" I cry "You get to have a meeting… but with lunch as well!"

"I'm meeting my daughter" he replies flatly. I do not quite know how to reply. My instinct is to look for the positives and point out all the good things that could come from this. But I know very little at all about the actual situation and Head Porter has so far been rather backwards in coming forward. The clear message is that this is none of my business. I shall keep a respectful distance until such time as it may become my business. So, I offer a different form of assistance instead.

"Why don't you take the afternoon off?" I suggest. "We don't have to tell anyone. I'll say you are at the locksmiths or something. Just pop back before the end of your shift looking harassed. No one will be any the wiser."

"That's kind, but no, I can't. I have a May Ball Committee Meeting this afternoon."

Ah, yes. The May Ball – the well-known tradition among the Colleges of throwing a formal event in June, but still calling it The May Ball.

"Gosh, yes, that's only a couple of weeks away, isn't it?" I say thoughtfully.

"I know, I know" mumbles Head Porter. "Anyway, I need you to hold the fort here while I do that. I suggest you get ringing round some local bands or something for Junior Bursar's party. That's only round the corner, too."

"You're right, I haven't done anything about that bloody party. I'll get on it." I go to leave Head Porter's office when I remember something. "By the way, who has access to master keys for the College?"

"Very few people," Head Porter replies. "You and me, obviously. Senior Bursar would have had a set. Then there's just The Master and Junior Bursar. Why do you ask?"

"I was thinking, whoever killed Senior Bursar needed to pinch the spare key to his rooms. Probably someone without access to a master key, I reckon."

"Good thinking, Deputy Head Porter."

I leave Head Porter's office, for some reason not entirely convinced that I have quite grasped the full story about the missing key. Something in my subconscious is niggling away at me, a finely honed instinct signalling that something isn't right. Given proper thought, no doubt it will come to me.

However, right now my focus should be squarely on Junior Bursar's retirement party. It should be, but it is not. Right now, my focus is keenly targeted on rectifying the troubling tea situation. Priorities, you see.

Things Of Significance

HEAD OF CATERING APPEARS TO be a man on the edge. On the edge of what, one cannot be entirely sure, but he is certainly teetering atop a precipice of some description. The Catering offices are often host to scenes of, shall we say, high-octane activity and enthusiastic discussions. The academic world runs on its stomach and the Catering staff are often at the sharp end of an ever more demanding Fellowship.

Head Of Catering is partially concealed by a colourful array of paperwork stacked up on his desk. I notice a small bead of sweat tracing a haphazard path from his right temple, the progress of which is only mildly hampered by a throbbing purple vein twitching erratically. At present, both his desk and mobile telephones are ringing, almost drowning out the near-incessant 'ping!' that heralds the arrival of a new email. Head Of Catering spots me lurking by his office door and waves me in.

"Hallo, Deputy Head Porter!" his greeting is surprisingly jaunty.

"Morning," I reply "Busy?"

"I'm a bit pushed, yes. What can I do for you?"

I am thinking that maybe I should come back later, when things have calmed down a bit. Then again, there is no telling when that might be.

"I just wanted a quick word about a thing or two," I say. "But I can come back, if you're busy."

"It's fine, it's fine, sit down" Head Of Catering indicates the chair opposite his and silences his telephones with a few swift jabs of buttons and switches. "What can I do for you?"

"Well, first and foremost we are clean out of English Breakfast tea in the Lodge" I start with the most pressing matter first. Head Of Catering chuckles.

"Oh! Well, that's obviously a disaster, Deputy Head Porter, I'll get that put right immediately."

"Glad to hear it," I reply, grinning from ear to ear "It's a bloody disgrace, I tell you."

Head Of Catering pulls a face that suggests he feels suitably chastised, before moving on to the other, less important, matter.

"So, I hear you've been lumbered with organising the party of the century, then?"

"Quite so. I've no idea why. It's all very odd. Still," I take a breath and settle into my chair "Chances are I'll get to go as a guest, so at least I will be able to enjoy whatever delicious treats Chef has prepared for the occasion."

"Blimey, lucky old you, eh?" Head Of Catering looks surprised. "You must be on the right side of somebody important."

"I'm not so sure about that," I reply.

I am keen to take up as little of my colleague's valuable time as possible, so get straight to the point and request a copy of the proposed menu and any recommendations Head Of Catering may have regarding entertainment and decor. He is cheerfully obliging, but I cannot help but get the feeling he is a little confused as to why this particular task has fallen to me. I proffer a clumsy apology regarding this fact, but he laughs and dismisses my plea. As we approach the end of the academic year, there are an inordinate amount of feasts and events to keep the poor chap on his toes. Not to mention the highly anticipated May Ball, followed shortly afterwards by the dizzying climax of College life – Degree Day.

As I return to the Lodge, clasping reams of helpful information and suggestions in my sweaty mitts, I am struck (as I often am) by a thought. As we approach what is undoubtedly the most exciting time in the academic calendar, I am heading towards a milestone of my own. My first complete academic year as Deputy Head Porter at Old College. This is a thing of significance. My heart swells a little as I muse upon this. There is even the prickling of a tear or two and the suggestion of a lump in my throat.

I swallow back any ideas of blubbing as I enter the Lodge, but obviously not quite as effectively as I had hoped. Porter regards me with mild panic.

"Are you alright, ma'am?" he asks "You look like you're about to cry."
Bugger.

"I am not about to cry," I reply, cursing my crackling voice for betraying my underlying emotions. "It's hay fever." Porter remains unconvinced. We are joined by a flustered-looking Head Porter. Of course, he is heading off to his 'lunch meeting.'

"I'll be as quick as I can," he mutters, his mind on other things.

"Take your time," I assure him.

"Deputy Head Porter, you look like you're about to burst into tears!"
Oh for goodness' sake.

"It's hay fever" I reply, bluntly. "Go on, get to your meeting."

Head Porter scuttles out of the Lodge and into the lively City streets beyond. Porter is chatting away happily at front desk to a couple of Bedders and I settle down at my desk to go through the paperwork Head Of Catering kindly provided. After a few minutes, I realise that nothing I am reading is actually registering in my head, so I push the papers to one side. Rather self-indulgently (and surreptitiously, I might add), I find myself poring over the very first entries of my Secret Diary. How naive and twee those early scribblings seem to me now. Two murders, a secret society and nine months later, Old College is almost unrecognisable from the fairytale world depicted in those first writings.

Recalling those initial thoughts and feelings on what was then such a strange new world is bitter sweet. In those early days – those early, ignorant days – my joy and appreciation of the history and magic of Old College was untainted and voracious. How quickly the rose tinted spectacles fell from my eyes, only for my more usual temperament of suspicion and cynicism to return to my everyday thinking. I sigh to myself. Has life and experience really made me this distrustful and acerbic?

Maybe.

But then I wouldn't mind betting the casual assassinations have something to do with it as well.

Out In The Midday Sun

I AM A BIG FAN of parties, it has to be said. Any kind of party, really. House parties, garden parties, dinner parties, parties to celebrate, to commiserate, to integrate – even parties for absolutely no reason at all. In one way or another, I have attended practically every type of party you could possibly think of. Even some you can't. So, on the face of it, being selected to arrange Junior Bursar's retirement do is not such a surprise. Although, quite how Junior Bursar knows about my extensive experience in this field I cannot say. In fact, I'd rather not know.

I have been summoned to The Dean's rooms by way of a very brief email, simply saying I should make my way there as soon as is convenient. It isn't especially convenient, what with Head Porter out of the Lodge and my myriad of tasks to attend to, but I fancy a change of scenery.

The sun is hot today and the possibility of summer is feeling ever more likely. This being England, though, I know not to become too optimistic about these things. As welcome as this shiny warmth may very well be, my Porter's uniform does not lend itself well to sunnier climes. My bowler hat does a fine job of shading my eyes from the bright rays, but it is also cooking the top of my head as it does so. I have every conviction that I could fry an egg up there, if I could convince it to balance.

As I traverse the bridge I gaze longingly into the waters below. Despite the knowledge that they are full of filth from The City and are home to creatures unknown, I have an urge to leap into their invitingly cool embrace, just for a second. An inadvisable course of action, for a whole host of reasons.

I pause on the bridge, as I often do, to watch the boats punting along and to listen to the whoops of delight and dismay from punters of varying degrees of proficiency. From the corner of my eye, I see Junior Bursar approach from the opposite cloister. I straighten up quickly and prepare my best smile.

"Good afternoon, Junior Bursar!"

He responds with a convincing-looking smile of his own, although he may just be squinting in the sun.

"And how are my party arrangements coming along, Deputy Head Porter?" he asks. I explain that they are progressing nicely. I have been successful in securing a celebrated local magician for the event, as well as ordering the balloons. This seems to delight the dear old chap. Talk then turns to the May Ball, an event I am anticipating with some trepidation and excitement. All the Colleges hold their own balls, but Old College's balls are rumoured to be among the finest. I shall not be attending as a guest as I shall be working, but I am ebullient to be a part of it all anyway.

"Can you tell me, Junior Bursar, why the May Balls are always held in June?" I ask him. It is something that has puzzled me and sometimes the only thing to do with a question is ask it.

"I certainly can, Deputy Head Porter" he replies. "May Balls are a relatively new addition to College life, having only been in existence since the 1830's. They were originally intended as celebrations following the May Bumps, so the name refers to that, rather than the month in which they are held."

Ah, yes. The May Bumps. A complicated series of inter-College boat races that amount to little more than messing about on the river, in my view.

"Thank you, Sir, that is very interesting" I reply.

Junior Bursar appears to be in the mood to stay and chat awhile, but I have to make my excuses to continue on my way to see The Dean. Junior Bursar gives me a thin little grin.

"Is the nature of your visit business or pleasure?" he asks. It takes me a moment to comprehend what he means, but I recover myself quickly. *Our pretend affair.*

"Purely business, this time round" I explain. Junior Bursar seems almost disappointed.

"I am sure you will have an enjoyable afternoon, nonetheless" he says, before clasping his hands behind his back and making his way jauntily towards the Porters' Lodge.

As I watch him go, it occurs to me that I think I shall miss the old bugger when he goes. Goodness knows, he has made my life difficult enough on occasions, but an affection of sorts has grown within me. I catch myself before I become misty eyed yet again and decide to head straight to see The Dean.

The heat must be getting to me.

The Master's Plot

THE DEAN IS IN AN excitable mood. I can tell that he has been mulling over something important, as there are various pockets of his rooms that have been tidied and organised to within an inch of their lives. I can even see some of the heavy wooden surfaces in some areas. A sure sign of deep thought when it comes to The Dean.

I have been sat on his battered leather settee for a short time while The Dean has been engaged in a lively sounding telephone conversation. It sounds lively from this end, certainly, although I doubt the poor caller on the other end has been able to participate much. The Dean has been deploying his much-vaunted communication style of holding both sides of the conversation at once, in order to ensure that everything that needs to be said gets said. And, presumably, that unnecessary things remain unsaid. It is amusing to watch him spring to his feet in order to pace the floor furiously, but is hampered by the cord of his desk phone pulling him back like a little plastic leash.

Eventually, The Dean replaces the receiver and sighs heavily, thrusting his hands into his trouser pockets.

"Everything alright, Sir?" I ask, with a smile.

"Let me tell you, it had better be alright or there shall be hell to pay!" he replies. Then continues, "I have ordered a new mortarboard for Degree Day. The outfitters on Prince's Street are not handling my request with the gravitas one might expect."

A new mortarboard! What a treat. Who wouldn't want a little hat with a tassel on top?

222

I wonder for a moment if this is the reason I have been summoned. Somehow I doubt it.

The Dean makes himself comfortable in his armchair, which is in a considerably better state of repair than the settee. I notice that the end table adjacent to it is stacked with Colin Dexter novels, specifically those relating to his famous literary creation 'Inspector Morse'. Research, perhaps? Very apt, if so.

"Now, Deputy Head Porter" he begins. "I have called you here as something very troubling may or may not be developing. Senior members of The Fellowship have been meeting with The Master recently, myself included naturally. Not unusual at this point in the academic calendar what with everything going on. But I fear I may have detected a sinister undercurrent."

"How so?" I ask. The Dean shifts uncomfortably, something I have never known him to do before. It makes me uneasy.

"The Master seems unusually fixated on next week's May Ball. More accurately, the roles that you and Head Porter will be playing during the event."

"Head Porter is meeting with the May Ball Committee as we speak," I say. "As far as I know, he will be coming in early to oversee the setting up and I will be working until late that night. As far as actual timings and responsibilities are concerned – we thought we'd just play it by ear."

"I get the distinct impression that The Master has something in mind. No offense, but The Fellowship are not usually very interested in what Porters get up to. He seemed very keen to be sure that you would both be there."

"What do you think he has in mind?" I ask, nervous. The Dean throws up his arms and shakes his head.

"I have no idea!" he replies. "But think about it – a masked ball, huge crowds of people, lots of noise and distraction… it would be a good opportunity for mischief making."

A masked ball? I must have missed that important element. That could certainly put a different slant on things.

This is very little to go on, but The Dean does seem genuinely unsettled and things capable of having that effect on him are few and far between.

He knows The Master far better than I do, so maybe there is cause for concern.

"I will be careful" I say.

"Of course, I shall be attending the ball as a guest," The Dean continues "But obviously I cannot guarantee that I can ensure your wellbeing all evening. I am concerned that you may be vulnerable."

Before I can reassure him that I have every confidence in my capacity for self-preservation, the door is flung open. A triumphant-looking Junior Bursar sweeps into the room.

"Ho, ho what do we have here!" Junior Bursar remarks suggestively.

"Deputy Head Porter is here to discuss elements of your party, old boy" The Dean replies, irritated. "Surprise elements, I might add."

"Oh. I rather thought you might be indulging in this passionate affair you seem so insistent on?"

"Business first," says The Dean. "I was just about to see Deputy Head Porter out. Take a seat, Junior Bursar, we shan't be a moment."

Taking my cue from The Dean, I rise with some effort from the settee and head for the door. My host follows swiftly behind. Once out on the landing, he grabs my arm.

"I'm serious about this, I am certain there is something afoot. I shall find out what I can before next week and let you know."

"Okay, Sir" I reply. I turn to go but something pops into my head. "And by the way, Sir, this is absolutely the worst affair I have ever had. Just so you know."

"Oh, bugger off and get back to work, Deputy Head Porter"

And with that, The Dean slams his door shut behind me and there is nothing left to do but to return to the Lodge.

All The Fun Of The Fair

OLD COLLEGE IS BUSTLING WITH activity as the preparations for the May Ball are now well underway. The growing excitement is tangible.

Since first thing this morning, Head Porter has been like a man possessed. The constant stream of people and vehicles into Old College has had him capering back and forth since the early hours. Even before I have finished my bacon roll, a fun fair (including bumper cars and a Ferris wheel) has rolled in and started setting up home on the immaculate lawns. I can see Head Porter wincing as the great lumbering machines leave their ugly tracks across what at any other time of the year is considered hallowed ground.

The strange custom of allowing none but The Fellowship to walk on the grass has long since lost its quirk, for me. Even I feel a shudder of revulsion, watching through the window at the jolly fair people in their hobnail boots, trampling and churning the delicate green blades that Head Gardener slaves over so diligently. I smile as I see Head Porter hopping and fussing around them, attempting to supervise their efforts but invariably just getting in the way. He is looking harassed and somewhat dishevelled. What that man needs, is a nice cup of tea.

Head Of Catering has done me proud and restocked the Lodge with English Breakfast Tea, two steaming mugs of which I am transporting out across the courtyard. Head Porter has removed his bowler and is wiping sweat from his brow, his face flushed in the already tepid morning air.

"Thank you," he says, receiving the tea with gratitude. "Honestly, the Ball gets more elaborate every year. Can you believe all this?!" He indicates wildly to the growing army of men and machinery gradually filling every spare inch of College ground.

"It's amazing," I reply. "It's hard to believe that The Fellowship would allow it, actually. It's certainly disruptive."

"The Fellowship like the May Balls," explains Head Porter "They are stunning events. Also, the tickets cost a fortune so they make a bit of cash for the College as well."

"Senior Bursar must have loved that," I say wistfully.

"Professor K used to really enjoy the Ball as well," Head Porter says. "In his younger days, of course. He had quite the eye for the ladies back then." I raise an eyebrow and a smile but say nothing more. I really miss Professor K.

Head Porter decides that we should take a tour of the grounds and inspect the progress of all the Ball-related business. Armed with just our cups of tea, we venture through the cloisters to see what might be occurring.

I am delighted and stunned that Old College still has the ability to both surprise and amaze me, even when I think it has no further fascinations to declare. The May Ball Committee (comprised of mainly third year undergraduates) have really surpassed my expectations. There is the fairground, of course, and all the appurtenances associated with it – candy floss and ice cream stalls, pop-up fast food emporiums and any number of games of chance and skill. But even more impressive is the elaborate main stage being constructed on the lawns beyond Apple Tree Court, backing onto the river. This is truly a structure of which any self-respecting music festival would be proud. I have been told by various people to really get my hopes up with regards to the musical performances. In years past, Old College has played host to some of the brightest lights in the music industry, as well as a carefully selected batch of the finest up and coming local artists. How exciting! This looks like a very professional set up indeed.

There are numerous smaller stages, dotted around the grounds, where smaller, acoustic acts will perform. They are surrounded by elegant little eateries, still being constructed, that will eventually be serving all kinds of delicacies for hungry Ball-goers to enjoy. There are several bars, of course – no Old College event would be complete without a seemingly endless supply of alcohol.

It's a lot to take in, on the first tour round, as well as there being so many things still to be done. I am suitably impressed, I must say. When you take into consideration as well, many of The Committee have been studying for and taking some of the most important exams of their lives, yet have managed to pull together all this with what can only be described as aplomb. They may drive me to distraction on occasion, but there's no denying that the students of Old College are an admirable bunch.

As we make our way back to the Porters' Lodge to replenish our supply of tea, I mention to Head Porter about The Dean's concerns. It was disconcerting to see him so unsettled. Head Porter listens carefully, his complexion fading to a pallid grey as he does so.

"This isn't good news at all, Deputy Head Porter" he murmurs. "What if The Master is involved with The Vicious Circle? We could be heading for an unfortunate accident, like Senior Bursar."

"Won't we be safe, with so many people around?" I ask.

"Don't be so sure," replies Head Porter "Sometimes the more eyes there are, the less they see. We'd best keep our wits about us."

This is shaping up to be a very interesting event indeed.

The May Ball – Part One

I AM LOITERING IN THE College kitchens and the atmosphere is something rather akin to Hell. Smoke, fire and steam choke the air, which is already thick with heat, grease and the colourful exclamations of the Catering staff. The May Ball is reaching its final stages of preparations and some most disturbing news has reached my ears. Because of the demanding schedule that comes with producing first-rate food for the Ball-goers this evening, the Catering Department will not be supplying the usual sumptuous spread at lunchtime. This, of course, is of great concern to my stomach and I so I thought I had better get to the kitchens to see if I am able to beg any scraps that might be going spare.

Chef has grudgingly agreed to box up a selection of 'seconds' from the Ball menu; a rather ragtag collection of odds and sods and unidentifiable items that are far from presentable. I am having a rummage through my edible treasure trove while Chef is hunting down some of the floppy cheese of which I am so fond. There are definitely some vol-au-vents lurking in there, the pastry casings collapsed and deflated so that their strangely hued contents are leaking onto the other food. I am sure I can smell tuna but I am not sure which bit it is meant to be.

Before too long, a beleaguered-looking Chef returns with a generous armful of my beloved cheese and what looks like a batch of bread rolls, too. His face is hot and red and contrasts beautifully with his immaculate whites. I am about to comment on this observation but quickly change my mind when I realise how bad tempered he appears to be.

"This should do you and the Porters for today," Chef says, unceremoniously dumping the cheese and rolls into my already burgeoning box. "You could probably get the lads from the hog roast to plate you up some grub if you lot get hungry later on." *What does he mean – 'this will do you AND the Porters'? I thought this was just for me. I really am not comfortable with sharing food.*

"Thanks, Chef, I'm sure this will do nicely" I reply.

"I don't mean to be rude, but if there's nothing else can you bugger off out of my kitchen please? I'm very busy!"

I take the hint and leave Chef and his team to their labours. Back at the Lodge I hover near to my locker, unable to decide whether or not to stash my hard-won (well, not really hard-won) rations or to share them with the Porters. Perhaps I'll just see if I can fit them in here...

"What are you up to, Deputy Head Porter?" with my locker door half open I am caught red handed by Head Porter.

"This is my lunch" I reply. "I'm just putting it in my locker."

"Don't put it in there, put it in the fridge!" Head Porter says "It'll get all warm and sweaty. The locker room smells bad enough as it is, without your lunch adding to it." I sigh. My plan is undoubtedly foiled. Once the Porters spot this in the fridge, undefended and alone, my little box will be raped and pillaged like a town beset with Vikings. It just seems so unfair.

My ill-gotten gains now languishing and vulnerable in the Lodge fridge, Head Porter has other matters for me to attend to. Apparently, a small number of unscrupulous students attempt to gain unauthorised access to the Ball each year. They hide in their rooms until the party is in full swing, then sneak down and join the revelry unnoticed and without a ticket. My mission (should I choose to accept it) is to check every single student room and remove anyone who doesn't have a ticket. It seems they will have to find alternative accommodation for the evening. This seems very unfair to me, these rooms are their homes after all. But I suppose we simply cannot have gatecrashers at the May Ball. I am sure that would be unseemly. Personally, I feel that the best bits of any party are the gatecrashers. But anyway.

The 'student sweep' of Old College is a truly epic and often hilarious task. I find cunning and ingenious students hiding in wardrobes, under beds and even in a cleaning cupboard. The whole experience feels like being in a rather large-scale farce, where secret lovers and inappropriate guests are badly hidden in almost every scene. I was particularly amused by the jovial, 'Aw, shucks you found me' reactions of my little masters of stealth when I did find them. There was no attempt at pretence or explanation, just a good-humoured acceptance that their devious plot had failed. How very sporting.

Before I know it, dusk is creeping across the pink-blushed sky and the Old College May Ball is only minutes from commencing. The whole place has been spectacularly transformed into a glittering, twinkling wonderland and I can feel my heart beating a little faster as I survey the impressive scene. The fairground waits in anticipation, its gaudy lights and music hoping to tempt the pleasure seekers. The courtyards all have chandeliers tethered in mid-air, throwing crystal reflected light onto what now appears to be a rich and magical mix of regalia and fantasy. If an elven princess had a twenty-first birthday party, this is what it would look like.

Head Porter motions for me to join him by the main door of the Porters' Lodge. Peering through the window I can see a glamorous and excitable bustling line of sequin swathed and bejewelled masked guests, eagerly waiting to start the Ball. Head Porter checks his watch.

"It's time," he says. "Are you ready?"

"I'm as ready as I'll ever be!" I reply.

I really hope I am ready for this…

The May Ball – Part Two

IF YOU HAD ASKED ME, before tonight, what my preconception of a masked ball would be I would have said something along the lines of the following – an opulent formal event where *soigne* ladies and gentlemen attired in their very best bib and tucker enjoy a sophisticated evening of sumptuous victuals and beverages, accompanied by suitably respectable entertainment. Well, what I would probably have said was 'a posh dinner and dance' but one must always make an effort with the written word.

The Old College May Ball has completely blown my preconceptions out of the water. Although the expected opulence and grandeur of the guests and the event is very much in evidence, the overall is setting is more like an upmarket festival. Everywhere there are bands, DJs and musicians offering every conceivable form of audio delicacy. For those of a more visual persuasion, circus performers gallivant throughout the grounds, performing great feats of contortion and breathing fire for the amusement of the masked revellers. There is even a smattering of well-known faces from the screen and stage, plying their trades to the great delight of an enraptured audience. If the Royal Family did Glastonbury, this is what it would look like.

The food and drink is free flowing, the evidence of which can be seen in the erratic balletic movements passed off as dancing by only the very drunk. I check my watch. The night is still young and I fear some of our celebrants may have peaked too early. The May Ball continues until dawn with a Survivors Breakfast served at six, some of the guests will be in a sorry state by then. An idle thought of how many pools of vomit will be produced throughout the evening makes me shudder. I am grateful that Head Of Housekeeping as deployed a team of her Bedders to handle such eventualities. Thank goodness for the Bedders. Apart from the Porter on duty, they are the only people I can recognise this evening. I have lost count of the amount of people who have greeted me but because of their finery and masked faces I haven't got a clue who any of them are. Except for The Dean, of course. He is unmistakable in any guise.

I have to keep checking my mobile as the noise is such that I cannot hear a thing. The fact that I am 'patrolling' the area by the main stage probably isn't helping. Let me reassure you that it was pure serendipity that my raised concerns for the security of the area happened to coincide with one of my favourite bands taking to the stage. Actually, there is a valid reason for me keeping an eye on this area. The main stage is by the river and Head Porter told me that people try to gatecrash the Ball by sneaking along in punts and scrambling up the riverbank. Quite a noble endeavour, I feel.

My phone is telling me that I have three missed calls from Head Porter. Pah. I shall have to find a quieter spot to call him back. I duck into one of the nearby staircases where the sounds of merriment are mercifully muted by the ancient walls of Old College. Head Porter answers my call on the second ring.

"Where are you, Deputy Head Porter?" he asks.

"I'm in N staircase," I reply. "What's up?"

"There's a fire alarm playing up in the boiler room basement. Porter has been down a couple of times already but I need him up here manning the Lodge. We should go and have a look at it."

"Alright, I'll meet you there."

I must say I haven't heard any alarms going off but then over this racket I am not in the least bit surprised. There is a fire panel in the Lodge which lights up and squeals annoyingly, it must have alerted Porter. The boiler room is situated in a basement at the rear of the College, far from the May Ball. It is quite strange to leave the glittering Wonderland party and return to the mundane drabness of the boiler room.

My boots send clattering echoes along the stairwell as I descend into the bowels of Old College. As I approach the door to the boiler room I see

Head Porter already waiting for me. He shakes his head in mock despair and unlocks the door.

"What a night to have a dodgy fire alarm," he says, opening the door and standing aside to let me enter "Tonight of all nights!"

"At least you can't hear them over the noise of the Ball" I point out.

"There is that, I suppose. Come on, let's have a look then."

Apparently, Porter had thought that the detector head was malfunctioning internally, as he could find no obvious reason for the alarm to keep reactivating. Head Porter locates the detector and starts searching around for some stepladders so he can have a poke around. I check the rest of the room for anything that might be interfering with the alarm. They are notoriously sensitive and changes in temperature or even stray dust clouds can set them off.

The boiler room is probably fascinating, if you are so inclined, but I find it a little unnerving. The great behemoths of ageing metal and piping that dwell in this industrial lair are distinctively off-putting with their strange smells and random gurglings. The over-sized dials and levers create the effect of being in a steam punk graphic novel. Which is quite exciting, in its own way.

Suddenly, I hear a loud thud.

"Head Porter?" I run back around to where I left him fiddling with the detector head. "Are you okay?"

Head Porter seems fine. He is just descending the stepladders.

"I'm fine, I can't find anything wrong with this thing. What was that bang?"

"I thought it was you" I reply. Head Porter looks momentarily distracted. He sniffs the air.

"Can you smell that?" he asks. It smells like burning.

"Oh gosh, there must be a fire down here after all!" I exclaim. A few wisps of oily black smoke appear in the air to confirm my suspicions.

"Bugger, this is a dreadful place for a fire" says Head Porter. "Quick, call the fire brigade. I'll ring the Lodge."

I try my phone but there is no connection this deep underground, not even for an emergency call.

"I haven't got any service!" I call out to Head Porter.

"Me either. Come on, I'll get the fire extinguisher, you can go up top and make the call."

We both hurry back to the door. Two small details make my heart leap into my mouth. The first being that the fire extinguisher is not in its cradle by the door. The second thing is slightly worse. The door appears to have been shut and locked behind us. Head Porter rattles the handle ineffectually.

"That must've been the bang we heard" he mutters "I'll unlock it."

By now, the oily wisps of smoke are becoming more akin to billows. The air is becoming scorched and acrid and I can feel myself start to panic, just a little bit.

"Come on, old chap get the door open" I try to hide the shaking in my voice.

"It's no good," Head Porter replies, his eyes wild with horror. "Someone has left the keys in the other side of the door. I can't unlock it."

The realisation that I am locked in a burning room with no way of summoning help takes several seconds to sink in. When it does, I feel a terror unlike any I have ever known grip my very being like a rusty steel animal trap. The sheer fear literally takes my breath away. But then that could be the smoke and fumes.

Fear and terror are no good. What I need are for my survival instincts to kick in. What I need is to get us *out*.

Don't Look At The Light

Head Porter and I bang furiously on the boiler room door, yelling at the very capacity of our lungs. The fact that our lungs are quickly filling with sebaceous and smutty air is a drawback, certainly. I do not think anyone can here us.

Think. How can we get through this door?

We abandon our tactic of shouting loudly as we realise that oxygen should be used much more wisely in the current circumstances. We need to get through that door.

"We could unscrew the hinges off the door" I suggest breathlessly.

"Have you got a screwdriver?" wheezes Head Porter.

Damn.

The boiler room is certainly living up to its name. Absurdly, I remember being in the kitchens earlier today and musing that it reminded me of Hell. That was a far, far less gritty version of Hell than the one I have before me now. The kitchens were like the cartoon Hell, with mischievous –looking red devils with pointy boots and a pitchfork, dancing around a few small, localised fires. This is something else entirely. The heat is becoming so intense that even breathing in and out results in searing pain.

Think. Think again.

They say that just before you die, your whole life flashes before your eyes. I suppose no one *really* knows, but there is a sensible-sounding explanation as to why this might happen. The theory goes that, in a desperate eleventh-hour attempt to save your life, your brain goes through each and every memory, trying to find information that might help you survive, based on the experiences you have gained from previous threats and so forth. Your mind becomes the survival encyclopaedia that your subconscious is hurriedly flicking through.

Well, my brain obviously hasn't got quite that desperate yet, as although it has already reached for the encyclopaedia it at least knows what chapter it should be looking up. This should save some valuable time.

I become partially aware of a sound in the room. A very loud sound. I can hardly string a cohesive thought together in this state. It takes me a few moments to recognise it. The fire alarm.

You need to stop thinking about silly things and concentrate on getting out of this room.

"I need to stop talking to myself"

"I said the fire alarm's going off!" says Head Porter "That's got to be a good thing." I admire his positive approach but I doubt anyone will hear it. Porter will hear the fire panel go off in the Lodge, but he's single manned and will probably think it's us trying to fix it anyway. How long before he comes to check on us?

"Get down, below the smoke" I say, grabbing Head Porter's arm and pulling him down into a crouching position.

The way I see it is that we have several problems here. The room being on fire is the most obvious one. The other is that we cannot open the door, which is also a bit of an issue. The other sticky wicket is that we cannot summon help. Or...

"I've got an idea," I say to Head Porter. Speaking is difficult now, every brief utterance sends tiny white hot daggers down my throat until they are stabbing at my lungs. "If we can break something down here, cause a drop in pressure or something – won't an alarm go off in the Maintenance office?"

"Smashing things up could make things worse," Head Porter points out. He notices the delicately singed soles of his shoes, defiant little whirls of pale grey smoke spiralling into the fetid air. "Let's give it a go."

I am afraid to say I am little help to Head Porter. The smoke and limited oxygen have become so disorientating I have no idea where to begin. Head Porter is surprisingly focused, however. I watch as he fights his way through the gloom with distinct purpose.

Every inch of my flesh is screaming at me to lie down on the floor and close my eyes. Great bursts of white-hot explosions detonate behind my burning eyeballs as if my brain is going into supernova. The brilliance of the white light is blinding me from the optic nerve outwards

Don't look at the light

I take a deep breath to clear my head but it turns out to be a very bad idea. My chest fills with choking blackness but the coughing fit that ensues as least thrusts me right back into the present…

You Can Keep Your Hat On

THERE'S ANOTHER NOISE. IT'S ANOTHER type of alarm.

And… sprinklers! Oh, the sudden sound of sizzling showers of water makes the world feel like a better place.

Just ahead of me is Head Porter, on his hands and knees making his way back towards me and the door. I crawl towards him, clumsily extending my arm in a rather pathetic gesture of encouragement. Beneath the thickening layer of smoke, our flailing hands meet awkwardly and together we shuffle our way back to the door.

While hardly a comfortable environment, the sudden and very welcome arrival of gushing arcs of water has improved morale, if nothing else. Head Porter and I adopt positions somewhere between a crouch and a huddle and hold hands.

"It's getting a bit warm in here, Deputy Head Porter" Head Porter points out, once again displaying his talent for spotting the obvious. "Do you think we should take our hats off?"

Had I enough breath in my body to laugh, I would have. A crackly snort comes out instead.

"Oh, come on Head Porter" I reply. "Things aren't quite that bad."

"Just out of interest, at what point do things get bad enough to take our hats off?"

"Things can never be bad enough to take your hat off," I say with some certainty "I'm not taking my hat off. You can bury me in this hat."

"I'm sure that won't be necessary."

A strange and rapid sensation of heavy shunting comes over me. Bewildered, Head Porter and I topple forward onto the ground. *Oh, God, this isn't how it ends, is it? Am I literally being shoved off the mortal coil?*

But it is not death that approaches. It is something somehow far more terrifying. It is The Dean.

"Bloody hell!" he says (well, that's not actually what he says but I am not prepared to repeat his exact phrasing).

The door bangs against my leg as it is flung back by The Dean. Instinctively, I scramble towards the opening as The Dean is battered back by an unexpected face full of smoke. Head Porter is right behind me as I crawl into the hallway, just as Head Of Maintenance comes careering around the corner at the far end.

"What happened?" asks The Dean

"Checking fire alarm. Got locked in" I splutter, the sudden influx of cleaner air evidently a shock to my system.

"But.. how…" The Dean is momentarily lost for words. That is even more memorable than being trapped in a burning room.

"The Fire Brigade is on the way," Head Of Maintenance comes to a breathless stop beside us "What the hell happened?!"

"Someone locked them inside, look" The Dean points towards the set of keys hanging in the lock.

The keys!

"Wait, grab that set of keys!" I croak. Head Of Maintenance hushes me and places my arm around his shoulder.

"Never mind that, we should get you two out of here…"

"I'll get the keys," says Head Porter, lurching towards the door. "Bugger, they're really hot!"

"Come on," says The Dean "You need to get to see Nurse"

"Whose keys are they, Head Porter?" I ask, ignoring The Dean. Head Porter is fumbling the smouldering keys on his cuff jacket.

"I'm not sure, I'll have to wait until they've cooled down."

"You two to the medical bay immediately!" The Dean has run out of patience. "Bring the keys with you, if you must."

The sequence of events that follow are somewhat hazy and something of a blur. But clear in my mind is the one thought that shines like a beacon in my mind.

The keys.

These keys are going to do more than unlock doors.

Aftermath

So my first May Ball experience at Old College wasn't quite what I was expecting. If not for The Dean, it would have been my very last experience. Of anything. Ever.

Junior Bursar has been good enough to allow Head Porter and I a few days off following our near-final trip to the Pearly Gates. Well, that is probably a little dramatic. Some smoke inhalation and a vague threat of soiled trousers (the latter relating to Head Porter more than myself, naturally) didn't do much to enhance the evening but we came out of it fairly well, all said and done.

By lunchtime of the second day of convalescence, I am bored. I am also willing to wager that Head Porter is bored, too. A few text messages confirm this and I decide to afford the old chap the pleasure of my company.

I have only visited Head Porter's house once and I wonder at first if I will be able to remember which one it is. A fear unfounded, of course, when I spot his immaculate front door, painted in the Old College colour of morro blue.

When he answers the door, there is a brief, strange moment where we both see each other for the first time without our Porter uniforms. Obviously, we are wearing other clothes instead. Head Porter, for example, is wearing jeans and a rugby shirt.

As our eyes meet we both realise that we are thinking the same thing and have a little giggle. *Ooh! I've never seen you with your clothes on! Hilarious.*

I am invited in and ushered straight through the kitchen and then out into Head Porters' garden.

The garden is quite surprising. It looks a little wild, but closer inspection reveals organisation, of sorts. I don't think I have ever seen so many things growing in such a small space. There is a bit at the back that looks like it could be a vegetable patch.

"So, how are you feeling?" asks Head Porter, handing me a mug of tea.

"Not bad, all things considered" I reply, taking the tea and chinking mugs with him. "I won't be attending any barbeques for a while, though."

"I'm with you there."

I take a sip of tea and my eyebrows rise involuntarily. It's pretty good tea.

"The bunch of keys hanging in the door. Do you know who they belonged to?" I ask.

"Well, I had to leave them at College so didn't get a proper look, but I'd say they were one of the Maintenance bunches."

"What, just a standard Maintenance bunch?" I must admit I am quite crestfallen. I was rather hoping they might belong to The Master, or someone exciting like that.

"Looks like." Head Porter replies. "I wonder which of our Maintenance guys is missing his set of keys?"

I take another, longer sip of tea. This doesn't sound entirely practical to me. Why would anyone from Maintenance want to lock us in a burning boiler room? Unless they were assisting *someone else*. Someone who would probably love to lock us in a burning boiler room. But who would want to do that? I need to work this out quickly, before whomever it is tries again.

"You haven't got anything a little… stronger, have you Head Porter?" I enquire innocuously, emptying the dregs of my tea onto what I suppose he calls his lawn.

"It's only lunchtime" there is an air of caution in Head Porter's voice. "But I have got the rest of that sherry from last time?" *On second thoughts…*

"Nah. It's okay," I say after some deliberation. "Probably best to keep a clear head. Right, well I reckon we should find out exactly who those keys belong to and take it from there?"

"Right. First thing tomorrow."

"Or we could pop in now?" Head Porter looks none too impressed with this suggestion. "Problem?"

"Oh. No…" I can tell that there obviously is a problem. I give him my best 'oh, really?' look. He caves in graciously. "I've just got the complete *Sharpe* box set. I was hoping to enjoy my last afternoon of recuperation in front of the box."

This is a lie. I know he does not have a DVD (or video, for that matter) player, nor any kind of digital or satellite equipment. Just that old, clunky television set in the corner of his sitting room.

"Oh. Alright then…" I reply "I'll just pop along there myself. I need to thank The Dean, anyway, for saving our lives. D'you think he knew we were down there?"

"He had dropped by the Porters' Lodge, looking for us" explains Head Porter. "Porter explained about the fire alarms and he came down to find us."

"Really? I wonder what he wanted" I muse. Head Porter shrugs.

"Ask him."

"I will."

A moment of silence falls between us and I am uncomfortable and a little hurt that Head Porter has been untruthful about his plans for the afternoon. Whatever, he obviously just isn't in the mood for investigating. *Unless he wants me to join him?* Hmm. Surely the investigation takes precedence over a twenty-year-old period drama, even if it has got Sean Bean in it. A rare, starring role for Sean Bean, where he doesn't die halfway through. He gamely stays alive for the whole sixteen episodes, would you believe.

"Okay then," I announce, eventually. "I'll get down to Old College, then."

"Well, if you're sure," says Head Porter. "Be careful, won't you, on your own."

"I shall be perfectly fine. I only seem to get myself into trouble when I'm with you!"

"Good point."

I step out of Head Porter's front door and into the street and turn to say goodbye. It has been a rather strange visit. The tea was nice, though.

"You know something, Head Porter" I say before I go. "I've been to your house twice now and we've even been out for s drink. Maybe it's time we called each other by our actual names?"

Head Porter just gawps back, confused. He splutters a little before finally getting his words out.

"I'll see you at work tomorrow."

Original Pranksters

It seems very strange to be heading into Old College on a day off. Without my College tie and bowler hat, I really do not feel like the Deputy Head Porter at all. It reminds me of non-uniform days at school, which always had a faint air of anarchy about them. It is quite astonishing what an outfit can do for your mindset. If the clothes maketh the man, what does a pair of jeans and a vest top make me? I dread to think.

I decide to make my entrance through Sprockett Gate, as far away from the Porters' Lodge as I can be. It's not that I don't want to see the Porters, rather I feel they would prefer not see me. It might make them a little nervous if I suddenly appear unannounced. Besides, Sprockett Gate is nearer to The Dean's rooms and the Maintenance department.

The atmosphere in Old College today is palpable; the courtyards and cloisters have a steady stream of excitable Third Years, organising their gowns and mortarboards for the main event of the week, nay, the entire academic year – Degree Day. Head Porter seems to be quite looking forward to this. He is not usually one for the great pomp and ceremony of many College events, but I can tell he is excited about Degree Day. I think that, quite often, the graduating students bring gifts to the Porters' Lodge – edible gifts, at that. Cakes, biscuits, chocolates… oh, I can only imagine! No wonder Degree Day is so popular. If there's one thing a Porter likes, it's a biscuit.

I am disappointed to find The Dean sadly absent from his rooms this afternoon. Maybe he is still chasing his new mortarboard. I decide to try Head Of Maintenance instead, when something catches my eye. I notice a very furtive-looking student poking his head around the door of the Computer Room. He looks a little pale and nervous, a sure sign of being up to no good.

I make my way over, my civilian clothing offering me a degree of camouflage. The young chap doesn't recognise me until I am right on top of him, by which time it is far too late for him to do anything clever. I have seen this lad before, he is a First Year student studying law, I believe. He is a friend of Hershel and Penelope, who I last saw following their soggy encounter with Hawkins College on The River.

"Hello, Darwin!" I say cheerfully. His little face falls through the floor. "What are you up to, then?"

Darwin quickly looks behind him, his panicky eyes imploring to some unseen companion in the room behind him.

"I'm not up to anything, Deputy Head Porter" he replies in a manner so unconvincing that it implies the exact opposite.

I smile sweetly and gently push back the door behind him. Helpless, he walks backwards clumsily as I advance on the Computer Room. Darwin starts coughing theatrically, as if to warn an accomplice. As it happens, this is a redundant gesture as I am happily striding through the room within seconds.

Ah. I might have known. My old adversary Hershel and his little friend Penelope are furtively switching off the computer monitors. "Good afternoon, my favourite students!" I announce. I turn to Hershel. As a Second Year, he is older than the other two and I rather feel he leads them astray. "What are we up to on this fine day?" Hershel goes to speak, but I cut him off "And don't tell me 'nothing' because we all know that's not true."

There is a little bit of a pause.

"You might as well tell her, Hershel" sighs Penelope. *Oh, this ought to be good.* Hershel holds my gaze with his own for a few seconds, but evidently either lacks the imagination or the compunction to come up with an excuse. He sighs, then switches on the nearest monitor to us.

"Alright, Deputy Head Porter" he says "You've caught us. We're preparing a prank for the end of term."

"I thought it was supposed to be graduates that did the end of year pranks?" I ask.

"Yes, but I thought we could play a prank or two and they would get blamed for them" is Hershel's reply. *Actually, that's quite clever. Rather wish I'd thought of it myself.*

"Go on then, what's the prank?" I say, intrigued. Hershel indicates the monitor he has just switched on.

"Try and use this computer," he says. I shrug and take hold of the mouse and try to launch the menu. Nothing. I click along all the icons at the bottom of the screen. Still, nothing. The files on the desktop don't seem to work either.

"You've broken the computer," I remark "Well done you." This is about as technical as I can get when it comes to IT diagnosis.

"Actually I haven't," explains Hershel. "What I did was to take a screenshot of the desktop, then hide all the icons and folders in a separate folder over here. Then, I set the screenshot as the desktop background, so it still looks the same but it's obviously only, like, a photo of it, do you see?"

Even I sort of understand this. People will be clicking on what they think are real icons, when actually they are all tucked away in this separate folder. Okay, that is actually quite an ingenious prank and it doesn't cause any harm, really. It will probably waste the time of a fair few students, and then eventually the IT chaps as well, but all in all a rather intelligent practical joke, I feel. And I'm not even really at work today, so probably none of my business anyway.

"Have you done this to all the computers in here?" I ask, looking round at the twenty or so machines in the room. Hershel looks at his feet.

"Yes" he replies, using his best 'little boy' voice. I bet that works a treat on his mother.

"It's pretty clever, actually, Hershel," I say, to his obvious shock. "And, it's quite funny too. I mean, obviously, if it gets back to The Dean that you've done this, you will be in big trouble. But he won't hear it from me, alright?"

Hershel and his two companions look relieved and a little surprised.

"Thanks, Deputy Head Porter" says Penelope "We really appreciate it, honestly." I wave away her platitudes with a flick of my wrist and allow her a little smile.

"I'm not even on duty today and quite frankly I've got other things on my mind. But if you lot get caught, I'm denying all knowledge, alright?"

My young charges seem quite happy with this result and I leave them to continue with their endeavours. As student pranks go, it's a fairly tame one. The vague concern niggling at the back of my mind is that Hershel did mention 'a prank or *two*'...

Ah, well. How bad can it really be? Not too bad, I'm sure. Probably. I hope.

Anyway. I need to track down Head Of Maintenance and find out about these keys...

Degree Day

After some considerable and epic undertaking (the likes of which had previously only been seen in the works of Homer), I was finally able to track down the suave yet elusive Head Of Maintenance. Not that he was able to enlighten me further in my quest to identify the owner of the set of keys that almost sealed the fate of Head Porter and myself. It seems that the Maintenance staff have a rather cavalier attitude to the keeping of keys, with the swapping and borrowing of each other's bunches being commonplace. It seems that no one even realised a set was missing. Naturally, Head Of Maintenance received a stern and solemn ticking-off, delivered with the kind of ferociousness you have come to expect from this Deputy Head Porter.

On today of all days, I do not trouble Head Porter with the disappointing news that we are no nearer to identifying our assailant. Moreover, I particularly do not wish to disturb him with the shocking revelation that his precious keys are not, in the Maintenance department at least, afforded the reverence and respect that he believes they deserve. Head Porter seems to have enough on his plate already.

And so Degree Day is finally upon us!

A time of great pride for tutors and students alike, this is the day when Old College finally reminds the world what it is *really* here for – academic excellence. It is all too easy to be distracted by the archaic and seemingly redundant ceremonials and practices, the enduring and intoxicating reverence of the past and the ornate pomposity (not to mention the odd corpse). I stand guilty as anyone of missing the point entirely. What Old

College does (and has done for over five hundred years) in a spectacular fashion, is educating and inspiring the finest young minds on the planet. Whether this is in spite of the aforementioned or because of it – well.

That really is none of my business.

Head Porter is in his element. The Porters' Lodge is a gleeful hubbub of proud families and relieved students, resplendent in their Sunday best and gowns, respectively. Smiling to myself, I watch the scene with interest. I note that Head Porter holds a certain charm for the families, the mothers especially. To them, he has played a vital part in the success of their talented offspring. The Porters are often the first port of call for a student in need of something. Anything. Such is the Porters' reputation for unerring wisdom and practicality that they have been called upon to deal with anything from a broken tap to a broken heart; to discuss everything from the rugby to the meaning of life.

It is a little bit like watching a famous celebrity (shall we say, Sean Bean?) being mobbed by a small group of very polite fans. Although red-cheeked and giggling, they are on their best behaviour for the man who runs the mighty Porters' Lodge. The Porters' Lodge – which has saved the lives, reputations and future prospects of students and Fellows alike for centuries. And, of course, he is loving every minute. If he was as personable to the Porters as he is to middle-aged ladies, we would be an unstoppable force. Still, he is getting better at that sort of thing.

I watch our soon-to-be graduates in their mortarboards and gowns, uneasy yet full of pride. You can see in their faces how the celebratory nature of the day is tainted with the realisation that it is now all over. Some may come back, of course, to pursue further studies. But many will be thrust into the sobering confines of reality, somewhere that is a very different place to Old College. Then again, they *will* have the piece of paper from Old College that will, hopefully, act as a golden ticket to an expectant world. And that, when it comes down to it, is what today is all about. Going to collect your piece of paper.

But this being Old College, there is far more to it than *that*. Apart from anything, it is a bloody excellent excuse for a good, old-fashioned academic knees-up. There will be food and, by God, will there be wine. Collecting the bits of paper is something resembling a Royal outing in itself. The Master and Head Porter will lead a procession of Fellows and students through The

City to Swallow House, a respectably sized building just beyond Hawkins College. A building seemingly used to hand out bits of paper, Head Porter did not elaborate further. The winding mass of students and Fellows, all in formal academic dress, must be quite a sight to behold. Not that I will get to see much of it, as I am informed that I am to walk at the back of the procession. Apart from being traditional, I am also required to ensure that no-one gets left behind or lost. Or run over. Pah. I'm looking forward to it anyway. Oh, and I'm not allowed to wave at people, either.

I check my watch and it would seem that the hour is almost upon us. I see Head Porter notice the time and take his leave of his audience. He collects his jacket from his office and comes to join me.

"Come on, get your hat on" he says. I dutifully do as I'm told. Head Porter sighs, irritated, and starts tugging at the brim of my bowler and tutting. "It's got to sit *properly!*"

"You've never been this fussy about my hat!" I complain, trying to bat him away.

"Well, you just look scruffy. There!" He makes a final tweak and seems satisfied with the result. "You'll need to get your jacket on, too. Come on."

I never wear my jacket. Especially in June. But, if the moment calls for it I shall not be found wanting. On goes the jacket and I follow Head Porter out of the Lodge and on to take our places in the procession.

As Head Porter strides away to the front, I loiter somewhat sheepishly at the back. Some of the families chat with me and even take photographs. I cheer up a little at my moment of minor celebrity. In fact, I am so taken with my posing and small talk that I almost miss the procession moving off. I bid farewell to my new associates and march along behind in what I hope is a graceful and dignified manner.

I had my concerns about a large and elaborately costumed procession promenading through The City in the middle of the morning. Clearly, though, the populace of The City is well versed in this historic event and despite the fact that no roads have actually been closed, no one impedes the well-worn route. There are many spectators, in fact, lining the streets, clapping and waving. The celebration of the academic achievements of these fine young folk reaches far beyond their own family and friends. The City as a whole applauds their efforts, for they know that they are the future.

I am more than a little miffed that I am not permitted to wave. It strikes me as unnatural not to return the wave of a complete stranger. I can smile, though. They can't stop me doing that. In truth, I can barely stop myself.

When we reach Swallow House and our young heroes-of-the-hour retire inside for the no doubt elaborate ceremony of collecting the reasonably sized bits of paper, the Fellows gather in a wonderful little side alleyway, aptly-named Scholars' Lane. Some have got hold of choc ices, the crafty devils. I spot The Dean reclining gracefully against the stone wall.

I subtly manoeuver myself so as to be placed directly next to The Dean, although not leaning against the wall. It is hardly my place to lean against the same wall as The Dean.

"Good show, wouldn't you say, Deputy Head Porter?"

"Absolutely, Sir" I reply. I reach into my back pocket and retrieve a carefully placed pouch of tobacco.

"Oh, not here, for goodness' sake" hisses The Dean.

"That Porter over there is having a smoke" I reply reproachfully, indicating a fine-looking gentleman wearing the colours of Wastell College.

"So he is," says The Dean. "I say, he's got a top hat on as well! fancy that!"

I admit I am a little jealous. I am immensely fond of my bowler but nothing quite beats a top hat. I had not considered it before but it occurs to me that I might look quite fetching in a topper.

"Well, that's just showing off" I reply curtly. "What are Wastell trying to do? Trying to start a hat war amongst the Porters?"

"We'll bloody well beat them at their own game. What beats a top hat?"

I think carefully for a moment. It's a tough one.

"A crown?" I suggest.

"A crown? Yes, that can be the only thing…" I can see the multitude of cogs turning in The Dean's mind. "Next term, all our Porters shall wear crowns, d'you hear? I'm not being outdone by bloody Wastell College…"

We are interrupted by shouting from the far end of the alleyway. I recognise Porter making his way towards us at a fair lick, especially for a Porter.

"Is that one of our chaps?" Asks The Dean, squinting at the earnest figure bowling towards us.

"I am afraid it is," I reply. "And he is running. This *cannot* be good news…"

The Best Laid Plans

PORTER REACHES US, SWEATY AND breathless. There is little point asking if he is alright; he clearly isn't. Porters are not designed to travel at anything more sprightly than a leisurely preamble. That is not to say that they don't, on occasion. Especially if last orders have just been called.

"What is it?" I ask.

"You're not going to believe this, Ma'am," he wheezes. "But there are these little exploding things in the Dining Hall. Head Of Catering is going *mental*."

Exploding things are never good news, even if they are little.

"Do you mean bombs?!" The Dean says, actually sounding quite excited at the prospect. Porter looks at him sideways.

"No, Sir, not bombs. Look, Ma'am, you'd better come and have a look." Porter gestures for me to join him. The Dean holds up his hand.

"If there are exploding things, I should be there," he declares.

"It's Degree Day and you're The Dean of College. You need to stay here," I tell him gently. "Besides, someone needs to let Head Porter know what's happening. Tell him I'll see him back at the Lodge."

"But I don't even understand what *is* happening!"

But Porter and I are already heading back to Old College at an impressive pace. Porter seems to have got his second wind.

Arriving back at the Porters' Lodge, the general atmosphere is far more sedate than when I left. Even the presence of Head Of Housekeeping does not seem to be causing too much of a stir. She has a clipboard and pen and is looking devastatingly efficient. Her brow is furrowed, but I sense she is positively thriving on the fumes of catastrophe.

"Ah, Deputy Head Porter!" She greets me with a chilling cheerfulness. "Now, don't you worry. My team have got everything under control. I have even had a pot of tea and plate of biscuits sent along to Head Of Catering, poor chap. He was beside himself. But the Catering staff are doing sterling work re-laying the tables and helping the Bedders fetch and carry fresh tablecloths and the like. I really have got everything covered."

"But what has actually happened?" I ask, silently relieved that Head Of Catering seems to have averted any major disaster.

"Well, if you ask me, it has all the gubbins of a student prank, I reckon."

Head Of Housekeeping explains to me that the ceremonial salt shakers have been tampered with. They have been loaded with ingredients designed to erupt when the vessel is shaken. One of the Gardeners thinks it is lemon juice and baking soda, separated by a scrap of tissue paper. This was once common practice amongst his school friends, apparently. A jolly jape which culminates in the top of the salt shaker flying off with a satisfying *pop!* Followed by the immediate arrival of a slithering, bubbling salty mess all over yourself and your lovely food. But it seems something went awry with this particular execution of this old schoolboy favourite. Best guess is that the tissue paper was not substantial enough and the divided elements rushed eagerly towards each other, like lovers in a cornfield.

A familiar *beep beep* resonates from my pocket. It's a text from Head Porter

DEAN SAYS COLLEGE UNDER ATTACK FROM TERRORISTS. EXPLAIN.

I reply

PRANK GONE WRONG. NO STRESS. CAN YOU DELAY THE RETURN PROMENADE?

JUST ABOUT TO LEAVE. BUGGER. WILL WALK SLOWLY.

I return my phone to my pocket.

"They're on they're way back. How close are you to being ready?"

Head Of Housekeeping assures me that the Bedders will have everything ship shape in the nick of time. However, she hurriedly returns to the Dining Hall, so her confidence is ambiguous. I decide to pay Head

Of Catering a visit, see if there is anything I can do. The thought that he has a pot of tea and a plate of biscuits in his office did not occur to me at all.

Head Of Catering appears stressed, but focused, as he is feverishly making notes at his desk. I notice crumbs on his tie and as mild panic builds in my stomach, I scan the area desperately looking for the biscuits. *Oh no! He's eaten most of them already.*

"Hallo, Deputy Head Porter" he barely lifts his head. "And before you start, I know you're only here because I've got biscuits."

Curses! My scheme has been foiled.

"I was hoping to be of some help, Head Of Catering" I reply, sounding as hurt as I can.

"I don't see how. Coming here and eating my biscuits isn't going to help anybody." Head Of Catering finally looks up from his scribblings and gives me a broad grin. "Look, I just need to delay the thing by twenty minutes or so and we'll be fine. I've been racking my brains, but the best solution I can come up with is to do what my wife does when she burns the first course at our dinner parties."

"And what would that be?" *This is going to be fascinating.*

"She puts some crisps and nuts out and gives everyone another drink." I am not sure quite how to react. Then again, they do say that the simplest ideas are the best. But on Degree Day? Head Of Catering leans forward, as if to impart some earth-shattering thing. "Actually, we've got some really nice crisps. Not so much in the nut department, but Chef has some frozen niceties that might go down quite well. We'll keep them out on the lawns with the champagne and nibbles until we're ready for them."

"My friend, you are a genius" I reply. Well, it's obvious that I'm not going to get a biscuit so I take to my feet. "I shall leave you to bask in the glory of your own brilliance."

"Thank you, Deputy Head Porter, I shall do exactly that."

"I don't suppose you've seen young Hershel around today, have you?" I ask as I turn to leave. Head Of Catering shrugs. He has had other things on his mind. "Okay. Have a nice afternoon."

I am making my way towards the rooms of a certain student acquaintance of mine, when I see a stiffly jovial Head Porter walking comically slowly alongside The Master, who is not doing a marvellous job of disguising his irritation. They have just entered Old Court and are making their way towards me, albeit incredibly slowly. It is rather reminiscent of being in a zombie film. Not that I've ever been in a zombie film, you understand.

Painfully aware that I should be at the very back of the procession, I tuck myself inconspicuously in a recess in the cloister. As the column approaches, I can hear Head Porter attempting to distract The Master with his own special brand of small talk. In all fairness, The Master does look very much distracted. They pass by, followed by The Fellows and then the students and I fall in a few steps behind the last, straggling graduates. I see them on to the lawns, where our proud degree-holders are reunited with their even prouder families, and The Fellowship are reunited with liquid refreshment. A resounding success for the Porters' Lodge, anything from here on in is Catering's problem.

Head Porter has obviously been nervously awaiting my return to the Lodge. I can see him pacing his office before I even reach the door. I step in and his eyes are immediately searching my face for something, anything…

"Well? Is everything alright?"

I sigh.

"Yep, it seems to be. Somehow. Nothing to do with me."

"It's just, The Dean was very certain about the terrorists."

I laugh.

"Tea?"

With a hot cup of strong tea, the world can look like an entirely different place. Now, sat in Head Porter's office, it seems like a brilliant place to be. Strange, perhaps, but one way or another the day as been an undeniable success. The failure of the prank was in fact what saved the day. I barely dare imagine the commotion if it had actually *worked*. I suppose it is not essential that The Dean hear about this little event, but I am not about to make that opinion widely known. Someone needs to sweat over this for a while yet. I never did get a biscuit, though.

"How did you find your first Degree Day, then?" asks Head Porter, sipping his tea. "Was it what you expected?"

"Well…" I take a few moments over my reply. "I can't say it was quite what I expected. To be honest, it was probably a fair bit more straightforward. I mean, despite everything, all we had to do was walk up and down a street, really."

"Not bad for a day's work, eh?"

Head Porter and I toast our small contribution to a magnificent day. I feel I should take the opportunity to congratulate myself while I can. Next week is the highly anticipated celebration of Junior Bursar's lifelong contribution to Old College. I suspect it may not be such a straightforward affair.

Final Touches

I HOLD IN MY HAND something quite magnificent, the likes of which would never have come to be my possession outside of Old College. Embossed in gold and black, the elegantly scripted card feels very significant in my hands. It is my very own invitation to Junior Bursar's retirement party.

It would be fair to say that I had been expecting this particular arrival, but that does nothing to dampen the thrill of spying it on my desk this morning. I have been as happy as a bee since then, but unfortunately I am resigned to keeping my enthusiasm to myself for now.

Head Porter, on the other hand, is reserving none of his feelings – especially those concerning his involvement with the carousing this evening. Junior Bursar has bequeathed him the dubious rank of Cloakroom Attendant and Head Porter will therefore be relegated to below stairs pursuits for the night. I have charitably offered to smuggle him what food and drink I can.

Although confident that there is nothing I have overlooked, my assurance that everything will go according to plan is vague. Despite my best efforts, I am unable to imagine *every* possible eventuality when it comes to Old College. The whole place seems to be governed by some doddering force of disambiguation. Almost *anything* could happen. But it will probably be splendid; I have found the perfect band for the occasion and Head Of Housekeeping has generously loaned me a couple of her Bedders to help with decorations. The magician will be arriving at nine thirty and Head Of Catering has been planning the victuals for weeks. As the supposed organiser of this retirement do, I have not really had to exert myself too vigorously in the business of organisation. But if anything at all should go awry, it will be my head on the block.

Head Porter is in his office, morosely filing receipts behind a seemingly deliberate pile of College magazines. As a barricade, it is ineffectual. I shall breach his defences.

"Would you like a cup of tea, Head Porter?" I ask. He huffs a little.

"Are you sure it's not a bit beneath you, Deputy Head Porter?" There is the very edge of malice in his voice. "Now that you're hobnobbing with The Fellowship?"

"Now don't be silly. Come on, I'm going to check on the Wide Gallery, you should join me."

"I'm busy" Head Porter is clearly not in the mood to be jollied along. I know better than to provoke the beast when he is this ill tempered, so decide to let him wallow in his pit for the time being. I am sure he will perk up later.

I am making my way across Old Court towards The Master's Lodge when I spot a familiar figure trudging towards me, the weight of several worlds and a moon on his shoulders.

"Afternoon, Hershel."

Hershel stops before me and gives me a hurt little look, before returning his gaze to his shoes.

"You told him, didn't you!" Hershel wails, still inspecting his footwear. What can be so interesting on his toes? A quick glance reveals very little.

"What are you talking about?" I ask him, concerned.

"The Dean! I've just had the hairdryer treatment about Degree Day."

"So it was you and the salt shakers, then?"

Hershel tersely confesses to his passing involvement with the suspected terrorist attack on Old College. It seems news of this has reached the ears of The Dean and now the ears of Hershel are in rather poor shape indeed. But none of that has anything to do with me. I suppose that The Dean has saved me a job, though, as I had intended to have suitably strong words with the young man myself. It would probably be a little unfair to pursue that now, given the circumstances. The Dean's input is more than adequate.

Having gone some way to reassuring Hershel, I continue on my merry way to The Master's Lodge. I do enjoying visiting The Lodge. Quite apart from the fact that it is a stunningly preserved historical masterpiece, the very knowledge of the hidden passageways and secret tunnels delights me beyond words. It is not necessary to travel them, only to know that they are winding and hiding all around me gives me a little tingle to the tips of my toes.

The Bedders really have excelled themselves. The somewhat heraldic theme of black and gold is continued throughout The Wide Gallery, with streamers and drapes placed sympathetically around the assorted antiquities. The additional décor has leant something of an air of the theatre to the numerous gold-framed portraits along The Gallery. The oil-painted subjects seem none the more cheerful for it, however.

A small stage area has been created at the far end and on approaching it I suddenly feel a shiver of dread. I really hope I've done the right thing about the band. *He did say he wanted a lively band. I distinctly remember him saying upbeat, dancing music.* Well. It is a little tardy to be worrying about it this late in the day. I have every certainty that Junior Bursar will be delighted with the Ska band I have hired for the evening.

I am congratulating the Bedders on their sterling achievements when Head Porter pops his read around the door. He looks a little more agreeable than he did earlier. I give him a wave and make my way over. He is giving me the little contrite look he reserves for times when he knows he should be penitent. The one where he tilts his head a little to the left and drops his shoulders slightly.

"I'm sorry I was so grumpy earlier," he says earnestly. "It was being daft. Is there anything you need me to do?"

I give him my second-best smile and shake my head.

"Thank you, but it's fine. Do you… do you need anything for your – um – area, this evening?"

"You could make sure I get some of the sausage rolls," suggests Head Porter. "I think that would be very helpful." I can tell that there is something else behind his words, something he really wants to say but isn't saying, for some reason. I look him straight in the eye.

"I can get you some sausage rolls, no problem" I reply. Head Porter cracks.

"Look, I'm just a bit worried, you know, so soon after the May Ball?" Head Porter moves closer and drops his voice to a whisper. "I just wish we could have, you know, stuck together tonight."

"Oh, don't worry about me I shall be absolutely fine!" I reassure him.

"I was more thinking about my own safety, actually, Deputy Head Porter. I mean, what if the… the people behind all this see me as an easier target? A soft option, maybe? I shall be all alone down there with the coats!"

I am not, under ordinary circumstances, an eye-roller. But on this occasion I feel that no other response will suffice. He was brave enough in the boiler room.

To assuage his fears, we hastily concoct a strategy. At the beginning and end of the party, Head Porter will be perfectly safe as the cloakroom area will be bustling with guests and their unwanted outer clothing. When everyone is safely ensconced in the Wide Gallery, we initiate a needlessly inconvenient 'checking in' system of meeting at the hallway staircase every twenty minutes, Head Porter at the foot of the stairs and me at the top from the door to the Gallery. A quick nod will confirm that all is well and we will return to our separate endeavours. If anything happens during the twenty minutes, well, I suppose he will just have to scream or something.

There. We couldn't be more prepared if we tried.

What could possibly go wrong?

Junior Bursar's Retirement Party

THE FACE STARING BACK AT me in the bathroom mirror is non too shabby, if I do say so myself. It has taken a fair bit of effort and determination to achieve that effect, but even so. I'm still not so sure about the hair. Should I try the parting on the other side? Hmm. Looks a little odd. Brush it back. Pah. I look like a heavily made-up lion.

Although still rather hesitant about my hair, the time for deliberation is over as I hear the *beep beep!* of Head Porter's elderly yet immaculate Ford Scorpio in my driveway. He has kindly offered to give me a lift, I suppose so that we might finalise our battle plans for tonight in a more discrete setting.

"Are you sure you won't be cold in that?" says Head Porter as I swing open the passenger door. I look down at my red halter neck dress and shrug. *I'm not taking a coat. Not tonight.*

"I think I'll be alright" I reply, climbing into my seat.

"Bloody hell, look at those shoes! How are you ever going to walk in them?!"

"Who d'you think you are, my father?" I snap back sarcastically, instantly regretting my turn of phrase. "Oh. Sorry. I didn't mean… it was a stupid thing to say."

Head Porter just rolls his eyes at me and smiles. I may have touched a nerve, though. The journey to Old College is certainly a quiet one.

By the time we arrive, Head Porter has abandoned his quiet contemplation and is regaling me with tales of caution and ever so slightly patronising advice. I rather think he is a little jealous. We are quite early, as

Head Porter needs to be in position before the arrival of first guests. I loiter with him in the cloakroom for a while, putting in place the final elements of our 'checking in' arrangement and idly wondering who will be the last Fellow standing at the end of the night. My money is on Chaplain, there is no time to ponder it further. It is time to join the party.

As I enter the Wide Gallery, a relieved sigh finds its way out of my lungs. This looks *fantastic*. In the muted glow of candlelight the adorned Wide Gallery is somewhat striking. It is almost reminiscent of some Arthurian drama, where knights and princes would bound through the doors at any moment. However, the chirpy, up beat rhythm from the Ska band at the far end of the room distracts from that general theme slightly.

I helpfully relieve a server of one of the numerous glasses of champagne he is carrying and look around for someone serving canapés. Head Of Catering promised there would be those little tiny toad-in-the-holes that you can eat in one bite. I am going to need one or two of those.

This is just *incredible*. I have always had envious intentions regarding the feasts and dinners and drinks receptions. I feel that I was born to go to feasts. Alas, it was not to be, but now – look at me now! Here I am at Junior Bursar's retirement party. I really hope he likes his party.

Soon after beginning my quest for tiny toad-in-the-hole, I come across The Dean. At first, I think he is distracted but then I notice he is intently watching the band. I see his foot tap once or twice.

"Good evening, Sir!" I raise my voice to catch his attention. "Enjoying the party?"

"Rather good, isn't it?" He replies. "But listen – I've been thinking about something."

Always excited to hear about what The Dean has been thinking about, I allow myself to be shuffled several feet away from our nearest fellow guests. He seems a good deal pleased with himself. In hushed tones, he shares with me his insights regarding our situation as he perceives it. He is convinced that those responsible for the deaths of Senior Bursar and Professor K will be in The Master's Lodge this evening. With every Fellow and senior member of College in attendance, it stands to reason that The Vicious Circle must be among them. But who?

"Can you two not keep your hands off of each other for a single moment?!" Startled by the sudden and, until just now, silent arrival of

Junior Bursar we spring apart quite involuntarily. "For goodness sake. If you must continue with your salacious activities, please at least refrain from indulging at my party. Thank you."

"Are you… having a nice time?" I venture politely.

"I am, actually" he replies, much to my relief. "Although I am not entirely taken with those miniature sausages in batter contraptions. I'm really enjoying the band, they more than make up for it."

Before I can say any more, Junior Bursar waves me along with him in the direction of the nearest glass of wine. I manage to catch The Dean's eye as I am led away. He is evidently furious. I am forced to look away by having a large glass of Chateauneuf du Pape thrust into my hand by a smiling Junior Bursar.

"Well, this isn't too bad at all, is it Deputy Head Porter?" His tone is conversational. A rarely used tone, in the case of Junior Bursar. "You have done a good job. Not just for tonight, either. So I want you to enjoy my party to the fullest capacity. You will not be expected in the Lodge tomorrow. Think of it as a token of thanks from me personally."

We chink glasses and drink deeply of the thick, smooth wine, which tastes all the sweeter for having those unexpected words swimming in my ears. *A 'thank you' from Junior Bursar. Now I really have seen it all.* He leaves me fighting to keep a soppy grin from my face and heads towards a gathering of Fellows who have collected several feet behind me. It must be time to check on Head Porter. I head towards the hallway.

Our check-in passes without incident, as do those that follow. Unfortunately, although the check-ins have been a resounding success, the bits in-between have been less so. Inspired by Junior Bursar's encouragement to let my hair down and emboldened by a general feeling of pride, I have made every effort to really get into the spirit of things. The spirits are a recent diversion, though. It's been wine up until then. Far too much of it and scant amount of canapés to compensate. There were not nearly enough canapés and not even any crisps at all. I mean, who has a party without crisps, right? Anyway… anyway.

The realisation that I am barely a few sips away from being a complete catastrophe nags unpleasantly, somewhere in the soup that was once my brain. I very, very carefully place my glass on the table, after only three attempts.

Not bad.

Motor functions still operating to some degree. What can rescue me from my stupidly self-inflected malaise? There is only one thing. The saviour of alcohol-induced idiocy since mankind first laid eyes on a pig. A bacon sandwich. Now. Think. Where would I find a bacon sandwich. In a room... a room with other food in it. A food room. A kitchen! The Lodge kitchen isn't even that far. It's just down there and along a bit.

Let's go.

What had I been saying earlier, about feeling so proud? And we all know what comes after pride. I stagger with as much dignity as I can muster to the kitchens, in the far reaches of The Lodge. The change of air has sharpened my senses a little, but only sufficiently enough to tell me that I am in no condition to cook. There is a good chance there might be some sort of leftovers nestling in the fridge so I continue on my way, stopping only to remove my shoes.

When I reach the kitchens, killer heels tucked clumsily under my arm, I am surprised to find the place in darkness. Catering must have gone home. My unfamiliarity with this room leaves me fumbling blindly for the light switch before realising why it is in darkness. Cold and spotless, the kitchens evidently have not been used tonight. Must have been brought over from the main Kitchens.

Still squinting from the sudden brightness, I gently sway towards the fridge, vainly hoping that something delicious is just sat there waiting for me. Heaving open what feels like the heaviest door in the world, I am bathed in the happy glow of the fridge light as its treasures are revealed to me. This is a fine hoard of booty indeed and I think I know how pirates feel.

But then, what I feel next is something else entirely.

From somewhere near the base of my skull a heavy, immobilising *thud* explodes, vibrating right through to the tip of my nose. There is barely time to register the howling ache to the back of my head before I don't feel anything at all.

And then, just...

Black.

End Game

A COOL, HARD SURFACE PRESSES against my cheek. There is a breeze. It feels like flying.

Somewhere far away, the rusted wheel that is my mind is beginning to turn once again. Fighting through an incessant cycle of blackness and white noise, I struggle towards consciousness.

As I haul myself from delirium and crawl gingerly along the shoreline of reality, I am beginning to feel nostalgic for the blackness and white noise. They, at least, were devoid of physical awareness. I now find myself especially aware of a hideously painful throbbing from the back of my head. I blink. Oh, how it hurts to blink. I seem to be slumped against a wall. This is no good. I need to move.

My arms feel like they have been replaced by sandbags as I grope around, trying to find a way of pulling myself up. Forcing my eyes to open results in the rapid liberation of my stomach contents, which hurtle downwards some hundred feet before colliding spectacularly with the courtyard below. The main component of this fluid offering being red wine, the scene below looks rather grim indeed. *Bugger. I am at the edge of the Flag Tower.*

Surprisingly, this little episode has perked me up somewhat. But as I place my weight on my hands and attempt to push myself up and away from the wall, I am shoved firmly back to the edge and I find myself admiring the courtyard once again. *Listen. I think someone is trying to push you off the Flag Tower. You might want to do something about that.*

I push again, harder this time, kicking out with what little energy I have in my legs. I wish I still had my shoes on. You can do a lot of damage with heels. Elbows flailing, I scramble to my feet, managing to glance a feeble blow across my attacker's cheek as I do so. It affords me the time and space I need to pull myself together and adopt a defensive stance.

With the Old College standard fluttering high above our heads against a twinkling night sky, my assailant and I stand and face each other. The distant throbbing of the Ska band mingles with the familiar sounds of The City when it stays up late. But I am barely aware of any of it.

"You were actually going to throw me off the Flag Tower, were you, Sir?"

"It would be a drunken accident. The misadventures of an inebriated young woman."

"Oh, really? And what about the great thwack to the back of my head? They will know it is an earlier injury."

"No one will question the coroner's report, Deputy Head Porter. No one ever does."

A silence settles between us as we stand face to face in the starlight. I must say I am rather impressed. Who would have believed that Junior Bursar would be capable of carrying me all the way up here?

"Deputy Head Porter I must tell you that I simply cannot be delayed here much longer. There is a plane flying to Tuscany tonight and I very much intend to be on it. Do you see?"

"What, do you expect me to throw my*self* off the Flag Tower?!"

Junior Bursar takes a few steps towards me and my whole aching body clenches as I stare into him, trying to see what is behind his eyes.

"You are proving a remarkably difficult person to kill, Deputy Head Porter" he says. There is a sigh, which although weary is brief. "And I am so glad that that is so."

Something passes between us that I cannot explain.

"I don't see why that should be," I reply. "You bloody well killed Professor K, didn't you? Do you really think I'm just going to put that to one side?"

"I didn't kill Professor K" says Junior Bursar, his words like lead. "You did."

The words sting me in a way no physical wound ever could. That saying about sticks and stones is misleading. Junior Bursar continues.

"You believed you were showing him a kindness by taking your own breakfast to him when he came out of hospital. Thought it would build up his strength, no doubt. Of course, it was prepared as such so as to have the absolute opposite effect. But then, it wasn't meant for him. Was it?"

"You mean you've tried to poison me as well?!" I realise that arguing with a Fellow is deemed to be poor manners but I'm feeling rather justified.

"If it is any consolation, Deputy Head Porter, Professor K was completely against the idea. He had become somewhat fond of you, it seems. But you were getting to be awfully knowledgeable about things you shouldn't be and the Professor and I had an agreement, you see."

Junior Bursar visibly slumps into something approaching resignation. In light of the fact that he has been keenly trying to murder me for several months, I see this as no reason to let down my guard. I say nothing, but strain my ears in eagerness to listen to him.

"For so many years The Vicious Circle went about its brutal way of protecting the reputation of Old College. Somehow thinking that hiding bodies under more bodies would preserve silence. And silence, indeed, was what they achieved – but preserve our reputation? Just because a bad thing is not known does it make it any the less wrong?"

"You intended to put a stop to The Circle?"

"Yes. We were adamant. Professor K and I shared a devotion to our beautiful institution and wanted her to be at peace. Using the dear Professor's extensive chemical expertise we intended to gently remove the remaining members and then quietly disappear to our twilight years."

"But why all the cryptic clues, than?" I ask, baffled. "Why did he want me to find out?"

Junior Bursar shakes his head first towards his feet and then up to the sky. He appears to bathe in the moonlight for a moment to compose himself.

"He could be sentimental fool, at times" Junior Bursar mutters. "He could never forget the peasants beneath the Porters' Lodge. He believed they deserved to be recognised, to be respected. They are, after all, the very thing that Old College is built on. Placed there by the Order of the Lesser Dragon, no less." *Which is why Old College is so named. In honour of the ancient order of founders.* "He had some notion that you would see to it, some way or other. He could never forgive himself for not having the courage to do so himself. He thought that maybe you would be braver."

"Maybe the guilt of his actions was sitting heavily with him?" I suggest.

"Well, maybe. I suppose that now we will never know."

"What about Senior Bursar?"

"He was to be our final duty," Junior Bursar explains. "With him gone, no further members of The Vicious Circle remain. We intended to poison him, of course, but with Professor K no long in situ as our resident chemist, I had to be rather more resourceful. It is well within my experience to tamper with a kettle and a plug. And the keys used by the Maintenance department are so simple to come by."

"And you locked us in a burning room as well. Fantastic."

"Such an easy undertaking, really. I typed the note requesting the replacement kettle myself. It was not difficult to keep up with events from then on. When the new kettle arrived the following morning, I merely had to wait until he made his first cup of coffee. I sent you that email shortly afterwards. While I was there, I placed a copy of the note from a memory stick into his documents folder. And there we have a simple accident with faulty electrics. No one need look any further than that."

"You can hardly believe that you can get away with this."

"Of course that is what I believe, Deputy Head Porter. I know it to be true. No one will listen to you. The influence of Old College reaches deep into the very mechanics of The City. The law is the law outside of our walls only. Do what you will, but do you not understand that ultimately Old College has been freed from the trappings of its bloodthirsty past? Professor K has not died in vain. The Vicious Circle has fallen."

Putting it like that, Junior Bursar almost seems to present a reasonable argument. But then, I have suffered a rather severe blow to the head.

"As I said, I have a plane to catch, Deputy Head Porter. You, on the other hand, have a nasty cranial injury. If I were you I would have someone attend to it. You must consider drinking less in the future."

Junior Bursar turns to go but I put out my hand to him.

"Hang on, there are questions…"

"They shall have to remain unanswered, for now" and he turns towards the staircase, nimbly darting across the tower and down into the spiralling darkness below.

I make after him, but pain and exhaustion drag at my heels. Descending the stone tower steps is nauseating beyond belief and I have to stop and sit down after three or four. I rest my head for a moment against the cool walls and allow a soothing fug of oblivion to envelop me for a short while.

I have no idea how long I am there before being shaken awake by a visibly panicked Head Porter. The Dean is with him, peering over his should in the gloom.

"Oh my God!" squeals Head Porter "Are you alright? What happened?!"

"Where is he?" I splutter "Where is Junior Bursar?"

"Half way to the airport by now, I fancy" replies The Dean "What has happened to your head? You look dreadful."

I reassure The Dean and Head Porter that I am no so bad, but agree to be seen by Nurse. In a midway state between what is real and what is not, I allow myself to be gently guided to the Medical Centre, where we await the arrival of Nurse. I try to impart the revelations from atop the Flag Tower but I am hushed into quiet by The Dean.

It will be several days before the three of us are able to confer on the events of Junior Bursar's retirement party, by which time the man himself is far beyond our reach. The Dean delights in enlightening me about how he reached the inevitable conclusion and how he and Head Porter mounted an eleventh-hour rescue mission to come to my aid. Apparently, it was the splatter of vomit in the courtyard that led them to the Flag Tower. It is a story I will share with you I am sure, but all in good time.

All things considered, I have reached the conclusion that I need a little time apart from Old College and the suffocating atmosphere it currently holds for me. Head Porter has told me I can take as much time as I need, so long as I promise to come back. Not for the first time, I entertain the notion of never setting foot inside the blasted place again. But I have tried that before. Somehow something always calls me back.

My place in the unspoken history of Old College is forever assured. My future remains uncertain.

Questions do not remain unanswered forever.

www.ingramcontent.com/pod-product-compliance
Ingram Content Group UK Ltd.
Pitfield, Milton Keynes, MK11 3LW, UK
UKHW021314210225
4708UKWH00031B/251